FINDING FOREVER

TREADING WATER SERIES, BOOK 5

MARIE FORCE

Finding Forever
Treading Water Series, Book 5
By: Marie Force
Published by HTJB, Inc.
Copyright 2020. HTJB, Inc.
Cover by Kristina Brinton
Print Layout by Holly Sullivan
E-book Formatting Fairies
ISBN: 978-1950654826

THE TREADING WATER SERIES

For all the readers who asked for Maggie's story over the last seven years, this is for you. Thank you for asking me to finish this series. You were right. We needed one more.

CHAPTER 1

*S*pring in central Tennessee happened suddenly. After weeks of seemingly endless rain, overnight the miles of rolling hills had turned emerald green, buds popped on the crepe myrtles, maples and oaks, and the sweet smell of new life filled the air. Forsythia, the first harbinger of spring, had exploded to yellow life weeks earlier than it did at home in Rhode Island and had been followed in quick succession by daffodils and tulips that filled lush flower beds with splashes of vibrant color. By the second to last week in May, the days had become longer and warmer, the rain less frequent.

Maggie Harrington took a mug of coffee with her when she walked across the driveway to the stables to see the horses. Having them nearby was one of the best parts of her new life running Matthews House, a shelter for women and children in crisis founded by her music superstar sister, Kate, and brother-in-law, Reid Matthews. Maggie had been crazy about horses all her life, and she'd missed being around them during the years she'd lived in New York City.

She found Thunder, the sleek, dark thoroughbred Reid had given Kate when they were first together more than a decade ago, in the paddock, turned out for a day of exercise and sunshine. The old guy gave a happy nicker when he saw Maggie coming, probably because he knew she always came bearing gifts, and trotted over to see her. Standing on the bottom rung of the white fence that surrounded the paddock, Maggie fed him apple slices and carrots, despite Kate's edict that he needed to lose some weight.

Maggie disagreed. At this point in his life, he ought to have whatever he wanted.

His velvety tongue swept over her palm, scooping up the carrots in one swift lick.

Maggie laughed. "Pig."

He snorted in response and nudged at her hand, looking for more. Kate swore the horse had human tendencies, and Maggie had to agree with her sister. In deference to her pregnancy, Kate had had Thunder moved to Matthews House so Maggie could exercise him while Kate couldn't. Maggie was already sad about the thought of Thunder going home after Kate had the baby and could get back to riding.

Maggie found a single sugar cube in her pocket and gave it to him, feeling guilty for playing favorites among the horses. After feeding apple slices to the other horses who came over to say hello and giving them each some attention, she headed back to the house to start her workday. If no new crises arose, she might get done with work in time to ride before dinner at Kate and Reid's.

The toot of a horn from a car coming up the long driveway stopped her from going inside. She recognized Ashton Matthews's sporty silver Jaguar. Ashton, who was Reid's son, was engaged to Maggie's sister Jill and served as the pro bono attorney for the shelter. And yes, her sisters were involved with a father and son. Their story began when Kate first met Reid as an eighteen-year-old chasing the dream in Nashville.

Tall, blond, broad-shouldered and handsome, Ashton emerged from the car, tucking a leather portfolio under his arm. He wore a tailored navy suit with a matching tie. "Glad I caught you. I'm on my way to the office and was hoping to talk to you for a minute." Since they got engaged last Christmas, Ashton had been living with Jill at her house on Kate's estate. Ashton and Jill were getting married in the Harrington sisters' hometown of Newport, Rhode Island, in late July.

"What's going on?" Maggie asked him.

Ashton had wanted to be part of the project at his family's home and had offered to handle any legal work involved. "I've got the background check on your horse-whisperer guy."

Brayden Thomas had come highly recommended and was due to arrive for an interview after lunch. She'd asked Ashton to run a check on him, the way he had every employee they'd hired over the last few months. That he'd had to come here personally to discuss the results with her didn't bode well. "And?"

"Everything came back okay, but there was one weird thing."

"What's that?"

"He has a juvenile record."

"What did he do?"

"No way to know. Juvenile records are sealed. I did a little 'extra' digging, or I never would've found it."

"Huh." Maggie tried to wrap her head around this unexpected development. Brayden had come so highly recommended. She hadn't expected to find any skeletons in his closet.

Ashton withdrew a printed report from his portfolio and handed it to her. "Whatever it was happened years ago. He's almost thirty. His adult record is clean. He has bachelor's and master's degrees from UT Knoxville in animal science."

Maggie had applied for and received a grant to run a therapeutic riding program for the children who came to stay at the shelter and had planned to offer the job to Brayden if the interview went well. She'd wanted the program to be separate from what Reid and Kate had done with Matthews House, something that was entirely her own initiative. After having studied equine therapy in college, she'd been determined to make it available to their clientele.

"What're you going to do?" Ashton asked.

"Have the interview and ask him about it, I guess." It'd taken months to find Brayden and then a week of back-and-forth messages to schedule the meeting. The thought of starting over to find someone else made her feel tired, and it was only eight thirty.

"That's what I would do. Maybe it's some foolish adolescent prank or something like that."

If it was anything more than that, Maggie would be reluctant to hire the man to work with the troubled children who would come through Matthews House.

Because Kate and Reid were personally funding the program, they were able to make their own rules and regulations for the program, but safety was their top priority. They'd installed manned gates to provide added security to their residents, many of whom had fled violent relationships. Keeping them safe had to also be Maggie's top priority.

"Good luck with it," Ashton said as he got back in his car. "I'll see you at dinner later?"

"I'll be there."

He waved as he turned the car around and drove off toward town, away from the house where he'd grown up. Reid had become a single parent when Ashton's mother was killed in a car accident when he was only two. Jill said Ashton had no memory of his mother except for the photographs his father had kept around the house and the stories his father had told him.

Maggie couldn't imagine what it'd been like for him to grow up without his mother. She'd spent three years without hers after an accident had left Clare in a coma. The day she'd unexpectedly recovered had been the best day of Maggie's life. Sometimes she still couldn't believe everything that'd happened after her mother's accident.

It had divided their lives into before the accident and after.

She shuddered, recalling the horror of the car hitting her mother, of Clare seeing it coming but not reacting, the sickening crunching sound at the moment of impact and the surreal, slow-motion flight of her mother's body into the air, her head connecting with the windshield with a sound Maggie had never heard before or since.

"Stop. Don't think about that." Easier said than done. Images from

4

that shocking incident were etched permanently upon her soul. They didn't torment her the way they had in the months after the accident. Time and therapy had given her coping skills that kept the distress at bay most of the time. However, this time of year always brought the memories back to the forefront, as the accident had occurred on a day much like this one. Shaking off the troubling thoughts, Maggie went inside, poured herself another cup of coffee and brought it with her to the office to start her workday.

She took a second to check her phone and found a text from her brother Eric, who would soon graduate from high school.

Help me. They're driving me nuts. I don't want to go to college this year. I need a break from school. Promise you won't tell? I have a secret!

Maggie wasn't surprised to hear of his lack of interest in college. He'd been less than enthusiastic when her dad and stepmother, Andi, had taken him to tour a few schools and had only applied under pressure from his parents, teachers and school counselors. He'd gotten into all five schools he'd applied to and had reluctantly committed to Northwestern in Andi's hometown of Chicago right at the deadline.

When have I ever told your secrets? Spill it!

I'm applying to the Peace Corps.

Whoa. That was huge news. *I LOVE that. I can see you doing that for sure.*

Really? I can teach ASL, he said, referring to American Sign Language. Eric had been born deaf, and Maggie had learned sign language from him and Andi. When Maggie had been unable to get a job as a family counselor after grad school, that skill had come in handy, as she'd been hired to provide sign language for criminal trials.

Really! It'd be such an adventure. Let me know how it goes, and when you're ready to pitch it to the parents, I'll help.

You're the best. LY

LY2. Keep me posted.

He replied with the thumbs-up emoji.

Maggie hoped Eric would be able to pull it off, especially since their dad was super gung ho about all of them going to college. She'd met plenty of people in college who didn't belong there and wasn't afraid to say so to her dad and Andi if it came to that. Perhaps Eric could take a couple of years to volunteer and go to college later.

Teresa, the overnight program manager, appeared at the door to Maggie's office a few minutes later. "Good morning."

"Morning. How are things?"

"All quiet. The McBride family had a good morning. Debbie had the kids up and ready for the bus stop."

"Did they have breakfast?" Two days last week, the McBride kids had gone without breakfast because they'd been running late to make the bus. Maggie had sent them off to school with granola bars and juice boxes.

"They did."

"Well, that's progress." In addition to providing emergency shelter, counseling and career services, their program aimed to help strug-gling parents learn skills and routines designed to prepare them to eventually live independently with their children. Some of the mothers needed this help more than others. One of the things Maggie had come to appreciate was how the more experienced mothers stepped up to offer wisdom and counsel to the younger ones, which gave them a community of support that would hopefully outlast their time at Matthews House.

"In other news, Corey is having pains. Could be Braxton Hicks. I've got her first on the list for Arnelle when she comes in."

Maggie was alarmed to hear that twenty-year-old Corey Gellar might be in early labor with her first child. She'd come to them via a referral from Davidson County police after they intervened in a domestic situation at her home. Her live-in boyfriend had been arrested for assaulting his pregnant girlfriend and was still in jail. "How far apart are the pains?"

"Twelve minutes."

"Damn it. She's only thirty weeks. Should we call for rescue?" These were the moments Maggie found most challenging in her new job. When did a situation become a crisis, and how did she know whether she was doing the right thing?

"Corey didn't think that was necessary."

"Okay," Maggie said, exhaling. "We'll see what Arnelle has to say."

Maggie's day spun out of control from there. When Arnelle determined that Corey could be in early labor, they called the rescue. Maggie ended up at the hospital with Corey until they decided to admit her to see if they could stop her labor. Maggie stayed until a friend of Corey's came to be with her.

"I'll check on you after a bit," she said to the petite young woman with blonde hair and fragile features marred by bruises that infuriated Maggie. How any man could hit a pregnant woman, she would never know.

Over the last few months, she'd had to take a mental step back from questions like that, or she'd go mad from the things she saw and heard on a daily basis. She would never understand how people could do such things to the people they loved, but it happened far too often.

Arnelle liked to say the crises kept them in business, which was sadly true. She also said dark humor was necessary to keeping one's sanity when working with families in turmoil.

As Maggie drove back to the house, down scenic, winding country roads, she had the window down and the stereo volume cranked up. Around here, country music was all the rage, but it wasn't her jam. She preferred her alternative playlist to country, not that she'd admit that to her sister Kate, one of country music's biggest stars.

For Kate, Maggie made a rare exception to her no-country-music rule. She loved Kate's work, as well as that of Kate's husband-and-wife mentors, Buddy Longstreet and Taylor Jones. Buddy, Taylor and their four children were family to Kate and Reid, who'd grown up with Buddy.

Maggie took the last turn before the security checkpoint where the handsome young guard waved her through, flashing a big smile. Xander was always friendly and flirtatious with her. However, she didn't encourage him because she was in no place to be thinking about men or dating or anything like that. The thought of it made her shudder in revulsion after what she'd been through with the last guy she'd dated.

She navigated the long lane that led to the Matthews estate, driving past the two-story Tudor-style guesthouse where Kate had spent her first night in Nashville, and pulled into her usual parking space behind the stables. Only as she walked around the stables and came face-to-face with a handsome man wearing well-worn denim and a formfitting Western-cut plaid shirt did she remember the meeting with Brayden Thomas that she'd failed to reschedule after Corey's early-labor crisis.

The photos she'd seen of Brayden hadn't done him justice. Tall and broad-shouldered, with dark hair and brown eyes, he looked like a movie-star version of a horse wrangler. He removed a battered tan cowboy hat from his head in a gesture of respect she found ridiculously charming.

"Are you Maggie?"

"Yes, that's me."

He stepped forward, hand extended. "Brayden Thomas. Nice to finally meet you."

She shook his work-roughened hand and met his intense gaze. Manners *and* eye contact, two things that mattered for people who worked in equine therapy. "You as well. So sorry to be late for our appointment. I had an emergency with one of the women."

"No worries. Arnelle told me what was going on. Gave me some time to look around. What a beautiful place you've got here."

"It belongs to my brother-in-law and sister, actually."

"Your sister is Kate Harrington, right?"

"That's right."

His eyes glittered with excitement. "I'm a *big* fan. I've seen her in concert five or six times. She's fantastic."

Maggie was never sure how she was supposed to reply when people praised Kate, so she said what she always did. "Thank you. We're proud of her."

"You don't look like her."

"Nope. I favor my dad, and she's our mom's twin. We do have the same eyes, though." Why was she telling him this stuff when she ought to be asking him how he'd landed in juvie?

"I had a chance to check out the stables, and they're some of the nicest I've ever seen. I'm really looking forward to hearing more about what you have in mind for the equine therapy program."

This would be a really great time to tell him you can't hire someone with a criminal record, Maggie. "As you know, most programs focus on children and adults with special needs. Here, it won't be about that so much as providing therapy and riding lessons to kids who've been through traumas and/or suffer from PTSD."

He nodded, listening intently to everything she said.

Maggie realized he'd begun moving toward the stables, and as if she'd been hypnotized or some such thing, she walked with him without having made the conscious choice to move.

"The kids have been abused, then?"

"Some of them were. Others have seen things that no child should ever see—parents overdosing, fathers beating mothers, mothers beating fathers, among other things that can't be unseen." Such as your mother getting hit by a car right in front of you...

"I see. My philosophy is all about building confidence. I tell the kids I work with if you can mount a thousand-pound animal and get him or her to do what you tell them to, you can do anything." He reached out to scratch the nose of a quarter horse mare named Dandy, who leaned into his caress. "It seems like that approach might be a good fit for the kids in your program."

It would be perfect. That was exactly what Maggie had dreamed of when she approached Reid and Kate about using a couple of the horses that were boarded at the Matthews estate for a therapeutic riding program. Once she hired someone to oversee the program, each horse would have to be evaluated for temperament and suitability.

Maggie had secured signed releases from the owners of the other horses, allowing them to be used for that purpose if it was determined their temperaments worked for the program. Most of the owners were friends of Reid's or Ashton's, so getting permission hadn't been difficult. In fact, the owners had been thrilled to know that their horses would help to make a difference for kids in need and get regular exercise, too.

"As I mentioned on the phone, it's important that I work closely with a counselor or therapist to tailor my program to the needs of each child."

"That's where I come in," Maggie said. "My undergraduate degree is in social work, and my master's is in family counseling." She'd busted her ass to finish both programs in just over five years at NYU.

His gorgeous face lit up with a warm smile. "That's an ideal fit for what I do."

For some reason, hearing him say the words *ideal fit* made Maggie feel like laughing. Yes, he was an ideal fit for her program, and the fact that he was to-die-for handsome didn't hurt anything, either.

"Are these the horses I'd be working with?"

Now would be the perfect time to tell him he couldn't work there. "They are. All but Thunder." She pointed to him. "He's getting on in years, and Kate thought it might be better not to have him be part of the program."

Brayden worked his way down the row of stalls, giving each of the horses a minute of his time and attention. Each of them responded favorably to him, even Lonnie, who didn't like anyone—or so it seemed. "Is Thunder in good health?"

"He's in excellent health and is gentle as a lamb."

"He'd be ideal for the program, but I understand if your sister doesn't want us to use him. In my experience, I've found that older horses are sometimes better for therapeutic riding. They've sown their wild oats, so to speak."

"I'm sure Kate would be open to discussing it."

He ran a hand over Thunder's elegant neck, and the horse nickered in response. "Did you get the info I sent about my PATH certification and insurance?"

She licked lips that'd gone dry as she watched him interact with the animals and noted how each responded to him with trust. "I did, thank you for sending them."

In addition to his obvious affinity for the horses, Maggie would have to be dead and buried not to also notice that he was, without a doubt, the best-looking man she'd ever met in person. He'd rendered her speechless and stupid in the head just by the way he interacted with the horses she loved like people.

He had a gentle, soothing way about him that would be ideal for the population of children he'd be working with. In fact, it was nearly impossible for her to reconcile the information Ashton had given her with the man currently standing before her.

Maybe he'd investigated the wrong Brayden Thomas.

That was possible, wasn't it?

She took a deep breath for courage and released it. "We ran a background check, which is customary with everyone we hire."

"Okay."

"We discovered you have a juvenile record."

"I do."

"Can you tell me what that's about?"

"Nope."

CHAPTER 2

*M*aggie was late for dinner, but that was nothing new.
She, who'd prided herself on punctuality in her old
life, was hardly ever on time in her new life. "Sorry," she said to Kate
when she walked into her sister's spacious kitchen.

Reid and Ashton were sitting at the bar devouring chips and salsa,
while Kate and Jill tended to the stove.

Kate kissed her cheek. "You haven't missed much." She glanced
toward the guys. "They don't speak until the first bowl of chips is
consumed."

"This is true." Jill kissed Maggie's other cheek. "How was your day,
dear?"

"Insane."

"Good insane or bad?" Kate looked at her carefully, the way she
always did these days, as if trying to see if Maggie was breaking under
the strain of her new job.

"Some of both." Maggie prepared a weekly status report that she
emailed to Kate and Reid on Fridays, updating them on each of the
residents and the efforts being put forth by the team Maggie had hired
to assist them. They'd settled on that plan so they wouldn't feel
compelled to talk about the facility every time they were together.

"Do you need us?" Reid asked.

"Not at the moment, but I'll let you know if I do."

"We're always here for you, darlin'. You know that."

"I do." Maggie smiled gratefully at her brother-in-law, charmed as always by his delightful accent and inherent sweetness. "You know I appreciate the support, but what I'd appreciate even more right now is a margarita. Make it a tall one."

"Coming right up." Jill fired up the Ninja and produced a yummy strawberry margarita that she garnished with a lime.

Maggie took a sip, closing her eyes as the heat of the tequila moved through her system, calming her after another crazy day. "That's delicious." When she opened her eyes, the others were looking at her with concern. "I'm *fine*. I love every second of it. It's just a lot, but I'm coping. I swear."

Although she'd interned for a year at a homeless shelter in New York while in college, she'd worked in the donation center and helped kids with their homework. Running the entire show was a whole other level of challenge, which she loved most days.

Kate and Reid exchanged glances that told Maggie they were worried about whether she'd taken on more than she could handle by making their passion project hers. She didn't want them worried. She wanted them to feel confident that they'd made the right choice by choosing Kate's inexperienced sister as their director.

Maggie appreciated that they were always far more concerned about *her* than the program itself, although they'd both given tons of time and attention to the program over the last six months. They'd chosen to be more hands-off now that Maggie was in charge, but had made it clear they were a phone call or text away if needed. Before she could think of something more she could say to reassure them, Jill's phone rang.

"It's Mom FaceTiming about wedding plans." The wedding, set for the last weekend in July, would be held at Infinity Newport, the hotel her dad's company had built on Newport's famous Ocean Drive. He'd met his wife, Andi, during that project, and she had later been appointed the hotel's general manager.

"You've got all of us for the price of one call," Jill told their mother, Clare, as she panned the gathering with her phone.

"All my girls together. I love it. How is everyone?" Clare had blonde hair and the same striking blue eyes as Kate and Maggie. Though now in her late fifties, she would say that Max and Nick, the sons she shared with her second husband, Aidan, kept her young.

"Maggie's stressed, Kate's huge and I'm great," Jill said.

"I know why Kate is huge—she's about to make me a grandmother, after all—but why is Maggie stressed?"

"I'm not." Maggie glared at Jill. "I'm just adapting to my new job and being responsible for twenty extra people. No biggie."

"She makes it look easy when it isn't," Kate said.

"Enough about them." Jill flashed a giddy smile as she waved her hand to dismiss her sisters. "Let's talk about *me* and my *wedding*!"

"See what you're marrying?" Maggie said to Ashton.

He grinned like the lovesick fool he was around Jill. "Isn't she *magnificent*?"

Maggie made barfing noises that had everyone laughing.

Jill flashed a huge, dopey smile at her beloved. "That earned you big points redeemable at bedtime, my love."

Ashton stretched and yawned dramatically. "I'm feeling really *tired* all of a sudden."

While the others laughed, Maggie experienced the oddest hollow feeling. Jill and Kate had their lives figured out, and she was still floundering. Granted, she was a few years younger than them, but still… Their delirious happiness had her wondering if she'd ever find what they had with Ashton and Reid.

For some reason, that had her thinking of Brayden Thomas. She wanted to laugh out loud at the trajectory of her own thoughts, but her family already thought she was on the brink of a breakdown. No need to give them proof.

While Jill and Kate talked wedding plans with their mother, Maggie checked the stove and stirred the chicken Kate had made for fajitas.

"How'd you make out with the horse whisperer?" Ashton asked.

"I'm not sure."

He offered her another margarita, but she declined. One drink was her limit these days. She never knew when she'd be called to deal with a new crisis and had to be ready—and able to drive. "What happened?"

"I mentioned that we'd noticed he has a sealed juvenile record and asked if he could tell me why."

"And?"

"He said, and I quote, 'Nope.'"

Ashton tipped his head inquisitively. "That was it? Just nope?"

"That was it."

"Huh, well, he's not obligated to share that info with you as a prospective employer. The more important piece of information, in my opinion, is the twelve-year adult record, which is squeaky clean."

"So you'd be comfortable hiring him based on that as well as numerous recommendations?"

"I think I would be."

"Even knowing there's something in his past that resulted in him being in juvie?"

"I don't know about you, but I'd hate to have things I did as a kid held against me as an adult."

"No kidding."

Ashton flashed a wicked grin as he leaned in. "What did you do?" Before she'd met Brayden Thomas, Maggie had thought Ashton was one of the best-looking men she'd ever encountered. Now the bar had been set even higher.

"Dream on. I'm not telling you."

"I'm sure you were a wild child," he said, laughing.

"I had my share of fun but never got into any real trouble. What was it my grandmother used to say? 'There but for the grace of God go I'?"

"Buddy's mom Martha says that, too."

"I guess the bottom line is we all have things we regret from the past. Brayden comes highly recommended and has a clean record as an adult. I called his references, and they raved about him. The last people said they only let him go because they lost funding for their program. I wanted to do a three-month probationary period, but Brayden said it's got to be all or nothing. If he's going to pull up stakes and move to the estate, he doesn't want it to be provisional."

"We can write his contract so he can be terminated at any time for cause."

"What does that mean?"

"That you can find fault with him for any reason you'd like and fire him."

"Is that fair?"

"It's fair to you. It gives you an out if he's not getting the job done or if other information comes to light. It's fairly common language in employment contracts. It'll also give him the right to quit at any time, with at least a week's notice."

"So we'd both have an out if we need it."

"Right."

The other employees she'd hired were regular full-time workers, not contracted. Ashton had recommended doing a contract with Brayden and anyone else who was brought in to oversee special programs.

"I'll put the contract together and shoot it over to you in the morning. You can run it past him, and we'll go from there. When he's ready to sign, send him to my office. We'll need witnesses, which my people can do."

"All right, thank you. I appreciate your help with this."

"No problem."

"Maggie," Jill said, "Mom and the boys want to talk to you."

"I'm coming." She spent the next few minutes catching up with her mother, stepfather, Aidan, Max and Nick.

"We can't wait to see you guys," Clare said.

"We're waiting for her to pop." Maggie glanced at Kate, who was on a chaise in the living room with her feet up and her husband by her side, as usual. "Any time now."

"Dad has a plane on standby to get us all there."

"Of course he does," Maggie said, laughing. Her dad, Jack, was nothing if not predictable when it came to his children.

"We can't believe Kate's going to make us grandparents!"

"She's taking the pressure off the rest of us." Maggie felt like she was light-years from where her sisters were, settling into marriages and families. She was still figuring out her own life, and after what'd happened in New York... *Stop. Don't go there.*

"How're things going with the job?"

"It's an adventure. Every day is different. Today, we were all about preterm labor. Tomorrow, it might be an outbreak of lice. It's never boring, that's for sure."

"Yikes. In case I haven't said it enough, I'm so proud of the work you're doing. You're helping to change lives."

"That's the goal. We'll see how it goes."

"Be confident, Maggie. Kate and Reid wouldn't have hired you if they didn't believe in you."

As much as Maggie wanted to believe that was true, she wondered sometimes if she would've had a prayer of landing this job if her sister and brother-in-law weren't the bosses. Probably not since she had zero experience in the field, but she was certainly acquiring on-the-job training on a daily basis. "Thanks for the pep talk, Mom. We'll see you soon."

"Can't wait. Love you, honey."

"Love you, too."

Maggie walked Jill's phone into the living room and handed it to her sister. "I'm not sure who's more excited about this baby, Kate, you guys or the Rhode Island contingent."

"It's probably a tie," Kate said. "She texts me every day to 'check in,' and so does Dad. Andi only texts once a week, so she gets the award for restraint."

"Our little one will be very well loved," Reid said. "That's for sure."

His accent was to die for. Maggie could easily understand how eighteen-year-old Kate would've been bowled over by the man who'd been a college friend of their father's. At the time, Maggie had been unable to imagine being attracted to a man so much older, but Reid was an exception to every rule, and he was hopelessly in love with Kate. That much was apparent to anyone who spent time with them.

They'd spent ten years apart before getting their second chance, and were deliriously happy together.

What more could anyone ask for than to see someone they loved as much as she loved Kate with a man who worshiped the ground she walked on? Both the Matthews men had become the gold standard in Maggie's mind, making most of the men she'd met since knowing them seem lacking in comparison.

A memory of Brayden Thomas's handsome face popped into her mind, reminding her she still needed to decide what to do about him. They'd left things open-ended earlier, and she'd promised to be in touch one way or the other soon. Normally, she'd run it by Reid and Kate to get their opinion, but the therapeutic riding program was her baby, and they'd tell her it was up to her to decide who was going to run it.

Besides, they had enough on their plates with the baby due at any moment without her adding to their concerns. Her job was to run the facility so they didn't have to be involved on a daily basis. No, this was her challenge, and she'd deal with it.

After a lively, entertaining and delicious dinner, Maggie kissed Kate's cheek. "I'm going to go. Thanks for dinner, you guys."

"We love any chance to have you guys over," Reid said.

Maggie rested a hand on Kate's explosive belly. "Call me—day or night. I'll come running."

"I will, don't worry. I can't do this without you and Jill."

"We've got you covered." Maggie and Jill had agreed to remain close by while the baby was born, but had declined Kate's offer to be in the room. They were both afraid of seeing things that could never be forgotten. "I'll check on you tomorrow."

"Hey, Mags?"

Maggie turned back to face her sister.

"If the job is too much for you, you're not under any obligation because it's us. You know that, don't you?"

"I do, and while I appreciate the out, I'm in for the long haul. No worries."

"If you need anything, darlin', you know where we are," Reid added.

"Thank you both. Don't worry about me. Stay focused on finishing cooking my niece or nephew."

Kate rested her hands on her huge belly. "That's about all I'm good for these days."

Maggie laughed at the bored-senseless face Kate made and went back to the kitchen, where Jill was locked in a passionate embrace with Ashton. "Get a room, will ya? Oh wait, you live together, so why you gotta do that here?"

"Don't be a grouch, Maggie," Jill said while gazing at Ashton's face. "I'm outta here."

"Drive carefully," Jill said.

"Bye, Maggie," Ashton said.

Maggie drove home through the darkness, thinking about her sisters and the happiness they'd found with Reid and Ashton. She'd never come anywhere near finding what they had. She thought she had once… Thinking about that—about him—made her ache, so she tried to never let her mind revisit that difficult time when she was in college and thought she'd found "the one," until he'd cheated on her and broken her heart. Sometimes, when she was with her happily-in-love sisters, it was hard not to think back to that heady first love, the one she'd thought would last forever.

Why was she thinking about that when she had so many positive things to focus on? Her new job, new home, new niece or nephew, the upcoming visit with the family and Jill's wedding next month… Life was good and busy and fulfilling. She had absolutely no reason to be dwelling on the past.

As she took the turn down the long lane that led to home, she vowed to stay focused on the present and the future.

She was done living in the past.

"Do you think Maggie's all right?" Kate asked Reid after he'd helped her change into a nightgown and get into bed. She was so big that she needed help with the simplest things these days. While she couldn't wait to meet her baby, she was also looking forward to not being pregnant anymore. How pregnancy was supposedly the most natural thing in the world was beyond her comprehension.

Wearing only boxers, he slid into bed and snuggled up to her. "She's adjusting to her new home and job, and there're apt to be some bumps along the way."

Kate had forgotten how to sleep without his arms around her, not that he could get them "around" her these days. "I worry that she wouldn't tell us if it wasn't working for her."

"She would."

"She wouldn't want to let us down."

"We'll keep an eye on her. Try not to worry." He kissed her forehead. "You want me to rub your back?"

"That's okay."

"I don't mind."

"I know."

"What's the matter, darlin'?"

"I'm so tired of being fat and gross, and I want to have sex with you, but I can't because of this ridiculous belly, and… Are you *laughing*? If you're laughing, I'm going to kill you."

"Well, first you'd have to catch me, and that's going to be a problem."

"I can't believe you're making fun of me when *you did this to me!*"

"I'm not making fun of you."

"Yes, you are, and I'm going to remember this when I'm no longer fat and you're the one who wants sex."

"Sweetheart, if you want sex, all you have to do is say so."

"We can't! I'll break you with this thing."

He shook with silent laughter.

"If you don't stop laughing at me, I'm going to divorce you."

"No, you aren't."

"Yes, I am."

"If you divorce me, you won't have sex tonight."

"Now you're just being mean to me."

He cozied up even closer, running his hand over the obscene bump and down to her leg. "My sweet, sweet love, I would never be mean to you, as you well know. If my baby mama is feeling needy, all she has to do is tell me, and we'll take care of that."

"The belly is massive."

"And your husband is endlessly creative." From behind her, he cupped her sensitive breasts and had her quickly ready for more.

Her body was an endless source of fascination to her as the pregnancy neared the end. Right when she would've thought sex would be the last thing on her mind, she found herself craving it. Kate had mostly kept that information to herself, because she feared her husband was put off by her obscenely large belly. She should've known better.

His hand slid down her front, gently sliding over the baby bump.

Kate shivered from the nearly painful need she felt for him.

Her nightgown slid up over her legs, which moved restlessly as she sought relief.

"Easy, sweetheart. Nice and easy."

She was so primed that all he had to do was slide his fingers over the tight knot of nerves between her legs to send her spiraling into an intense orgasm.

"Mmm, I do so *love* pregnant Kate. We may have to do this baby-making thing again very soon."

Kate groaned. The last thing she wanted to think about right now was being pregnant—again. She already knew if they were going to have two, the second one would have to happen soon. Only when they discussed having children did the significant age difference between them matter. The rest of the time, she hardly ever thought about it.

She had learned that having an older, more experienced husband had its advantages, such as when he artfully entered her from behind and had her screaming out his name before a second, even more powerful orgasm ripped through her.

"God, yes… Kate." He held her tight against him as he found his own pleasure, surging into her and then going still behind her.

They were quiet for a long time as their bodies cooled and throbbed with aftershocks that she felt everywhere.

"Feel better?" he asked in the Tennessee drawl that had gotten her motor running for him from the first time she ever met him. In all the years they'd spent apart, one of the things she'd missed the most was the melodic sound of his voice.

"Much." Her eyes were so heavy, she could barely keep them open.

"Any time you need me, you know where to find me."

She squeezed the hand he'd placed on the swell of her abdomen. Their baby chose that moment to let them know he or she was awake.

Reid's low chuckle made her smile. "I'm afraid our little one is going to be a hellion."

"If not a hellion, perhaps a kicker on the football team."

"Or a star soccer player."

"Or a prima ballerina."

"Or a star gymnast, a downhill skier, a distance runner…"

Kate drifted off to sleep to her favorite sound in the world—her husband's voice.

CHAPTER 3

$\mathcal{M}$aggie knew what it was like to wait on tenterhooks to hear if a job offer was going to materialize, so she planned to call Brayden Thomas first thing the next morning so as not to drag out the waiting for him. She'd tossed and turned all night, running the various scenarios through her mind, and had decided that while he might have committed a crime as a juvenile, she couldn't— and wouldn't—discount the sterling professional reputation he'd built for himself in the ensuing decade.

At eight o'clock, she put through a call to him and had to leave a message on his voicemail asking him to get back to her when he could. After ending the call, she felt oddly let down that she hadn't gotten to talk to him. "Stop being stupid," she muttered as she turned her attention to her email while she waited for Teresa to come by with the morning report.

Teresa came in ten minutes later with coffees for both of them. "Morning."

Maggie had told Teresa that she could get her own coffee, but the older woman said she enjoyed taking care of people. Working nights at Matthews House was her "retirement" job. So Maggie let Teresa take care of her. Teresa had short gray hair, warm brown eyes and an endless well of compassion that made her popular with the moms.

"Morning. How's Corey?"

"I checked with the nurses' station this morning, and they were able to stop the contractions. They'd like to keep her for another twenty-four hours, just to be sure. Her friend stayed with her, and she knows to call when she's ready to come back."

"Well, that's a relief. How's everything else?"

"Quiet."

"Quiet is good."

"Agreed. The McBrides had another good morning. The kids made the bus with breakfast and time to spare."

"Two days in a row. Is it too soon to call it a streak?"

"Let's not get ahead of ourselves."

Maggie laughed.

"What's up with the hunky cowboy? The moms are talking about him."

For a second, Maggie didn't know who she meant. "You mean Brayden Thomas?"

Teresa eyed her over the top of her coffee mug. "Is that his name?"

"Uh-huh."

"And he's the therapeutic riding guy?"

"Right."

"Are you going to hire him?"

"I hope so. I'm waiting for him to call me back." Maggie wanted to ask Teresa's opinion of Brayden's sealed juvenile record, but had to respect and protect his right to privacy. So she didn't mention it. Sometimes, being an adult and an employer was hard. This was one of those times. She was going to have to trust her own gut—and Ashton's input—where Brayden was concerned.

Teresa gave a detailed report on the status of each resident. "And now I'm heading home to get some sleep."

"Have a good day. I'll see you tomorrow."

"Bright and early. Text me if there's any news on Corey."

"I will. I'll go see her today."

24

"That's nice of you. I'm sure she'll appreciate it. All righty, I'm out."

"See you." After Teresa left, Maggie dove into the reams of paperwork that were part of running the program. On any given day, she dealt with schools, hospitals, police departments and the state Department of Children's Services. That last one gave her the most angst. Inspectors showed up without warning to check on children who were under their auspices. Maggie lived in fear of something going wrong with one of those inspections, even if it would be no fault of hers if it did.

Matthews House provided food, shelter, clothing, career counseling and long-term housing assistance. Upon entering the facility, parents signed a waiver Ashton had insisted on that absolved Matthews House, the Matthews family and all employees of any responsibility for the residents or their children. In other words, it was up to each parent to care for their own children within the safe, nurturing environment provided by the facility.

Maggie had joined an online community of shelter employees in which she'd been advised not to make their facility so inviting that residents would want to stay forever. The goal was to help them get their lives stabilized by giving them a place to catch their breath and figure out next steps, but it was intended to be temporary shelter.

One family, the Rosses, would soon be moving into an apartment of their own after a two-month stay at Matthews. They were the first of what she hoped would be many success stories of families returning to independent living. Once a family completed the Matthews House program, which also included family counseling, parenting classes when needed and financial planning, they were given a stipend to help secure an apartment.

In planning for the opening of Matthews House, Reid and Kate had consulted with numerous experts and tried to think of everything needed to help families in crisis. They had a wide variety of resources available to Maggie and the staff, as needed, including substance abuse and domestic violence counseling.

As she checked the ever-evolving program website and made a list of needed updates, she had the feeling she was being watched. "Good morning, Travis."

"Good morning, Ms. Maggie. Can we go see the horses today?"

She glanced at the adorable four-year-old boy. He had light-brown skin, curly dark hair and chubby cheeks that gave him the look of a cherubic elf. When he and his mother, Kelsey, first arrived, his little face had been covered with bruises and his brown eyes had been dull and lifeless. Watching him—and his mom—learn to smile and trust again had been among the most rewarding experiences of Maggie's life. "We absolutely can go see the horses. Does your mom know where you are?"

"I told her I was coming to see you and the horses."

"Then that's what we must do. Let's get them some treats." Maggie followed Travis into the kitchen, where he went straight to the fridge to get the bag of carrots while Maggie cut some apples. She loved how comfortable the child was in his temporary home and enjoyed the time she spent with him while the older kids were at school.

"You're sure you told your mom where you were going, right?"

"Yes, ma'am."

As they were leaving the kitchen, one of the other moms was coming in. "Travis and I are heading to the stables if Kelsey is looking for him."

"I told her this time, Ms. Maggie. I promise."

Smiling, Maggie held out her hand to him.

He took her hand and half dragged her out the door.

When she'd conceived of the therapeutic riding program, it had been with children like Travis in mind, children who'd seen and experienced traumatic events and needed to rebuild their self-esteem and confidence. In the stables, they encountered Derek, the elderly groom who'd worked for the Matthews family for years overseeing the horses and stables. He had white hair and the leathery complexion of a man who'd spent his life working outdoors. For years, Reid had tried to talk him into retiring with a full pension, but Derek had said he'd die of boredom.

Derek shook hands with Travis. "I was wondering when you were going to come visit."

Travis lit up at the sight of Derek, who was very good with the children.

"Did you bring treats?"

"Yes, sir."

The child's manners were, as always, delightful. "I've got a stall I need you to help me clean. Are you up for the job?"

"Yes, sir!"

"Let's get to it, then."

While listening to Derek guide Travis through the cleaning of stalls, Maggie visited each of the horses, gave them carrots and attention and an extra snuggle for Thunder, who was missing Kate. "We'll get out for a ride this week," Maggie promised him.

Thunder responded with a nicker that made Maggie laugh. They had no doubt a human was trapped inside the horse's gorgeous body.

Her cell phone rang, and when she saw the number on the screen, an odd zing of adrenaline went through her, making her heart beat faster. Before she could take the time to process what the hell that was about, the phone quit ringing. Maggie was about to call back when it rang again. She jumped on it.

"Maggie Harrington."

"Hey, this is Brayden Thomas. Sorry about the first call. I'm driving and hit a dead zone."

"No problem."

"I'm returning your call."

"Right, well, I'm hoping you're still interested in the job at Matthews House."

"I am."

"Excellent." Maggie ran through the salary that would be paid through the grant, not that he needed to know about those details, as well as the benefits Reid and Kate offered to all their employees.

"That sounds great. I should mention that I have a weeklong trip planned with some friends at the end of this week. I can either start before that or after it. Whichever you prefer."

"Before is fine with me. The other apartment over the stables is available for your use."

"That'd be great. I have my own horse, too. I assume I can bring him and board him on the property?"

"Yes, of course. I'll mention that to Derek, our stable manager, who lives in the other apartment."

"Great. I'll head there later today, then."

Like *today*? "Great."

"I'm looking forward to working with you and the residents."

"Likewise. I'll look for you later."

"I'll text you my ETA when I have it." He was relocating from the Chattanooga area, where he'd worked for a horse farm.

"Sounds good. Safe travels." Maggie stashed her phone in her back pocket and went to find Derek and Travis.

"He's a heck of a hard worker," Derek said of Travis, who was raking the stall with fierce determination.

"I can see that. We'll have to put him on the payroll at this rate."

"What's a payroll?" Travis asked.

"It's the word businesses use to describe how they pay their employees," Maggie explained.

"So it's like money?"

"It *is* money."

"I like money."

Maggie and Derek laughed.

"You keep up the good work, and I'll make sure you get a little green stuff," Derek said.

Travis gave Derek a high five. "Yes!"

Maggie made a mental note to spot Derek some petty cash to pay for Travis's help. "Are you guys set for the next little while?"

"Yes, ma'am," Derek said. "I'll bring him back in when he's done."

"Have fun."

"We will."

"By the way, I wanted to let you know I've hired Brayden Thomas to run our equine therapy program."

"Glad to hear it. Seemed like a nice young man."

"He'll be bringing his horse with him."

"We'll make him feel welcome, ma'am."

"Appreciate that."

Maggie went back to the main house, amused at being called ma'am by a man fifty years older than her, but since moving to Tennessee, she'd learned not to question the manners of Southern gentlemen. She appreciated the attention Derek gave to each of the children, who were fascinated by horses the way she'd been as a child. She'd begged for riding lessons at eight. Her parents had finally relented when she turned nine, and she'd been hooked ever since.

One of the things that had most appealed to her about this job opportunity was the close proximity to horses and the chance to ride any time she wanted. Although, as it had turned out, she was far too busy to ride most days. If she got to do it once during the workweek, that was a great week. Despite the frenetic pace of her days, the move to Tennessee had been a good one. She loved the job, the horses and having her sisters nearby.

Her biggest challenge was protecting her own heart from some of the horrible things that happened to the people who came to them for help. She'd had the same issue when she'd provided interpretation for the hearing impaired at criminal trials in New York. Some of the things she'd seen and heard then would stay with her forever.

It was a relief to be away from that and other things she'd left behind there, things she tried not to think about so she could stay focused on the present rather than the past. Too bad that was easier said than done sometimes. Some things could never be forgotten.

CHAPTER 4

*M*aggie's day got busy when a new family arrived via Uber, in need of temporary shelter because the mother's cancer diagnosis made it impossible for her to work during treatment. After getting a call from a local social services agency, Maggie was ready to meet Trish Lawson and her three children, Lily, Jimmy and Chloe, ages six, five and two. She set up the children to have snacks in the kitchen so she could meet with Trish in the conference room they'd made out of the former dining room. Maggie could hear Trish's sobs as she approached the conference room.

Maggie ducked into her office to grab a box of tissues and brought that and the coffee Trish had asked for when Maggie offered her something to drink. "Here we go," Maggie said, trying to project cool competence in the midst of Trish's despair.

"Thank you."

At about five-foot-five, the woman's lovely light-brown face was streaked with tears, and the scarf on her head had slid to the left side, making her look lopsided.

Maggie wanted to put her arms around her and tell her everything would be all right, except she'd learned not to make promises she couldn't keep. She had no way to know if everything would work out for their clientele. All she could do was give them her very best effort during the time she had with them.

Trish dabbed at her eyes with a tissue. "I'm so sorry."

"Please don't be. We're here to help."

"Thank God for that, because I didn't know where else to turn. I heard about your program from a friend, and when the landlord told me to be out by today or he was bringing the police, I had nowhere else to go. I contacted one agency, but they couldn't take us all. They referred me to you."

Maggie handed her another tissue. "I'm very glad you came here and that we had an opening available for you and your children."

"I never thought this would happen to me," she said softly. "I had a decent job. I paid my rent every month and took care of my kids. But when I got sick with ovarian cancer... I just couldn't keep up."

"Of course you couldn't. No one could."

"My friends have helped so much, but none of them have room for four of us, and my family lives in Texas. My doctors are here. I just... I don't know..."

Maggie put her hand over Trish's. "Take a deep breath. You and your children are safe here."

Trish broke down into deep sobs.

Maggie got up to hug the other woman. "Our staff nurse, Arnelle, will be able to help you with side effects of treatment, coordinating with doctors and anything else you need."

Trish clung to her. "Thank you so, so much. You have no idea what a godsend you are to me."

Over the next hour, Maggie went back and forth between checking the children, who were now in the playroom with several of the other kids and their mothers, and helping Trish complete intake paperwork. By the time she got them settled in their room upstairs, it was after three o'clock, and her plan to visit Corey in the hospital before dinner was in jeopardy.

She would go later.

While she had one minute to herself, she sat in her desk chair and closed her eyes, breathing through the emotional storm that each new heartbreaking story brought into her life. She loved the job, loved the people, loved the challenge, loved that she was making a real difference for people in crisis. But sometimes… Sometimes it was too much for her to handle. Not that she would ever admit that to anyone.

God forbid Reid and Kate ever have second thoughts about giving her the job of a lifetime. She wanted to make them proud and help as many people as she could.

The sound of a throat clearing had Maggie opening her eyes to find Brayden Thomas standing in her doorway.

"Sorry to interrupt."

"You're not. I was taking five after a difficult intake."

"No need to explain yourself to me." Holding the worn cowboy hat in his hands, he looked ridiculously large and hopelessly sexy standing in the doorway. "I was told to come check in with you."

Maggie pulled herself together and stood. "Yes, I can walk you through the onboarding process." She reached for the clipboard she'd put together earlier and set him up in the conference room. "Can I get you anything to drink?"

"Some water would be great."

"Coming right up." She checked on the children in the playroom on the way to the kitchen and was pleased to see Trish's children happily playing with the wide assortment of toys that Reid and Kate had sprung for. They'd spared no expense when it came to ensuring the children had everything they could possibly want. Maggie had joked that the playroom resembled an FAO Schwarz store. Every one of the children who walked through their doors marveled at the toys in that room.

Kate had said that shopping trip had been among the most fun things she'd ever done.

Maggie took a tall glass of ice water back to the conference room. "Here you are."

"Thanks a lot." Brayden drank half the glass in one big gulp. "Starting to get hot out there."

It's starting to get hot in here, too, Maggie thought, holding back the ridiculous need to giggle like an eighth-grade girl.

The man was too handsome for words. In addition to broad shoulders, he had silky dark hair that had a tendency to slide down over his brow, golden brown eyes and lashes every woman she knew would kill for. His cheekbones were prominent, his jaw chiseled and covered with the perfect amount of stubble. As he filled out the forms, Maggie discovered he was left-handed, and his plush lips moved adorably as he wrote. Shifting her gaze to his right hand, which was flat on the table, she noted that his hands were as big as the rest of him.

"I feel like I'm being watched," he said without lifting his gaze from the paperwork.

Maggie's face went warm with embarrassment. "Sorry. I was thinking about something else." *Liar.*

"I can bring these in to you when I'm finished if you have other stuff to do."

"Sure. Thanks." Mortified, she got up and left the room. So far, he'd caught her taking what looked to be a nap in the middle of the workday and had called her out for staring at him. "Great way to start a professional relationship."

"What was that?" Mitch, the cook, asked as he came in the kitchen door carrying shopping bags. He made dinner for the residents each evening and provided instruction for those who wished to learn basic cooking skills. In his mid-fifties, Mitch was retired from the Marine Corps and wore his gray hair in a buzz cut.

"Just talking to myself."

"First sign of senility."

"Very funny."

"Heard you're bringing in some more testosterone."

"You heard right."

"He's some kind of horse whisperer or something, right?"

"That's what they say. I've hired him to run a therapeutic riding program for the children."

"It'll be good for the kids to have access to that. The things some of them talk about…" He shook his head. "Hard to hear."

"I know. If you need support—"

"I'm okay. I just worry about them, about the long-term fallout."

33

"We'll do everything we can for them, now and into the future. My sister and brother-in-law want Matthews House to be a long-term source of support for our families. They have so many plans to expand into scholarships and other forms of support long after they've moved on from here. We're going to be there for them, Mitch."

"It's a really good thing y'all are doing here. I'm glad to be part of it."

"We're happy to have you. I'll let you get back to work."

"It's taco night," he called over his shoulder as he continued toward the kitchen. "The kids will be happy. It's their favorite."

Maggie smiled. Happy, safe kids were what they were all about. Her cell phone rang, and she took the call from Jill. "Hey."

"What's up?" Jill asked.

"The usual chaos. You?"

"Wedding madness. I think Mom is more excited about this wedding than I am."

"That's absolutely not true."

Jill laughed. "She and Andi are having too much fun planning it." Their mom was working with Andi, who, as the manager of the Infinity Newport Hotel where the wedding would take place, was seeing to most of the details herself.

"Can a person have too much fun?"

"If they can, Mom is."

"Well, good for her," Maggie said. "Whatever she wants, right?"

"You said it."

Ever since their mother had miraculously recovered from a three-year coma that doctors had once said was irreversible, her daughters had indulged her every whim. They were so damned happy to have Clare back in their lives, they didn't care what she asked of them.

"I'm calling to remind you about the interview tomorrow."

For a brief second, Maggie's brain went completely blank as she stood in her office, facing the window that looked over the back side of the vast property. "Uh, what interview?"

"Maggie! Come on! You said you'd do it with us. We're counting on you."

The details came back to her all of a sudden, a sit-down with one of the local news shows with Kate and Jill. Apparently, people were interested in how Kate Harrington had both her sisters working with her in Nashville, and Kate had agreed to the interview, provided they got it done before the baby arrived. "Stand down, Counselor. I said I'd do it, and I will." Even if it would require hair and makeup before noon, something that rarely happened these days.

"They're coming to Kate's at ten tomorrow."

"I'll be there."

"At nine, for hair and makeup."

"Yes, ma'am."

"Ashton said you found someone for your therapeutic riding program?"

"I did. He's starting today."

"Congratulations, Maggie. You worked so hard to make that happen. I'm happy for you."

As the baby sister of two insanely accomplished women, Maggie basked in the glow of her eldest sister's praise. "Thanks. I'm excited about it."

"It's such an amazing thing you, Kate and Reid are doing there."

"Mostly them. Without their support, I couldn't do what I do."

"It's mostly *you*, Maggie. They would say the same thing. Don't sell yourself short. You're changing people's lives with that program."

"That's the goal."

"You sound down. What's wrong?"

"Nothing at all. I'm not down. Just busy."

"You swear? You'd tell me or Kate or both of us if you weren't okay, wouldn't you?"

"I would."

"Promise?"

"Yes, Jill," Maggie said, exasperated. "I promise. I'll see you in the morning."

"See you then. Love you."

"Love you, too." She ended the call, muttering about overprotective older sisters who felt the need to constantly mother her. That, too, was a holdover from their mother's accident, when Jill and Kate had become much more than older sisters to Maggie. They, along with their stepmother, Andi, had been the ones to see Maggie though adolescence, puberty, her first period, her first date and many other milestones.

They were much more than siblings to her, and she was so happy to be able to see them all the time again. She loved them even more than the horses. "But sometimes they drive me crazy with their mothering. I have a mother. I have *two* mothers, counting Andi."

From the doorway came the deep sound of a male clearing his throat. Maggie closed her eyes and counted to five. Dear God, now the man had heard her talking to herself, too? She opened her eyes and turned to him, forcing a smile. "All set with the paperwork?"

To his credit, he didn't mention what he'd overheard. "Yes, ma'am."

"No, sir."

"Ma'am?"

"You're not going to ma'am me." She glanced at his paperwork, which listed his date of birth. "You're four years older than me. I'm *Maggie*. Not ma'am."

"Sorry, ma'am… Er, I mean Maggie." And the accent… Sigh. It was on the same dreaminess level as Reid's and Ashton's. God help her, but he was temptation personified.

Maggie scowled at him, trying to maintain some semblance of professionalism. "Being called ma'am makes me feel like I'm eighty."

He smiled, and holy wow. That smile took him from handsome to staring-at-the-sun gorgeous.

She blinked, forcing herself to act somewhat professional in the face of unreasonable male beauty. Taking the clipboard from him, she put it on her desk. "Let me show you to your accommodations." She gestured for him to lead the way, and after locking her office door, she followed him to the driveway, where a huge black pickup truck and horse trailer were parked.

They walked to the stables, where Maggie introduced Brayden to Derek.

"Welcome," Derek said as the two men shook hands. "I'll get you set up with a stall for your horse."

"That'd be great. Thank you."

"My pleasure."

Maggie gestured to a set of stairs. "The apartment is up there."

She led the way up the stairs, aware of him behind her and thankful for the jeans she'd splurged on in New York that flattered her figure, even as she told herself to quit having such stupid thoughts in a *professional* situation. Hadn't she learned her lesson with the last guy she'd met through her work?

The memories came over her in a flood of images, things she would never forget. She shuddered in revulsion, and for a terrifying second, she feared she might be sick in front of her new employee. At the top of the stairs, she paused, took a deep breath, tried to find her equilibrium.

"Are you all right?" Brayden asked.

Damn it, Maggie thought. The last thing she needed was a new employee seeing her undone over things that happened months ago and should've been long forgotten by now. It'd been a while since she'd awoken in a cold sweat after having dreamed about that night and months since she'd moved hundreds of miles away from *him*. Why was *he* resurfacing now, in the middle of an ordinary workday?

"Yes," she said, "I'm fine."

Taking another deep breath, she released it and gestured to the door on the right. "Derek lives there. Your place is here." She opened the door on the left side of the landing and led the way inside to a cozy studio apartment with a combined living area/kitchen, a bathroom and bedroom. "It's not much, but it's clean, and the furniture is new."

"It's more than enough for me. I don't need much."

He was so tall, he could reach up and touch the seven-foot ceiling. The small apartment seemed smaller with him standing in the living area.

She handed him a set of keys. "You'll find sheets and towels in the bathroom closet, and there's a laundry room off the kitchen that you're welcome to use."

"Sounds great. Thank you."

"I'll leave you to get settled. Let me know if you need anything."

"I will. Thanks again."

Maggie went down the stairs, eager for some fresh air and a moment alone to recover her equilibrium. Why now? Why when she was showing Brayden to his quarters had those memories popped into her mind to remind her that she could run but she could not hide from the nightmare she'd left behind in New York? Tears burned her eyes as she walked to the back side of the stables to a well-worn path, beaten down by years of feet and hooves traversing it.

She put her head down and walked toward a meadow that Kate had told her was among her favorite places on the vast property. In the distance, Maggie could see the windsock that marked one end of the runway and the hangar where Reid and Ashton kept their Cessna. When Maggie had fallen off a ladder and been badly injured years ago, Reid had flown Kate home to Rhode Island to be with her.

Keep thinking about things like that, how surprised she'd been to see Kate there when she woke up from hours of being unconscious, how her mother, stepmother and sisters had helped her with everything for months as she grappled with two broken arms. *Think about that.* At the time, Maggie had thought having two broken arms was the worst thing that would ever happen to her. She'd since learned it could get so much worse.

Think about the boys... Eric, John and Rob, who were her father's sons with Andi, and Max and Nick, her mother's sons with Aidan. Her brothers had brought her endless amounts of love and joy, especially Eric, who was not only her brother but one of her closest friends. The two of them had shared a special bond since Andi and Eric first came to live with her family, and that bond had only deepened over the years.

Maggie told herself to think about John and Rob, who were in the thick of their Little League baseball schedule and full of excitement about each game. John was a pitcher, Rob a catcher, the two of them the stars of their team.

And Max and Nick, who were getting so big and always wanted to talk to Maggie when she FaceTimed with their mom. They didn't understand why she didn't love skateboarding and hockey as much as they did.

Whenever the memories of that night returned to haunt her, she tried to power through them, to think of the people she loved, the new niece or nephew who'd be arriving soon and her many blessings. If only she could blot out the things that haunted her, including the vision of her mother being hit by that car all those years ago and one horrific night now seven months in the past, but still far too present for her liking.

Maybe if she'd told someone…

"No. I'm not telling anyone. What good will that do? It wouldn't change anything, and it would only upset the person I tell. I need to just stop thinking about it, put it in the past where it belongs and move the fuck on."

Maggie screamed with frustration, thankful for the vast open space where she could vent to the passing breeze without fear of being overheard.

CHAPTER 5

*S*tanding at the window that overlooked the rolling hills of the Matthews estate, Brayden watched Maggie walk away. Hands tucked into the pockets of her denim jacket, shoulders rounded, she projected the aura of having the weight of the world on her slim shoulders.

He hadn't gotten that vibe from her in their previous meeting. If anything, she'd impressed him with her calm competence in a job that probably took a lot out of her emotionally and physically. He understood that dynamic, having worked with kids in crisis for much of his career. They could break your heart with their pain as much as their resilience.

She'd left a whole other impression on him after their first meeting, one that had given him pause about taking this job. For days afterward, he'd thought about the most striking blue eyes he'd ever seen, as well as her lovely face and long dark hair that she'd worn tied into a messy bun. She'd had an all-business way about her during the interview, but her compassion for the population she served had come through in the way she'd talked about the facility and what she, her famous sister and brother-in-law hoped to achieve there.

Other than those incredible blue eyes, Maggie looked nothing at all like her sister, whose career Brayden had followed from the start. Working for Kate Harrington, albeit indirectly, was a huge honor and part of the reason the job had interested him so much.

He'd been attracted to Maggie as a man from the first time he met her, and that attraction had initially given him pause about taking the job. The last thing he needed was personal drama in the place where he worked and lived. However, despite the sterling reputation he'd developed in his field, Matthews House had been the only offer he'd received during several months of interviewing. Declining the job wasn't an option.

Brayden's last job had ended abruptly when the program lost funding, and after casting his net in a hundred-mile radius over the last few months, he'd come up dry. He'd heard about the opening at Matthews House through the grapevine and had jumped on the opportunity. Funding wouldn't be a problem at this place, not with Kate Harrington and Reid Matthews backing it. The former developer was nearly as well known in Tennessee as his wife was.

Brayden watched Maggie until she was out of sight and then turned to take another look at his quarters. The apartment was small, but clean and nicely furnished. Best of all, it was free and offered as part of the job, along with boarding for Sunday Morning, his beloved quarter horse.

He sat on the unmade bed and released a deep breath that was equal parts relief and anticipation. After suddenly losing his job two months ago, he'd been getting increasingly more nervous as the weeks went by without finding something new. The savings account he'd worked so hard to grow had taken a big hit from paying to board Sunday while he job hunted. He'd had a lot of interest from a wide variety of employers, but none of them had openings available.

The call from Maggie had solved a huge problem for him, not that he'd ever tell her that. She was under the impression that she'd gotten someone who was in hot demand, not a guy down to his last couple thousand dollars. He was determined to make the therapeutic riding program at Matthews House a huge success for her and the children, and when the time was right, he wanted to talk to her about possibly expanding the program to other children in the community.

Despite his successes, he carried a deep well of insecurity about his chosen career path, especially when it took months to land a new position. He certainly hadn't expected that when he found out his other job was ending abruptly. The long job search had given him far too much time to question every choice he'd ever made, every fight he'd waged to live the life he felt called to. He'd sacrificed a lot to follow his dreams, and the period of unemployment had seriously messed with his sense of security and purpose. That, coupled with the sudden loss of his mother and biggest cheerleader, had rocked him to the core.

Standing, he vowed to shake off the insecurity and to move forward. This was the start of a whole new opportunity with a well-funded program that was already getting rave reviews from the social services sector. He'd asked around before he accepted the job, wanting to be sure the program was solid. Everyone he'd talked to said they'd heard great things about Matthews House since it had opened in March.

So he'd snapped up the job and was determined to make it work, which was why he absolutely could not be having inappropriate thoughts about his new boss.

Brayden went down the stairs to get Sunday Morning settled in her new home. First, he had to ask Derek where he wanted Brayden's horse to live. He found Derek supervising a little guy as he raked hay in one of the empty stalls.

"Hi there," Brayden said when he approached them.

The child dropped the rake and ran to Derek, hiding behind him.

"Hey, Brayden."

Brayden leaned forward, trying to catch the child's gaze, but he was looking down at the ground. "Good to see you again, sir. Who've you got there?"

"This is Travis. He's a very good worker if you ever need help with your horse."

"I always need help with my horse. How long has he worked for you?"

"Just about a week now," Derek said, "but he's become a key member of the team."

"Good to know."

The little boy peeked out from behind Derek, taking stock of the newcomer.

While Derek kept an arm around the boy, Brayden squatted to put himself at the child's level. "Hey, Travis, I'm Brayden." He extended his hand to the child, who looked at his hand for a long moment before he reached out to shake it. "It's really nice to meet you."

The child took back his hand and looked down at the floor. Baby steps.

"Do you like to ride horses, Travis?"

His gaze flipped up, filled with raw yearning that touched Brayden deeply. "I think so."

"You don't know?"

Travis shook his head.

"Have you ever ridden?"

He shook his head again.

"Well, we'll have to change that. What are you doing later today?"

Travis glanced up at Derek, seeming to gauge the more familiar man's reaction.

"My horse, Sunday Morning, loves to take little boys just like you for rides. Would you like to do that?"

He looked at Brayden with big, solemn dark eyes and nodded.

"What do you say?" Derek asked.

"Please and thank you," Travis said quickly.

"We'll have to ask your mom first. Do you want to go get her while I unload Sunday Morning and get her settled?"

Travis nodded again and was off like a shot toward the house.

"Never seen him move that fast," Derek said, laughing. "He's a good little guy. Quiet, but well behaved."

"Do we know his story?"

"Only that he and his mom left an abusive relationship. Had bruises all over his face when he first got here."

Brayden processed that information with the usual feeling of dread when he considered what the child had probably been through. He'd worked with a lot of traumatized kids in his career, and it never got easier to hear about what they'd endured, especially in light of his own history. "Will the mom allow him to ride?"

"I'm sure she will. She's been very supportive of him working in the stables with me. It's taken a few days, but he's starting to talk more than he did at first."

"Good to know. Where can I put Sunday?"

"Third stall on the left, across from Thunder. He's Ms. Kate's pride and joy. He just came in from sunning himself in the paddock."

Brayden went to take a look at the stall and took a second to say hello to Thunder, a dark-coated thoroughbred with wise eyes and a gentle demeanor. "Hey, guy," Brayden said, caressing the gorgeous horse's nose. "I hear you're the star around here, huh?"

"You got that right. Ms. Kate and Ms. Maggie are crazy about him. He gets a lot of attention, well, a little less since Ms. Kate has been expecting. She moved him over here so he could get lots of attention from Ms. Maggie, but Ms. Kate still visits him on the regular."

"So she comes by the house?"

"Oh, yeah. She and Mr. Reid are hands-on benefactors, although Ms. Maggie is in charge. They come once in a while."

Brayden tried to imagine what it would be like to actually *meet* Kate Harrington.

"A little starstruck, are you?" Derek chuckled as he followed Brayden to the trailer, where they worked together to unload Sunday.

"I love her music. I can't believe I'm actually working for her."

"She's good people. You'll like her. I have to admit, I was a little shocked when she and Mr. Reid first got together."

"Because he's so much older than her?"

"Yeah, but when you see them together... Well, it's obvious they're both exactly where they belong."

"Seems that way from what I've seen of them on TV and stuff."

"They're very happy, and their little one is due any time."

They got Sunday settled in her new home, filled her water, gave her a leaf of hay and left her to get acclimated while Derek showed Brayden the tack room, where there was already a spot labeled with Sunday Morning's name. Something about that small gesture made Brayden feel very much at home.

"Feel free to make use of anything you need."

Brayden shook his hand. "Really appreciate your help."

"Happy to have you on the team. You can park the rig around back. There's plenty of space out there. Let me know if you need anything else."

"I will. Thanks again." Brayden spent the rest of the afternoon unpacking his truck and settling into his new home.

Travis came out with his mom, Kelsey, to meet Brayden.

"I understand you offered to let him ride your horse."

He couldn't help but hear hesitance in the woman's voice. "Yes, ma'am. I'd be happy to teach him everything he needs to know."

"I'm a little reluctant to let him get hooked on riding when I know I won't be able to afford it after we leave here."

"He'd be welcome to come back to ride with me any time he'd like to."

Travis tugged on his mother's hand. *"Please*, Mama. Can I?"

Kelsey's eyes glistened with unshed tears. "Y'all are so kind. I've never encountered so much kindness."

"We're here to help in any way we can."

"Thank you so much." She squatted to talk directly to her son. "Mr. Brayden is in charge. You do whatever he tells you to do, and you mind your manners. Understand?"

"Yes, Mama."

She kissed his cheek. "Go ahead, then. Have fun and be careful."

Over the next half hour, he went through each step of the saddling process with Travis, teaching him the names of the various items and showing him how to use them. The child was a quick learner and asked numerous intelligent questions that impressed Brayden.

He helped Travis into an age-appropriate helmet before giving him a leg up into a child-sized saddle. While Kelsey watched from the fence that surrounded the paddock, Brayden led the horse around in big circles, letting the child get a feel for the mare.

"You're doing great. Sunday likes you."

"How can you tell?"

"She's got her head up, her tail is moving and her steps are lively. She's enjoying this as much as you are."

"This is the best day of my whole life."

That right there was the kind of comment that made this the most rewarding career he ever could've chosen to pursue, not that there'd ever been a question in his mind about the right path for him.

After at least fifty circles around the paddock, he showed Travis the steps of removing the saddle and let the little guy carry it to the tack room, where he hung it on the hook below Sunday's name. "You did a great job. Next time, I'll show you how to groom her. I'm going to take her for a ride before I do that."

"What do you say to Mr. Brayden?" Kelsey asked.

"Thank you so much, Mr. Brayden."

"You're very welcome. We'll do it again soon, okay?"

Travis nodded and ran off toward the house.

"Thank you again," Kelsey said. "I haven't seen him smile like that in a long time."

"Hope you got some good pictures."

"I did."

"Have a nice evening."

"You, too."

As the sun headed for the horizon, he put his saddle on Sunday and headed out for a ride, since they both needed the exercise.

They set out on the path behind the stables and followed it for miles through lush, rolling green hills that made up the Matthews property. Fields of wildflowers added splashes of color to the vista. His mother would know the name of every one of those flowers. Brayden never had been able to remember them, despite her trying to teach him.

And now it was too late. His heart ached from the fresh loss of the woman who'd given him everything she could, who'd stood by him through the worst of times. He was still trying to figure out his place in a world that no longer included her.

As always, he and Sunday were in perfect harmony as they moved together as one being. She was the best horse he'd ever had, in many ways his soul mate. They understood each other in a way he'd never achieved with anyone other than his mother. She had encouraged him to follow his dreams no matter where they led.

Tears filled Brayden's eyes. How could she be gone just like that with no warning that life as he knew it was going to change in an instant?

The same week he'd lost his job, the police had come to tell him she'd been killed instantly in a car accident. Even two months later, he still couldn't believe she was really gone. He still reached for the phone every day to call or text her and had to remind himself she wasn't there. Lost in his thoughts and mired in relentless grief, he rode much farther than he'd intended to. Darkness was falling by the time he turned Sunday to head back toward the stable. He slowed their pace in deference to the falling light so there was no chance she could be injured.

That was his greatest fear now that his mom was gone, that something would happen to the other woman in his life. It was him and Sunday against the world. He was nearly back to the house when another horse and rider came around the stable, heading toward him and Sunday.

He brought her to a stop as Maggie came alongside them, riding Thunder. Brayden noticed the smooth way she handled the large horse and the confidence with which she rode. Her long dark hair was pulled back into a ponytail that was almost as long as Thunder's tail. The hairstyle made her look ten years younger.

"Did you have a nice ride?" she asked.

"I did. Beautiful property."

"It's gorgeous. I love it here. I wondered if I would, having been raised on the coast."

"Where?"

47

"Rhode Island. Newport area."

"Fancy."

She shrugged. "It's home. What about you?"

"Right here in Tennessee." He glanced at the sun firing the horizon. "You're heading out late."

"Just going for a short one so Thunder can stretch his legs. I'd better get to it. Are you all settled in?"

"Yes, thanks. Good to go."

"There's dinner in the main house if you're interested. Make yourself at home."

"Thanks very much."

"I'll see you in the morning." She nudged Thunder forward, and he took off, apparently eager to move.

For a long time after she left, Brayden kept Sunday on the path facing sideways so he could watch her go. He told himself he was watching the horse, but when he was still there ten minutes later, he had to acknowledge that he found the rider every bit as stunning as the horse.

CHAPTER 6

*M*aggie was late getting to Kate's the next morning. By the time she arrived, Kate and Jill were already through hair and makeup, while she looked like she'd just fallen off the turnip truck. That was nothing new. She'd spent her entire life trying to catch up to her older sisters. "Sorry I'm late. Rough morning at the ranch."

"Everything okay?"

"It is now." She didn't want to talk about several of the kids getting into a hair-pulling fight at breakfast or how Brayden Thomas had intervened before she could and diffused the situation with calm resolve that had further impressed her. She didn't want to talk about the uncomfortable attraction she felt for her new employee, because it was inappropriate for her to think he was hotter than the sun. "Where do you want me?"

"This way." LeAnn and Marcy had done Kate's hair and makeup for years, so both were familiar to Maggie.

"Ladies, you have a big job to do here," Maggie said gravely.

"This is nothing." LeAnn put a cape over Maggie's shoulders. "We've seen much worse."

Maggie laughed. "Good to know it can actually be worse."

Over the next twenty minutes, the two women brought about a minor miracle. By the time they were finished, Maggie's dark hair was shining and straightened and her makeup subtly but artfully applied.

"Thank you for making it so I won't embarrass my sisters."

"No chance of that, honey," Marcy said. "You're a stunner. Those eyes of yours and Kate's are to die for."

"They come right from our mom."

"Bluest eyes I've ever seen."

Jill came into the master bedroom as LeAnn was removing the cape. "Are you ready?"

"As ready as I'll ever be." Maggie followed Jill to the massive great room that had been transformed into a TV studio with cameras, lights and wires running every which way. Three chairs had been positioned together with Kate in the middle, Jill to her right and Maggie to her left.

"You girls clean up rather well," Kate said when they were miked and seated.

"Thanks to your glam squad. This," Maggie said, making a circle around her head, "would never be possible without professional intervention."

"What she said," Jill replied.

"You guys are selling yourselves short. You don't need any help being gorgeous."

"Said the one who falls out of bed looking like a star every day of her life," Jill said.

Maggie laughed. "Right?"

"That is not true. Ask Reid."

"Ask Reid what?" he said when he came into the room.

"Whether Kate rolls out of bed every morning looking like a supastah," Maggie said, affecting a New England accent.

"She always looks like a supastah."

The sisters busted up laughing at him trying to do New England with his Southern twang.

"Are they laughing at me?" Reid asked the amused cameraman.

"I believe they are, sir."

"Hmm, they do that a lot. Good thing I'm not easily offended."

"You know we love you, honey," Kate said, sending her husband a warm smile that turned into a grimace.

"What?" Reid asked, immediately on alert.

Kate rested a hand on her huge belly. "Just an odd twinge."

"Another one?"

Gritting her teeth, Kate nodded.

"How long have you been having 'twinges'?" Jill asked.

"Since yesterday afternoon," Reid said, his gaze laser focused on Kate.

"Probably just more of those hideous Braxton Hicks contractions," Kate said.

Maggie glanced at Jill, wondering if Kate was in labor and didn't realize it. After this damned interview was done, they were calling the doctor.

Lila Johansen, a local news personality Kate had befriended over the years, came breezing in with her team of associates trailing behind her. One of them carried a clipboard, another toted a large cup of coffee.

Did it really take multiple people to tend to the newswoman? Maggie thought that was a ridiculous waste of resources, but kept the thought to herself. She had found that since she'd been working at Matthews House, she had far less patience for excess, waste, privilege. So many people needed so much help to survive. She was happy to be part of the solution these days, but more attuned than ever before to the many injustices the less fortunate faced on a daily basis.

Lila flashed the smile that'd made her a local celebrity. "Hello, ladies, you're looking gorgeous." Every one of her red hairs was perfectly in place, her makeup flawless.

Maggie was glad she didn't have a job that required her to look perfect all the time. She wouldn't be able to do it.

Lila bent to hug Kate and whispered something to her that had Kate smiling.

"Any second now." Kate placed a hand on her big belly. "I can't believe you're making me do this when I look like a whale."

"You look beautiful as always, and since you're taking the next year off, it's now or never."

Kate was so excited about her year off, and Maggie was proud of her sister for standing up for the life she wanted. After busting her ass in the music business for more than a decade, she deserved a break. What good was all the success and money if she didn't take some time to enjoy it?

Kate's break also meant one for Jill, who traveled with Kate.

Jill still had plenty to do running Kate's business, which required management even when the star took time off, and she was also going to be working with Ashton at his entertainment law firm in town.

"If y'all are ready," Lila said, taking a seat across from the sisters, "we'll get started."

When she began the introduction, her Southern accent disappeared. "I'm so excited today to have music superstar Kate Harrington and her sisters, Jill and Maggie Harrington, with me today for the first sit-down interview the three of them have ever done together. As many of you know, Jill is an attorney who oversees her sister's business, and Maggie has recently joined the family business as well. Ladies, thank you so much for being with us today."

"Thanks for having us," Kate said.

"Kate, you're due with your first child very soon. How're you feeling?"

"I'm feeling huge and ready to pop. I can't wait to meet this little person."

"Do you know what you're having?"

"I don't. My husband and I wanted to be surprised."

"Speaking of your husband, Reid, our viewers are fascinated by your story. Can you share a bit of that with us?"

Maggie had to fight the urge to roll her eyes. Was there anyone who followed Kate's career who *didn't* know their story by now?

"We met when I first came to Nashville, but I was just eighteen and about to launch my career. The timing wasn't right for us. When we reconnected ten years later, that was it. We've been together ever since."

"And, Jill, you're marrying Reid's son, Ashton, in July. Sisters married to a father and son. You don't hear that every day."

Jill smiled, accustomed by now to the question. "No, you don't, but that's what happened to us. Ashton and I were thrown together so often, we decided we should get married, too."

Lila laughed. "I'm sure it was more complicated than that."

She doesn't know the half of it, Maggie thought. Their relationship had been adversarial before bickering turned to love.

"Actually, my relationship with Ashton isn't complicated at all," Jill said. "I can't wait to marry him next month."

"Your wedding is being held in Newport, Rhode Island, correct?"

"That's right. My sisters and I are from there originally and still have family there."

"And, Maggie, you're now working for the family business here in Tennessee. Can you tell us about Matthews House?"

"Reid, Kate and Ashton have opened the Matthews family home to women and children in crisis, and I'm thrilled to be the director overseeing this important initiative. Since we opened in March, we've had ten families come through, one of which is about to move into a new apartment later this week. We hope to continue that track record with all the families who come to us for help."

"What an amazing idea. Kate, can you tell us how it was decided to open Matthews House?"

"We wanted to do something with Reid's family home, which was sitting empty except for the stables. When it was brought to our attention that there was a shortage of local services available to women and children in crisis, we couldn't think of a better use for the Matthews family estate. Maggie has done an outstanding job getting our program off the ground and serving the families in residence as we help them to put their lives back together."

"What an important and much-needed effort. What are some of the services you provide at Matthews House, Maggie?"

"We offer everything from career counseling to parenting courses to financial planning. We've recently hired an equine therapy specialist who'll be working with the children, and we're very excited to offer that opportunity to our clientele."

"It must be very satisfying work."

"It is, even if at times it can be heartbreaking, too. I like to think we're helping to make a difference in the lives of people who've had a variety of difficulties."

"Kate, you must be happy to have both your sisters working with you."

"I couldn't be happier. The three of us were close growing up, and Jill and I were thrilled when Maggie decided to join us."

"Kate, you've decided to take this next year off from recording and touring to stay home with your little one. Of course we're hearing from your fans who're concerned that you may be leaving the business altogether. What do you have to say to the people who're worried they've heard the last of you?"

Kate laughed. "Well, they haven't heard the last of me, but after more than a decade of writing, recording and touring, I needed a break to recharge my creative and physical batteries. The time away has already been very good for me, and with the baby coming, I'm extending it into next summer, when I may tour again on a limited basis. I'm mostly trying to find some balance between work and the rest of my life."

"Totally understandable. A career like yours takes a lot of time and energy."

"It does, but I don't want anyone to think I'm ungrateful for the amazing career I have. My fans are so supportive, and I'm thankful for every one of them. I think more than anything, I've had to concede that I'm not a machine who can go at top speed all the time."

"No one can do that, and you're wise to take a break rather than make yourself ill."

"I did make myself ill with pneumonia and didn't take the time I needed to recover from it, which led to the infamous swan dive on stage. That was a real wakeup call for me."

"That was scary for everyone who loves you."

"It was scary as hell," Jill said. "I'm really glad that Kate decided to take some time for herself after that. She's been pushing so hard for so long that something had to give."

"You must hear the rumors that fly about you."

"I do," Kate said, sighing, "and they're hurtful. I've never touched any kind of drugs, and it's a big deal for me to have champagne on New Year's Eve."

"She's a total lightweight," Jill said, laughing.

"I am," Kate said. "I always have been, which is why I barely drink. I had pneumonia and went back to work too soon. That's the truth, and when people post accusations about drug use and other lies online, I wonder if they realize there's an actual human being on the other end of those accusations. Some would say I'm asking for it by choosing to lead such a public life, but really, I choose to perform my music, not be ripped apart online. I understand these things are part of the times we live in, so I try to stay far away from the negativity and focus on the things that matter—my family, my friends, the music."

"Sounds as if you've got your priorities in order."

"That's the goal."

"Well, on behalf of your legion of fans, I wish you the best year ever and early congratulations on the arrival of your little one."

"Thank you. I'm nervous and excited at the same time."

"Thank you for being with us today, Kate, Jill and Maggie. We appreciate you taking the time from your busy schedules."

"Thanks for having us," Jill said.

"And we're out." Lila stood to shake hands with each of them. "Thanks, guys. That was terrific. The fans will be thrilled to see you, Kate, and to find out more about your sisters. We're hoping to air it later tonight."

"Thanks again, Lila," Kate said.

Jill gave Kate a hand standing up, and the three of them went into the kitchen while the TV people took down their equipment.

"Um, guys?" Kate said.

Jill and Maggie turned to her.

"Don't freak out, but if you could please tell Reid I need him to get me to the hospital, like *now*, that'd be great."

CHAPTER 7

*T*he next few hours were a blur for Maggie as she and Jill supported Kate and Reid through the early stages of labor. When she and Jill had declined to be in the delivery room for the baby's arrival, Kate had called them wimps. However, Maggie was one hundred percent sure she'd made the right decision, especially after watching Kate suffer through early labor until she reached the point where she could push.

That's when Jill and Maggie had run for their lives to the waiting room. Maggie took advantage of the opportunity to visit Corey, who was in the same unit, still being closely monitored. The goal was to give the baby another couple of weeks to develop before being born.

"I'm *so* bored," Corey moaned. The young blonde woman's hair was messy from being in bed, and her hazel eyes were rimmed with red from lack of sleep and probably a few tears. "They let me up only to use the bathroom and shower once a day, and they're making me stay because my blood pressure has been so up and down."

"It'll all be worth it to have a healthy little one."

"I know."

Maggie had wondered about the baby's father and Corey's family, but the young woman had been reluctant to share anything about her past when she first arrived at Matthews House.

"Hey, check it out!" Corey gestured to the TV where the interview Maggie and her sisters had done earlier was airing. "You're on TV."

"Oh yay." It was so weird to see herself on TV. Maggie was used to seeing Kate all the time, but not herself or Jill.

"It's so cool. I hope I get to meet Kate while I'm staying with y'all."

"She's going to be pretty busy having a newborn for the next little while."

Corey nodded and seemed to fade a bit at the mention of having a newborn.

They watched the interview together, and Maggie was relieved that she hadn't embarrassed herself or her sisters. She sent a text to the family group chat to tell them the interview had aired and to look for it online.

Maggie spent another hour with Corey before heading back to the waiting room to try to get some sleep.

At four o'clock the next morning, Jill woke Maggie to let her know the baby had arrived and was eager to meet her aunts. "She's here," Jill said.

"She's a she?"

"She is."

As she followed Jill into Kate's room, Maggie stretched the kinks out of her neck caused by sleeping on a stiff love seat in the waiting room.

Sitting up in the hospital bed, swaddled baby in her arms and her husband next to her with his arm around her, Kate looked as happy— and as tired—as Maggie had ever seen her.

"Come in," Kate said to her sisters. "Come meet Poppy Harrington Matthews."

"Poppy," Jill said with a sigh. "I *love* that."

Maggie loved it, too, but the huge lump in her throat made it impossible for her to say anything, so she squeezed Kate's shoulder as she gazed down at her sleeping niece.

"I'm so glad you like it. We settled on it early on for a girl, and we kept coming back to it."

"Don't forget how much you love the flower poppies, too," Reid added.

"That, too," Kate said, smiling at him.

"It's perfect," Maggie whispered, blinking back tears. "And so is she."

"How do you feel?" Jill asked.

"Like I got sawed in half in one of those magician boxes and put back together all wrong."

"Ouch."

"Your sister was incredible," Reid said, seeming to battle his own emotions. "She was a warrior and never gave up until our little angel arrived."

"Couldn't have done it without you, babe," Kate said, gazing up at him.

"Mom and Dad are dying for us to FaceTime," Jill said. "Are you up for that?" Their parents had asked them to call the second the baby arrived, no matter what time it was. Knowing Clare and Jack, they were both up pacing as they waited to hear from them.

Kate grimaced when she shifted to find a more comfortable position. "Sure."

"Was it as bad as you thought it would be?" Maggie asked.

"I'll never tell. I want to have nieces and nephews."

"So it was horrific," Jill said.

"I never said that!"

Jill called their mother while Maggie called their father. Both picked up right away, as if they'd been staring at their phones willing them to ring. Knowing them, they had been.

"The gang's all here," Jill said, laughing as Aidan squeezed into the frame next to Clare, and Andi did the same next to Jack.

"We're dying over here," Jack said. "What's the verdict?"

"Reid and I are pleased to introduce you to Poppy Harrington Matthews." Kate angled the baby so they could see her face.

"Poppy," Clare said softly. "We have a granddaughter! I'm a grandmother! How dare you do this to me?"

Everyone laughed. No one was more excited to be a grandmother than Clare had been in the last few months.

"Congratulations, guys," Jack said, his voice wavering. "She's beautiful."

"We can't wait to meet her," Clare said. "We'll be there tomorrow."

"Looking forward to seeing you all," Kate said. "Poppy can't wait to meet you, either."

"You look beautiful, Kate," Andi said.

"Doesn't she?" Reid asked. "You'd never know what she just went through."

"Thanks, guys. You're good for a girl's ego. Aidan, will you let Grammy and the rest of the O'Malleys know that Poppy has arrived?"

"I already hit the group text, and congrats are flooding in. Colin is calling me Gramps."

Everyone laughed at that.

"Are you guys ever going to forgive me for making you grand-parents?"

"We already have," Jack said.

MAGGIE DROVE BACK to Matthews House as the sun was coming up, casting a warm, rosy glow over the rolling hills. She couldn't stop yawning as she drove and had the windows down and the music blasting to keep herself awake. She had a *niece*! Poppy. Maggie loved the baby's adorable name so much.

She hadn't expected to be so emotional over the baby's arrival, but today reminded her of the day her twin brothers had arrived, on the same day her dad had married Andi. She'd felt all the same things then —elation, joy, love, excitement… It was almost too much to process, she thought as she navigated the winding driveway that led to home.

At some point in recent weeks, Matthews House had begun to feel like home to her, which she hadn't realized until this very moment. She parked her car behind the stables and came around the corner to the driveway in a sleep-deprived daze to smack into an immovable object that knocked her right off her feet.

Maggie landed hard on the ground with a loud *oof*.

"Oh my God! I'm so sorry!" Brayden Thomas towered over her. Apparently, he was the immovable object she'd crashed into, and dear God, he was gorgeous in the morning, with scruff on his jaw and a plaid work shirt rolled up to reveal strong forearms. As he held out a hand to help her up, Maggie noted the perfect fit of his faded denim jeans. Yum.

A second after the thought popped into her mind, she chastised herself for thinking such things about her employee. *Knock it off.*

He gently pulled her to her feet. "Are you all right?"

Maggie immediately released his hand to brush the dirt and grass off her clothes, the same clothes she'd left wearing this time yesterday. Figured she'd run into him looking like death warmed over and in bad need of a toothbrush, a hairbrush and a horizontal surface. She ran her fingers through her hair and tried to find a shred of composure.

"I'm so sorry," he said. "I wasn't watching where I was going."

"Not your fault. I wasn't paying attention, either."

"Is everything all right?"

"Everything is wonderful. My niece, Poppy, was born early this morning." Why was she telling him?

His face lit up with a warm smile. "That's awesome. Congrats. How's your sister?"

"Tired but thrilled. Just like me. It's been a long night."

"You look really nice for someone who's been up all night."

For a moment, Maggie was struck dumb with pleasure from the unexpected compliment. Then she remembered the hair and makeup from the day before. "I did an interview with my sisters before Kate went into labor. That seems like a week ago, but it was just yesterday, thus the hair and what's left of the makeup." *Oh my God, quit babbling. He doesn't care about your hair and makeup.*

"I saw it last night. It was good."

"Oh, thanks."

"Derek asked me to drive the van to the bus stop this morning. Hope that's okay."

"No problem. Is everything all right with him?"

"He thinks he might have the stomach flu, actually."

Maggie had a brief, horrifying visual of the stomach flu whipping through the house. "Oh, the poor guy. I'll check on him later."

The kitchen door opened, and a gaggle of mothers and children emerged, the children carrying backpacks and lunchboxes.

Maggie was happy to see the McBride children and their mother among the group.

"I'd better get the van," Brayden said. "Get some rest."

"Probably not happening until later. Let's talk after lunch about getting your program started."

"Sounds good. I'll come find you."

Something to look forward to, Maggie thought, before again reminding herself that she could *not* lust after her employee. She wished she could attribute her lustful thoughts to being sleep-deprived, but she'd had the same lustful thoughts yesterday when fully rested. The man was gorgeous. She'd have to be dead not to notice that, and since she wasn't dead, she noticed him. So what? It didn't mean anything.

"Keep telling yourself that," she grumbled as she went inside.

"You say something, Maggie?" Mitch asked from the kitchen.

"Talking to myself."

"Ah, gotcha. You just getting home?" he asked with a teasing grin.

"I am. My sister had her baby early this morning."

"Oh, that's wonderful news. What did she have?"

"A girl named Poppy. She's perfect."

"Congratulations, Aunt Maggie."

"That's the first time I've been called that."

"Won't be the last."

Teresa came into the kitchen. "Did I hear you say the baby came?"

"Yes, Poppy arrived early this morning. She's absolutely perfect."

"That's fantastic! Congratulations."

"Thank you. I feel weird accepting congrats when I didn't do anything."

"You became an aunt today. That's a big deal."

"It sure is. Thanks."

After a quick trip to her apartment to brush her hair and teeth and change her clothes, Maggie shared the news with everyone she encountered over the next few hours. Friends from home, college and New York lit up her phone with a flurry of texts after Kate's team released the news about Poppy's arrival.

She was drinking a cup of coffee when another text arrived from the last person she ever wanted to hear from again. *Heard the news about your sister's baby. Congrats.*

Maggie choked on the mouthful of coffee and nearly vomited from the revulsion that overtook her at the sight of his name on her screen. How was he still able to contact her? She'd blocked him, hadn't she? Her hands shook as she tried to find her contacts to check. It took longer than it should have to locate her contacts and find his name still there. How could his name still be there? How could he think it was all right to send a casual text as if they were still friends?

She found the link to block him and pressed it firmly before dropping the phone on her desk and covering her face with her hands as a torrent of unwelcome thoughts and memories swamped her tired brain, leaving her devastated all over again.

Approaching footsteps had her scrambling to wipe tears from her face and control her rampaging emotions.

"Um, is this a bad time?" Brayden asked from the doorway.

Once again, he'd caught her in a less than professional state.

"I can come back later."

Maggie forced herself to rally, to stuff the traumatic memories back into the box where she kept them sealed off so she could function. "No, it's fine. Come in." She took a deep breath and held it for a second before releasing it slowly, trying to center herself and find some calm amid the storm raging inside her.

Apparently, she failed miserably.

"What's wrong?"

Maggie stared up at his handsome face and couldn't form a single sentence. Words jumbled about in her brain, but she couldn't make sense of any of them. Between the exhaustion and the reopening of a still-healing wound, she had nothing.

"You want to ride?"

Maggie nodded. She wanted that more than anything.

"Let's go."

Somehow, she managed to stand, to follow his direction to get her boots and meet him at the stables, where she stood idly by like a helpless fool while he quickly and efficiently saddled his horse and Thunder before leading them both outside.

"You need a leg up?"

Shaking her head, she swung herself up into the saddle and immediately found the calm she'd been unable to locate until now. Riding Thunder always made her happy and settled her in a way that nothing else could. Since her horse Destiny had died years ago, Maggie hadn't been able to bring herself to look for a new one. When she'd come to Tennessee, she'd immediately bonded with Thunder, which had worked out well since Kate had given up riding while pregnant.

Maggie followed Brayden around the stables to the same well-worn path she'd traversed the night before. They rode for miles in quiet communion with the horses and the natural beauty of the Matthews estate. She appreciated that Brayden didn't try to get her to talk. He simply kept her company as they rode toward a wooded area she hadn't yet explored.

They slowed the horses as they continued toward the woods.

"Have you ridden in there before?" he asked.

"Not yet. I had a phobia about going in there alone."

"Too much *Little Red Riding Hood* as a child?" he asked, cracking a small grin.

"Something like that."

She'd encountered her own version of the Big Bad Wolf, this one wearing a Brooks Brothers suit and Italian loafers. The memory sent a shudder through her.

Maybe it wasn't such a good idea to ride into the woods with another man she barely knew. How could you know which ones were trustworthy and which ones weren't? "Let's stop here," she said, her voice sounding higher than usual and far more uncertain than it should have, which infuriated her.

Right when she wanted to be projecting a serious, professional demeanor, her insides felt like they'd been put through a paper shredder. Goddamned Ethan and the freaking text that had set her back months.

When they reached the creek that ran through the property, they dismounted to let the horses drink.

"I want you to know…" Maggie said the words before she thought them all the way through.

"What do you want me to know?"

"That I'm not always a hot mess at work. Just when you're around, or so it seems."

He laughed. "No judgment. I promise."

"Thank you, but still… I wasn't sleeping the other day. I often close my eyes when I'm thinking."

"What happened today?"

"Something I'd much sooner forget."

"Ah, yeah, I know how that is."

"Do you?"

He nodded.

Maggie wondered if he was referring to whatever had happened to land him in juvie, but she couldn't ask. He'd already put that off-limits. "After Kate's baby was announced, I got a text from a guy I thought I'd blocked. Someone I *should* have blocked." Why was she telling him this? What was it about him that made it so easy for her to talk to him?

"Oh damn. That sucks."

"You have no idea how much that sucks."

"I hope you've blocked him for good this time."

"Hell yes, but I can't believe that all this time, he was right there in my phone, able to pop in any time and remind me of why I can't bear to hear from him. I feel like I've been walking around with a grenade that's had the pin pulled and could've blown up at any second."

"You must've been pretty rattled after whatever happened if you forgot to block him."

"I was. Rattled, that is. Still am if a simple text can screw me up all over again."

"There was nothing simple about that text, which he must've known."

"Yeah, he knew that."

"I'm sorry he ruined such a happy day for you."

Maggie forced herself to raise her chin, to keep soldiering on the way she had for months now. "He hasn't. I won't let him steal this day from me or Poppy."

"Good," Brayden said.

"Thanks for suggesting a ride. It helped."

"It always helps."

"You want to have our meeting out here?"

"Works for me." He went to his horse, opened a saddle bag and pulled out a sheet that he spread on the ground. "Have a seat in my office."

Maggie smiled. "What else have you got in there?"

He waggled his brows. "Wouldn't you like to know?"

Yes, I would like to know. I'd like that very much.

Brayden sat next to her on the sheet, which he'd positioned so they could keep an eye on the horses.

Thunder wouldn't go anywhere without her. She assumed his horse was the same. "What's your horse's name?"

"Sunday Morning."

"I like that. Where did she get her name?"

"My mom's favorite song was 'Easy Like Sunday Morning' by the Commodores. She used to play it all the time. It was the first song I ever knew all the words to."

"You said 'was' her favorite song. Did you lose her?"

He nodded. "Somewhat recently and very suddenly."

"Oh God. That's awful."

"It's been rough."

"What happened?"

"Car accident."

Maggie gasped as memories of an accident she wished she could forget assailed her. "I'm so sorry, Brayden."

"Why did you suddenly go completely pale?"

"Did I?"

He nodded.

"My mom was hit by a car when I was nine. I saw it happen."

"Oh damn, Maggie."

"Yeah."

"Did she... Was she..."

"She survived it but was in a coma for three years."

He snapped his fingers. "I've heard this story. I saw your sister on TV years ago. She talked about how that accident changed her life and her family's life."

"It sure did, but we were talking about you and your mom. I didn't mean to hijack the conversation."

"You didn't. It's fine. I'm sorry that happened to your mom."

"I'm sorry for what happened to yours."

"Thanks. I'm still trying to wrap my head around the fact that she's really gone."

"I'm sure. It takes a while for things like that to sink in."

"So I'm told."

Maggie turned so she could see him. "If you... If you want to talk about it with someone who gets it, I'm around."

"Thanks. That's really nice of you." He took a moment and seemed to make an effort to shake off the grief. "I meant to tell you I signed the contract at your lawyer's office yesterday. He said he'd get the signed copies to you."

"He's not just my lawyer. He's also my future brother-in-law. He's marrying my sister Jill in July, and his dad is Kate's husband."

"Ah okay. Well, let me tell you what I've got planned for the kids, and you can give me a yay or nay." They'd talked in higher-level specifics during the interview process and had agreed to get further into the details once he was on board.

"You're the expert. I'm not going to micromanage you."

"Still, I'd like your approval."

"Okay, I'm listening."

CHAPTER 8

"First thing, I assess the horses to determine which ones would be best for the program," Brayden said.

"I've identified a number of horses that I think would be ideal, but I'll defer to you on that. I also secured an insurance policy just for this program."

"Good. I was going to ask about that. The first week or so with the kids is all about acclimating them to the stables, to being around the animals and learning the rules. I teach them about respect and safety, about understanding the horse's physical and emotional cues. Once I feel they have a good understanding of the basics, I'll teach them about the tack and how to prepare a horse for riding. They're involved in every aspect and will saddle a horse ten times before they ever ride one."

Maggie found herself mesmerized as he explained his process in a calm, even tone of voice that projected quiet authority.

"They'll learn how to feed and water them, how to lead them properly, how to approach them, how to touch them. The goal is that by the time they're finally astride, they won't be afraid. They'll have become accustomed to being around the horses, hopefully tuned in to their various quirks and the need for safety at all times. After they ride, they'll learn how to care for the horses and put everything away where it belongs." He glanced over at her. "Does that sound okay to you?"

"It sounds amazing. It's just what I had in mind for this program."

"The goal is to show them they're part of something bigger than themselves. Research has shown that equine therapy can help children and adults cope with a wide variety of emotional and physical traumas. Not only does it give them a new hobby, but it also instills self-confidence, which is often lacking in people who've suffered trauma."

"Yes, I learned about it in a class I took in college, and I've been a fan ever since. I wrote the grant that's paying for the program here."

"Oh, I didn't realize the program was funded by a grant."

"Reid and Kate were willing to fund it, but I wanted to keep it separate from the larger program. This is my baby."

"Ah, gotcha. Okay. Is it okay to call or text your cell if I need you for anything?"

"Of course," Maggie said, her heart fluttering. *Stop it. Just stop. He's your employee.* "I use my phone for work."

Brayden typed something into his phone. "I sent you a text. Now you have mine, too."

"I already have yours from your application."

"Oh, right."

They sat in silence for a long time, watching the horses, enjoying the quiet, peaceful sound of the gurgling creek, the buzz of insects and the sweet smell of the grass.

"I love it here," Maggie said.

"I can see why. Is that an actual airfield we can see from the house?"

"It is. Reid and his son, Ashton, are both pilots. They keep a plane in the hangar."

"That's cool."

Maggie looked over at him. "Thank you for this. I really needed it."

"Can I say something that might be totally inappropriate in light of the fact that we only just met and I work for you?"

"You work *with* me, and yes, speak freely."

"I'm a really good listener if you need someone to talk to who isn't going to judge or condemn or question or do anything other than just listen."

His kind words brought tears to her eyes, which she instantly brushed away. "I suck at being a boss."

"What? No, you don't."

"Yes, I do," she said with a low chuckle. "So far you've seen me appearing to nap at work, caught me staring at you and made me cry by being nice to me."

"Don't forget the talking to yourself."

Maggie covered her face with her hands.

Laughing, he nudged her shoulder. "None of those things are fatal flaws in a boss. Trust me, I've had much worse."

She dropped her hands and glanced at him. "Sorry to hear that."

He shrugged. "Sometimes people suck."

"Yes, they do." Maggie knew she absolutely should not confide in this perfect stranger who now worked for her, but there was something about him that had her wanting to tell him. Perhaps it was the same something that made horses trust him so implicitly. "There was a guy in New York, a lawyer I knew through work. I was a court interpreter for the hearing impaired."

"Wow, that's a cool job."

"My brother Eric is hearing impaired. I learned so I could communicate with him and turned it into a career after grad school when I couldn't find a job in family counseling." She pulled at some grass to have something to do with her hands. "The guy, Ethan, he always made a point of finding me, flirting with me and asking me out. I had him pegged as a hopeless flirt and a player, so I resisted for months before I finally agreed to dinner the week before Christmas. We had a nice time, and I was surprised that I actually liked him more than I thought I would. After dinner, he insisted on seeing me home. I thought he was being a gentleman, but..."

Brayden's hand covered hers, giving a reassuring squeeze that reminded her that he was right there, which helped her to find the words to finish the story.

"When I opened my apartment door, he pushed me in ahead of him, closed the door and locked it. It happened so fast, I didn't even realize what was happening until he was on me. In the struggle, I dropped my keys—and my pepper spray was on the keyring—my phone, everything I had that could help me."

A sob erupted from her throat, the horror of it washing over her with new revulsion, as if it had happened yesterday rather than months ago.

Brayden sat up, put his arm around her, silently encouraging her to lean on him. "Is this okay?"

She nodded. The relief of telling someone was so profound that Maggie forgot about him being her employee and took the comfort he offered so willingly.

"I fought him. I'd had self-defense training in a previous job, and I knew where to hit."

"Good," Brayden said, running his hand over her back in soothing circles.

"I got him in the groin with my knee, pushed him off me and ran from my apartment. I didn't have anything with me, not my phone or purse or a coat. I just walked for hours before I could bring myself to go home to see if he was still there. I know I should've called the cops, but I was afraid it would be his word against mine and that he'd have the advantage because he was a well-known defense attorney."

"I can see why you'd think that."

"With hindsight, I can see I wasn't thinking straight. I never should've gone back there alone, but without my phone, I had no way to get in touch with anyone, and besides, I didn't want anyone to know what'd happened."

"I'm terrified thinking about you going back there alone after what he'd done."

"I barely remember doing it, but I do remember being so scared. The door was ajar, the lights were on, but thank God, he was gone. I found my keys and the pepper spray my dad had given me when I moved to the city, even though it's illegal there, and I kept it in my hand as I went through every inch of the apartment while keeping the door open, just in case.

"That must've been so scary."

"I was shaking the whole time."

"Of course you were."

"When I realized he was truly gone, I closed and locked the door and then sank to the floor and sobbed for hours. I couldn't move."

"I'm so, so sorry that happened to you, Maggie."

She wiped tears from her face. "Thanks for listening."

"Did you report him?"

"No, and I hate myself for that, but I was convinced he'd find a way to turn it all around on me. The next morning, I called my boss and quit my job so I'd never have to see him again. When I came here for Christmas a couple of days after this happened, I heard what Reid and Kate had planned for Matthews House and jumped at the chance to be their director, even though I'm probably not the best person for the job."

"Why would you say that? It's obvious you care so much about the clients and the program."

"I do care, but I'm figuring it out as I go. Sometimes I think they might've been better served by someone who's more experienced."

"I think they're being very well served by you, and the rest of your staff thinks so, too."

That was news to her. "How do you know that?"

"I did my due diligence before taking the job. I talked to people when I came for the interview, before you got back from the hospital the first day I was here. I wanted to make sure it would be a good fit for me before I agreed to it."

"Oh."

"You're doing great, Maggie. The residents know how much you care, and that's the first key to success in this field." He gave her shoulder a gentle squeeze. "You couldn't tell your sisters what happened?"

She shook her head. "I just couldn't bring myself to ruin Kate's wedding last Christmas, then Jill and Ashton got engaged, and everyone was having such a good time being together. It was the first time our entire family was together for Christmas in years."

"I'm sure they would've wanted to know you were suffering."

"They would have, but I didn't want to revisit the whole thing. I still don't."

"Could I say one more thing?"

She grunted out a laugh. "Since I've spilled my guts all over you, you can say whatever you want."

"You really ought to tell someone."

Maggie raised her head from his chest and looked up at him. "I just did."

MAGGIE'S STORY left Brayden feeling deeply unsettled for the rest of the day. After returning to the stables, he'd offered to care for both horses since he could tell she was wrung out after their conversation. She'd gratefully accepted and had headed inside to get some much-needed rest.

Then he'd taken care of feeding the rest of the horses and cleaned the stalls he hadn't gotten to earlier since Derek was still not feeling well. Maggie had said she hadn't gotten a chance to check on the older man.

"I did," Brayden had told her. "He's okay. He ate some soup that Mitch sent over and is feeling better."

"That's good," she'd said.

He'd sensed she hadn't had the bandwidth for anything but good news about Derek.

Hours later, he was alone in his apartment, trying to watch a movie, but all he could think about was her being attacked by that guy in New York and how the asshole had gotten away with it. Combating injustice was a central theme of his life. It had caused him trouble more than once, and if he wasn't careful, it could cause him trouble again.

Maggie's situation was none of his business beyond what she'd already shared with him. He needed to remember that and be thankful she'd chosen to share it with him, because keeping something like that to herself for all this time hadn't been healthy for her.

When he'd said she ought to tell someone, he'd meant the police. Telling him was an important step in her recovery, but he wanted her to have justice, too, although he understood her reluctance to report it.

"Not your business, man," he muttered as he stared at the TV with eyes that saw nothing but sweet, lovely Maggie being attacked by a man who'd gotten away with it.

Brayden picked up his phone and opened the message screen. He looked at it for a long time before he entered Maggie's name into the address line.

Just checking to see if you're okay. This is Brayden BTW.

He read and reread the text several times before he hit Send. And then he put his phone aside and told himself to butt out of her life and her business. She'd shared with him in a weak moment brought on by unexpected contact from the douchebag who'd attacked her. Otherwise, she probably never would've told him.

An hour after he sent the text, he was still telling himself he needed to respect her privacy and give her some space. But he wanted to go over there, knock on her door, make *sure* she was all right and hadn't been retraumatized by talking about it.

"*Fuck,*" he said on a low growl as he ran his hands through his hair with rough impatience. He had no idea what he should do.

No, wait, that wasn't true. He knew exactly what he should do, and fuck all the reasons why it might not be wise.

He pulled on boots, tucked his phone into his back pocket and went across the yard to the kitchen entrance.

Inside, Mitch was standing guard over something on the stove. The guy was scary intense and an excellent cook, from what Brayden had experienced thus far.

"What's up?" Mitch asked.

"Is Maggie around?"

"I haven't seen her. She probably crashed after the sleepless night."

"Yeah, I'm sure. Would it be okay if I knocked on her door? I need to ask her something."

Mitch directed a steely stare in his direction, but Brayden refused to blink. He was determined to check on her, even if it started tongues wagging in the house. Brayden was more concerned about her than he was about idle gossip.

"Sure," Mitch finally said. "Third door on the left."

"Thank you." Feeling the heat of Mitch's stare on his back, Brayden stepped into the hallway and went to the third door on the left. He hesitated for a moment before raising his hand to knock.

No response.

He knocked again, louder this time.

The door flew open, revealing a sleepy-eyed Maggie, her long dark hair a wild nest around her head. "What?"

"Sorry to disturb you. I wanted to check on you to make sure you're, you know, all right after we talked earlier."

"I'm all right."

"Okay. Sorry again to wake you."

"It's all right. I had to get up anyway."

"I'll, um, I'll go, then." He started to walk away.

"Brayden."

Turning back, he raised a brow.

"Do you want to meet my niece?"

The question stunned him, so much so, he waited too long to reply.

She cringed. "Never mind. That's weird. I know. I'm weird sometimes. And I'll just shut up now."

Ridiculously charmed, Brayden smiled. "I'd love to meet your niece."

CHAPTER 9

*M*aggie drove them to Kate's, all the while wondering what the hell she'd been thinking when she'd invited Brayden to go with her. Kate probably wouldn't want a stranger in her house the night she brought her baby home, but the words had been out of Maggie's mouth before she'd fully thought them through.

Her emotions were a jumbled-up mess after the roller-coaster ride of the last twenty-four hours. She knew she ought to regret the way she'd unloaded on Brayden earlier, but she didn't. Not at all. Rather, she felt relieved. She'd told someone. Finally. And he'd provided the perfect amount of support and outrage.

She took a tentative glance at him in the passenger seat. "I want to thank you for listening before."

"I'd say it was a pleasure, but I hate what happened to you."

"Obviously, I need you to keep it to yourself."

"Of course. I'd never repeat something like that."

"Thanks."

"How do you feel after talking about it?"

"I was just thinking that I expected to feel regret, but relief is the prevailing emotion. I feel bad that I dumped my shit on you when you work with me—"

"Can we just get past that? You're in charge around the house. No question. But I run my own program, so technically, you're not really my boss. You're letting me run my program in conjunction with yours."

Maggie chuckled at his logic. "That's very clever thinking."

"If it makes it possible for us to be friends, then let's run with it."

"You want to be friends?"

"I sort of thought that's what happened out there today. Two people who didn't know each other a few weeks ago got to know each other, shared some personal shit and offered support to each other."

"The support was kind of one-sided."

"Not entirely. I haven't told too many people about what happened to my mom. I appreciated being able to tell you that. And I suspect you don't invite just anyone to come with you to your famous sister's house."

"I've never brought anyone with me."

"See? We're already friends. So quit acting like you're the boss of me."

Maggie laughed. "Insubordinate already. I see how this is gonna go."

"You found me out."

Maggie continued to question the wisdom of inviting Brayden to come with her. Would Kate be pissed that she'd brought a stranger to her home on this of all nights? Ugh, probably... Shit. Well, too late to back out now.

And why had she invited him anyway? He'd been so sweet to come check on her, and the invitation had popped out before she'd taken even a second to ask whether it was appropriate. Hopefully, Kate would forgive her.

The trip from Matthews House in Brentwood to Kate's place in Hendersonville was about thirty minutes, most of it on I-440. As Maggie took a right onto the dirt road that led to Kate's estate, she glanced over at Brayden. "I don't need to worry about you becoming a crazy stalker or anything, do I?"

His low chuckle made her smile. "As I've mentioned, I'm a huge fan of your sister's music."

"Are you going to be able to hold it together?"

"Doubtful. I'm probably gonna fangirl all over her."

Maggie groaned dramatically. "You'll have to stay in the car, then. She just had a baby. She's not open for fangirling tonight."

"I'll see if I can control myself."

And he was funny. "You do that."

Maggie wasn't surprised to see Jill's Mercedes parked outside, but she hadn't been expecting Buddy and Taylor's Range Rover.

Uh-oh.

"This house is incredible. Is it a log cabin?"

"Yep, and an A-frame. When everyone came for Christmas last year, Reid built a mini version of the house that they call the bunkhouse. Wait till you see it all in the daylight. It's awesome." And Maggie realized she'd just inferred that he'd be coming with her again sometime. Great. "Um, how do you feel about Buddy Longstreet and Taylor Jones?"

"Is that a rhetorical question?"

"Unfortunately, no."

"I'm going to lose my shit."

"Brayden! Come on! You have to hold it together. Act like you've been there."

"I've never been anywhere with Kate Harrington, Buddy Longstreet *or* Taylor Jones except for a massive stadium with fifty thousand other people."

"Do I need to have you wait in the car?"

His low laughter pleased her. She liked making him laugh. "Nah, I'll behave."

"Promise?"

"I promise."

Maggie sent him a wary look, trying to decide if she could trust him.

He laughed again. "Swear to God on a stack of Bibles. I'll keep it cool, even if I'm freaking out on the inside."

"All right, then." Maggie got out of the car and waited for him to follow her into the mudroom. "Hang here for one second. Let me scope it out."

"Yes, ma'am."

"Don't call me ma'am."

"Sorry, ma'am."

Maggie bit her lip to keep from laughing and tried to glare at him, but apparently, that fell flat, because he laughed.

"Go on. I'll stay here until you tell me the coast is clear. But hurry up. Buddy, Taylor and Kate are in there." He shivered dramatically.

"I'm going to kill you." Maggie realized she'd never been this comfortable with any guy so soon after meeting him. She took that startling discovery with her into the kitchen, where Reid, Ashton and Buddy were gathered, beers in hand.

"Hey, Maggie." Reid came over to kiss her cheek. "Now the gang's all here."

"How're they doing?"

If it was possible for a man to glow with happiness, Reid was incandescent, even if dark circles smudged the skin under his eyes. "Absolutely fantastic. Kate's a trouper. You'd never know she just had a baby. And little Poppy is delightful."

"I'm going to go in and say hello."

"Please do. They're in the great room."

"I, ah, I brought Brayden, our new equine therapy guy. I left him in the mudroom until I made sure that Kate doesn't mind."

"She won't mind," Reid said, laughing. "Release the guy from time-out."

Maggie returned to the mudroom and gestured for Brayden to follow her into the kitchen. "Brayden Thomas, this is my brother-in-law, Reid Matthews, my future brother-in-law, Ashton Matthews, and our friend Buddy Longstreet."

To his credit, Brayden kept his shit together as he shook hands with each of the men and congratulated Reid on his new baby. To Buddy, he said, "I'm a huge fan."

"Thanks so much," Buddy said. "You from around here?"

"I am," Brayden said. "Grew up outside of Nashville."

Maggie released a deep breath when she saw that Brayden was going to keep his promise to behave in front of the celebrities and went into the great room to find Kate on the sofa, surrounded by Jill, Taylor and Taylor's daughter, Georgia, who was holding Poppy.

"Welcome home, Kate and Poppy." Maggie looked over Georgia's shoulder at Poppy, who was sleeping. "God, she's a cutie."

"Isn't she?" Like her husband, Kate glowed with happiness even if she, too, looked exhausted.

"She's *so* good." Georgia, who would soon be eleven, had her mother's long dark hair and Buddy's wicked grin and was clearly besotted with the new addition to the family. Buddy and Taylor had mentored Kate since her earliest days in the business. Kate had considered them and their four children to be her Nashville family for years.

"Give Aunt Maggie a turn, Georgia," Taylor said.

"No, that's fine," Maggie said. "I don't want to disturb her."

"We have to go soon anyway. School night."

Georgia made a face at her mother. "It's a special occasion."

"Will you remember the special occasion at six o'clock tomorrow morning when I'm dragging your carcass out of bed?"

"She's very abusive in the morning," Georgia said.

Maggie and her sisters laughed.

"Our mother was, too," Jill said. "We did not do mornings well in our house."

"Glad it's not just my kids," Taylor said.

"Definitely not," Maggie assured her.

"I want to be homeschooled," Georgia said.

Taylor snorted with laughter. "Your daddy says you'd be the dumbest girl in Tennessee if we tried to homeschool you."

"That's true," Georgia said, as the others lost it laughing again.

"I can say that about myself," Taylor said, "but you…"

"Yeah, yeah, I know. I'm not allowed to say you guys are too dumb to be my teachers. I get it."

"Four kids, and the last one is going to kill me," Taylor said, shaking her head as her eyes danced with amusement.

"You love me."

"Someone has to."

"Um, you guys," Maggie said hesitantly. "I brought a friend with me tonight. He'd love to meet you and Poppy, Kate, if you're up for it. I know it's not the time, but somehow I found myself inviting him and, well…" She stopped talking when she noticed they were staring at her in fascination. "What?"

"You're stammering over a guy," Jill said.

"I am not! I'm stammering because I invited him without really thinking of all the reasons why tonight wasn't the best night to bring him here…"

"Whoa," Kate said to Jill. "This is *huge*. Go get him."

"Never mind," Maggie said. "You can meet him another time."

"Are you going to make me get off this sofa?" Kate asked. "Because I will if I have to."

Maggie rolled her eyes at her sister. "Drama queen. I'll get him, but don't make anything of it. He works for us, for crying out loud."

"Um, we're not the ones making something of it," Jill said. "For the record."

Sometimes Maggie couldn't stand having older sisters who didn't let her get away with anything. Her whole life, she'd felt like she was scrambling to catch up to them—one of them at the top of her Ivy League classes in college and law school, the other a crazy-talented musician, singer and songwriter. And when it came to busting balls, Maggie still felt like the underachieving little sister next to the two of them. They always saw right through her. Every time.

Resisting the temptation to get into a verbal sparring match with Jill that she would lose because, hello, *lawyer*, Maggie went into the kitchen, where Brayden had been given a beer. The men seemed to have immediately accepted him into their tight-knit tribe, which gave Maggie an odd feeling that she couldn't quite describe.

"Do you want to meet Kate and Poppy?" she asked him.

"I'd love to."

Filled with misgivings—what in the hell had she been thinking when she invited him here?—Maggie led him into the great room,

81

where the others waited eagerly to meet the man whom Maggie had stammered over. *Ugh.* She hadn't been thinking. After Ethan's text earlier, her brain had been scrambled, leading her to confide in *her new employee* and invite him to a family event.

She really had no business trying to be anyone's boss. Clearly, she sucked at it.

"Brayden, meet my sisters, Kate and Jill, as well as Taylor and her daughter, Georgia. And, of course, the star of the day, Miss Poppy Harrington Matthews."

"Great to meet you all." To Kate, he added, "Congratulations."

"Thanks," Kate said. "Great to meet you, too. We've heard wonderful things about your work."

"That's nice to hear." Maggie could see him making an effort not to be starstruck while meeting two of the biggest names in the music business.

Of course, Kate and Taylor were used to people being bowled over by them. Maggie had been flummoxed the first time she met Buddy and Taylor, but by now, she was used to being around them.

He glanced at Poppy, still out cold in Georgia's arms. "She's gorgeous."

"Thank you," Kate said. "We're madly in love."

"I can see why."

"How're you feeling, Kate?" Maggie asked.

"Tired, sore, elated, relieved that it's over and it all went well."

"Ready to do it again?" Jill asked.

Kate groaned. "Shut your filthy mouth."

"What?" Jill asked, laughing. "You said you were having two in two years because Reid is getting old."

"I don't want to talk about that tonight."

"On that note, I think I'll rejoin the guys in the kitchen," Brayden said. "So nice to meet you all, and congratulations again."

"Thank you, Brayden," Kate said. "Nice to meet you, too. Happy to have you on the Matthews House team."

"I'm very happy to be there. Thanks for the opportunity."

"All thanks go to Maggie. Your program is all hers."

"That's what I heard." Brayden gifted Maggie with a warm smile and returned to the kitchen.

For long moments after he walked away, the others were quiet, each of them giving Maggie inquisitive looks.

"So, um, that's Brayden, the horse guy."

"Uh-huh," Kate said.

Another long silence.

"Isn't anyone going to say it?" Georgia asked. "That guy is hot AF."

"I'm almost afraid to ask what AF stands for," Taylor said.

Georgia grinned. "Hot as—"

Taylor's eyes went wide. "Stop! Not in front of Poppy."

Georgia rolled her eyes at her mother. "Puhleeze. She's not even a day old. We can still swear in front of her."

"No, we can't. I blame the older ones for ruining her."

"Back to Brayden," Georgia said. "Hot AF to the one millionth power."

Maggie felt her face get very warm and probably very red, too, and wanted to swear in frustration. Rather than swear in front of the baby, though, she shrugged. "I hadn't noticed."

The other women dissolved into hysterics, even Georgia, that traitor.

"Like hell you didn't notice," Jill said between gasping laughs.

"Shut up," Maggie hissed. "He'll hear you."

"Oh, relax," Kate said. "He won't know why we're laughing."

"Sure, he won't. He leaves the room, and you lose it laughing. Why would he think that has anything to do with him?"

They made a pathetic attempt to pull themselves together.

"So, Mags," Kate said. "That's Brayden the horse whisperer."

"I believe we've covered that already."

"What we haven't yet covered," Jill said, slipping into lawyer mode, "is why he's here with you."

"I asked him if he wanted to come meet you guys. That's all there is to it."

"Huh," Jill said. "Interesting."

Maggie stood up. She'd hoped for a chance to hold Poppy, but she wasn't sticking around for an inquisition. "Gotta run."

"You just got here," Kate said.

"Big day tomorrow. Lots going on." Maggie ran her fingers over Poppy's soft cheek, careful not to disturb her. "She really is perfect."

"Thanks, Mags. You don't have to go. We won't bust your chops. Too much."

Maggie was torn between wanting to get out of there and wanting to hold the baby.

Taylor helped to make the decision for her when she told Georgia to turn Poppy over to Maggie because they needed to get going.

Maggie held out her arms, and Georgia reluctantly transferred the baby to her. She snuggled the baby into her chest while gazing down at the perfect little face, remembering other babies who'd come into her life—her baby twin cousins, Owen and Olivia, now twelve, and her identical twin brothers, John and Rob, who were turning eleven this year.

They'd grown up fast, and this little one would, too.

Gazing down at the baby's perfect little face, Maggie was thankful she'd be close by for Poppy's childhood, even if Poppy's mother and aunt were a pain in Maggie's ass.

CHAPTER 10

*B*rayden couldn't believe he was standing in Kate Harrington's kitchen having a beer with Buddy Longstreet. On the scale of surreal days, this one ranked right up at the top of the list, beginning with the conversation he'd had with Maggie earlier.

He couldn't stop thinking about what she'd told him or how angry it had made him on her behalf.

"Have you worked with horses a long time, Brayden?" Ashton asked.

"All my life. My grandfather had a horse farm, and we lived on the property. I learned everything I know from him."

"Maggie is excited about the equine therapy program," Reid said.

"It can be hugely beneficial for children—and adults—who've suffered trauma or struggle with physical or emotional challenges."

"That sounds amazing," Buddy said. "Important work. Makes what I do seem stupid in comparison."

"Your music brings pleasure to a lot of people," Brayden said. "As I mentioned earlier—huge fan. Maggie told me I needed to behave around the stars, but I gotta say, that's easier said than done."

"You're holding up admirably," Ashton said, making the others laugh.

"Freaking out on the inside," Brayden said.

"I knew Buddy before he was a big deal," Reid said. "Trust me. He ain't nothin' special."

"Thanks, brother," Buddy said with a guffaw.

"You two are brothers?" Brayden asked.

"From another mother," Buddy said. "My mama was his family's housekeeper. Reid and I grew up together in the same house. He was the one with the silver spoon in his mouth."

"You had a mouth full of bullshit," Reid said. "Still do."

Brayden laughed at their exchange.

"That may be true, but the silver spoon here financed my first demo," Buddy said. "Gave me a huge leg up in the business. I wouldn't be where I am today without him."

"Yes, you would," Reid said. "Nothing could've held you back in those days. You were on fire with ambition."

"He never wants to take credit for the role he played, but it was—and is—significant."

"For what it's worth," Ashton said, grinning, "he's my godfather, and I don't think he's any big deal, either."

"Wow," Buddy said. "I'm feeling the love tonight."

"Our job is to keep you humble," Reid said.

"Good luck with that," Taylor said as she came into the kitchen with Georgia. "Buddy and humble are two words rarely spoken in the same sentence."

"This is a rough crowd," Brayden said, amused by them.

Buddy raised his beer in Brayden's direction. "You see what I deal with? It's not easy being me."

"Oh puhleeze," Taylor said. "Who has it better than you?"

Buddy put his arm around his wife. "Nobody on God's green earth."

"You know it, baby."

Ashton made barfing noises.

"Oh, listen to you," Buddy said. "Mr. Madly in Love and not afraid to show it."

"You got that right, old man."

Buddy scowled at Ashton. "Who you calling old?"

"Aw, my baby's gonna be fifty-one soon." Taylor caressed Buddy's back. "He's feeling a little sensitive."

"He's a big, fat baby," Georgia said bluntly.

"I'm in the biggest fight with all of you people." Buddy grabbed the black cowboy hat he wore all the time from where it hung on a chair and headed for the door. "Brayden, it was nice to meet you. Hope to see you again."

"Same," Brayden said, still dumbfounded by this entire evening.

"Great to meet you," Taylor said. "Don't mind us. We're family. Family is mean."

"It's all good," Brayden said, laughing.

"Let's go home, Georgia Sue."

"Don't call me that!"

The door slammed shut behind them.

"Ah, the tween years," Reid said.

"What're you talking about?" Ashton asked. "You had it made in the shade with me. I bet little Poppy in there will be the one to give you a run for your money."

"Don't speak that way about your baby sister," Reid said with a playful scowl for his son.

Ashton smiled. "You'll be too old to do anything about it anyway."

Brayden choked on a mouthful of beer.

"So rude," Reid said, grinning. "I plan to live long enough to watch you chasing *your* teenagers."

Ashton raised his bottle to his father. "We'll be chasing them together."

Reid touched his bottle to Ashton's. "That we will. I'd better check on my baby mama and make sure she's not overdoing it."

After Reid left the room, Ashton turned his attention to Brayden, his friendly smile disappearing. "I'm an attorney. Do all the legal work for Matthews House."

Brayden wasn't sure why Ashton was telling him that. "Oh."

"I did the background check on you before you were offered the job."

He refused to squirm or otherwise show any reaction. "Okay."

"Just thought I'd mention it." Ashton pushed off the barstool he'd been sitting on and tossed his empty bottle into a recycling bin located under the countertop. He left the room without another word.

Brayden wondered why Ashton had felt the need to put him on notice. Maggie had already told him they knew he had a juvenile record. He was under no obligation to share the details of his sealed record with anyone. Those records were sealed for a reason—so kids wouldn't be permanently penalized for childhood mistakes.

Not that he considered what he'd done a mistake. He'd done it on purpose and would do it again under the same circumstances, even knowing the consequences. Despite repeated efforts, he'd never been successful in getting his record expunged, due to the nature of his crime, or so he'd been told.

Ashton could watch him all he wanted. That was fine with Brayden. He had nothing to hide. He'd been hired to do a job, and he would do that job to the best of his considerable ability.

It might be a good idea, however, to curb his growing interest in the beautiful woman who'd hired him. If her brother-in-law had reservations about him, he'd probably expressed them to Maggie, too. So why had she hired him anyway?

As if he'd willed her, Maggie came into the kitchen, casting him an inquiring look. "Did they leave you all alone?"

"It's fine. I don't want to intrude on family time."

"I'm ready to roll. Got an early morning."

"I'm ready when you are."

"Let's say our goodbyes."

He went with her into the enormous great room to say goodbye to the others. His gaze was drawn to the stone fireplace that was the focal point of the room. Somehow, the room managed to retain its coziness despite its size.

"You'll be here tomorrow for dinner, right?" Kate asked.

Maggie nodded. "That's the plan."

"Brayden, you're welcome to join us. The grandparents are coming to meet the baby."

"Thanks for the invite, but I'm headed out of town late tomorrow. It was great to meet you all."

"Likewise," Jill said, speaking for the others. "Hope to see you again soon."

"You, too." He shook hands with Reid and Ashton and followed Maggie through the kitchen to the mudroom.

"Thanks for bringing me," he said as Maggie drove them back to Matthews House. "It was nice to meet them all."

"They liked you."

"How could you tell?"

"They were themselves in front of you. If they aren't comfortable around someone, they tend to clam up."

"Yeah, they didn't do that."

"You can take that as a compliment," she said.

"Buddy and Reid were telling me how they grew up together."

"Right. Buddy is Ashton's godfather and is like an uncle to him. Ashton handles all the legal work for Buddy's company. Jill is working with him part-time now that Kate has decided to take a break from touring."

"Will she go back to it?"

"I'm sure she will eventually. But right now, she wants to be home with Reid and Poppy. They'll probably have another baby pretty quickly, not that she wants to talk about that today."

"How many years between Reid and Kate?"

"Twenty-eight."

"Wow."

"Yeah, they first met when she was eighteen and he was forty-five. He was a friend of my dad's from college, and he was supposed to 'keep an eye on her' while she tried to break into the music business."

"Holy cow. Your dad must've freaked when he found out they were involved."

"That's putting it mildly. It was a really rough time. They ended up

89

breaking up, but she never forgot him and vice versa. Ten years later, she went looking for him, and they've been back together ever since."

"That's quite a story."

"Kate would tell you love is love, and age is just a number."

"How old is Reid?"

"Fifty-six."

"I never would've guessed that."

"Buddy says he's an ageless freak of nature."

"They're funny together."

"Yes, they are."

"I haven't met a lot of celebrities in person. I didn't expect them to be so…"

"Normal?"

"Yeah."

"A lot of people say that when they meet them. Buddy says they're regular people. Put their pants on one leg at a time like everyone else does. He says a few other things that aren't fit for repeating, but that's his take on things. Taylor is always after him for his colorful language."

"He's a cool dude. I liked him. I liked them all. Ashton, though… He's a bit intense, huh?"

"How do you mean?"

"He made a point of telling me that he's a lawyer and did the background check on me."

"Ugh, he did not!"

"Yes, he did."

"I'm sorry about that. He shouldn't have done that."

"He was putting me on notice that he knows I've got a past. I get it."

"Still… It's not up to him to do that."

"He's looking out for you, I think."

"I'm a big girl. I can take care of myself."

"You've proven that." Brayden wasn't sure if he should refer to what she told him earlier, but he wanted her to know that he admired her for escaping her attacker—and for putting a hurt on him.

"I've had a lot of regrets about that night. I never should've let him walk me to my door."

"Maggie, come on. That's not your fault. The guy was an attorney you knew from work. You shouldn't have had anything to fear from him."

She shrugged. "Still. I was caught off guard, and after living in the city for years by then, I knew better than to let that happen."

"You defended yourself, and you got away. That's what matters. You know that, don't you?"

"Still working on that, but thanks for listening. It really helps to have told someone."

"I'm glad you told me, and feel free to talk to me about it any time you need to."

"Thanks," she said with a deep sigh.

"Why the sigh?"

"I've crossed quite a few boundaries and muddied the personal and professional lines pretty badly on your second day with us."

"Fuck that. Who cares about the lines? I'm going to do a fantastic job for you regardless of whether we're friends or not. We're going to be living and working in close proximity. I'd much rather be friends than not be. This isn't corporate America, Maggie, and we both know exactly what our jobs are."

"When you put it that way," she said with a laugh, "it seems kind of dumb to be worried about it."

He flashed her a teasing grin that he hoped she could see in the darkness. "It is dumb."

She laughed. "Gee, thanks. It's just that this is my first time being completely in charge of something, and I'm trying to do it right."

"You care so much about the people you're working with and for. That's how you do it right. Don't get caught up in worrying about things that don't matter. You have enough to worry about just getting through the day."

"That's true. Thanks for being so cool. I appreciate the support."

"You got this. You're an outstanding boss lady."

"That's nice to hear, but I'm still learning. Got a long way to go."

"You honestly think you'll ever reach the point in this job when you can say, 'I've got this. Nothing surprises me anymore.'?"

"Probably not," she conceded. "It's something new every day."

"Exactly."

Maggie's phone rang, and she took the call from Teresa on the Bluetooth. "Hey. I've got Brayden with me."

"Hi there. Just heard that Corey's baby is arriving tonight by C-section."

"Is anyone with her?"

"The nurse said that one of Corey's friends is there."

"Oh good. Do you think I should go?"

"You could probably check on her in the morning."

"Okay, I'll do that. Did they say anything about what to expect for the baby?"

"Just that the baby will be taken right to the NICU."

"Right, well, I'll be back at the house shortly."

"See you then."

"Did you just tell her you went somewhere with me?"

"Crap, I did." She grimaced. "Oh well. I had to since she needed to know I wasn't alone. Client privacy and all that."

"How far along is Corey?"

"Thirty weeks. They were hoping for a few more."

"There's so much they can do for premature babies these days."

"Right. It's still so stressful."

"I know."

The house was mostly dark when Maggie drove to her parking spot behind the stables. "Thanks for coming tonight."

"Thanks for asking me." They got out of the car and walked around the stables, where they would part company. "Hey, Maggie? Why did you? Ask me to go, that is."

"I, um, I don't know exactly. I thought you might like to meet them, I guess."

"I did like meeting them. I liked hanging out with you, too, so thanks again. Sleep well."

"You, too."

Maggie walked away, and he waited for her to get inside. He stood there for a long time thinking of her and the things he'd learned about her during that momentous day before he headed for his place.

CHAPTER 11

a t seven o'clock, after passing a restless night in which her mind spun the way it had in the early days after Ethan attacked her, Maggie dragged herself into the shower. She figured the spike in anxiety had come from sharing what'd happened with Brayden. And why had she done that, exactly? Why had she invited him to come to Kate's with her? Why did she find herself thinking about him in all manner of ways that could complicate things for both of them? Getting involved with someone at work was always risky, but it was even more so when you worked and lived in the same place.

Say she allowed herself to develop this interest in Brayden. Say it went somewhere and then it went bad. That would be a mess for both of them and everyone else they worked with, which was the best reason she could think of to put up a firewall, to keep things friendly and cordial, but professional. She could do that. Of course she could. With both her sisters nearby, it wasn't like she was desperate for friends or entertainment in her new town.

Her sisters were part of her everyday life, and yet... The first person she'd told about Ethan had been Brayden.

After puzzling over the why of it as she dried her hair and got dressed, she still had no real answers other than that he'd been there after she received that disturbing text and had offered comfort. If she'd been with Jill and Kate when Ethan texted, she probably would've told them. But she'd been with Brayden, someone she barely knew, and for whatever reason, it had been easier to share it with him than it would've been to tell her sisters.

Maggie knew she ought to take a closer look at why she felt that way, but she had too many other things to do at the moment, starting with going to check on Corey and the baby. First, she had to touch base with Teresa to make sure everyone was off to school.

She went into the kitchen, where Mitch had a pot of coffee made, and helped herself to a cup, pouring in enough cream to make it palatable.

"What's for breakfast today?" Mitch asked her.

"How about some oatmeal?"

"Coming right up."

"Have I mentioned that you're one of the best perks of this awesome job?"

"Only every morning since I started," he said with what counted as a big smile for him, even though his face barely moved.

While Mitch made the oatmeal, Maggie took a coffee to Teresa, who was in the main office, typing on a computer.

"Morning," Maggie said, handing her the steaming mug.

"Hey." She gratefully received the coffee. "Bless you."

"How're things?"

"A quiet night, and everyone made it to the bus stop on time."

"Excellent. Any word on Corey?"

"She had a good night, and the baby is holding his own."

"Ah, so she had a boy. I'm headed there this morning."

"The nurse said she's very emotional, but I suppose that's to be expected. Hormones added to the upheaval she's been through and an early delivery."

"It's a lot."

"She'll be glad to see you."

"Oatmeal is ready, Maggie," Mitch called from the kitchen.

To Teresa, she said, "I'll check in later."

"Sounds good. I'm off tonight, so Cecilia will be covering."

"Got it. Enjoy the night off."

"I'll spend most of it asleep, I'm sure."

With a laugh, Maggie went to eat breakfast and was on her way into town a few minutes later. A truck from one of the local lumber-yards passed her going toward the house, delivering the supplies Brayden had ordered to build a platform for his program that would allow the children to safely mount the horses.

He had assured her he could build the platform himself, having secured plans online and seen many of the platforms in use over the years.

Maggie had left it in his capable hands. She would also be hiring part-time staff to serve as spotters and escorts, which were required as part of the program. She hoped to attract high school students who wanted to earn some money and get work experi-ence. The ad would be going live later in the day, and she expected to get a robust response due to Kate's involvement with the program.

Kate was a deity to teenage girls.

Maggie laughed at that thought. It still amused her, even after all the years her sister had been a big star, that people fell over them-selves to talk to her, to have any contact whatsoever with her. The news of Poppy's birth had probably set the internet on fire.

She got to the hospital at nine thirty, and after a stop in the gift shop to get flowers and a balloon, she took the elevator to the mater-nity ward. At the nurse's desk, she showed her Matthews House ID and asked for Corey.

"Room three twelve," the nurse said. "On the left."

"Thank you."

Maggie went into the room, put the flowers on a table and found Corey resting on her side, her face wet with tears. Judging by Corey's red, raw eyes, she'd been crying all night.

When Corey saw Maggie, she tried to sit up and winced in pain.

"Take it easy." Maggie helped the young woman get settled with pillows behind her. "How do we turn down the TV?"

Corey pressed buttons on a hand controller that brought the TV from blasting to a normal volume.

"That's better. How're you feeling?"

"Horrible, like I've been stabbed. I can't stop crying, and my boobs are killing me."

"It's the hormones."

"That's what the nurses said. They're so nice." More tears filled her big eyes. She looked so young and frightened.

"And the baby? How is he?"

"They said he's doing all right, but he'll be here awhile. He's so small. Just over three pounds." She swiped at more tears.

"What can I do for you?"

"The flowers are pretty. Thank you."

"They're from all of us at Matthews House."

"Everyone is so nice." She hiccuped on a sob. "I don't know what I would've done without y'all."

"Is there anyone I can call for you?"

She fiddled with the blanket. "I've been trying all morning not to call Trey."

"The baby's father?"

Corey nodded. "I thought I should at least tell him the baby came, but…" She closed her eyes and took a deep breath. "He doesn't deserve to know."

"After he hurt you, you mean?"

"Yes. He's the reason the baby came early. I know it's because he pushed me down those stairs."

Maggie handed her a tissue. She hadn't heard that he'd pushed her down stairs, and the information infuriated her.

Corey mopped up tears and blew her nose. "Even knowing that, why is it that I want him more than anyone else right now?"

"Because you loved him before you found out who he really is."

"I always knew who he was, and I loved him anyway. It's my fault."

"What is?"

"That the baby was born early. I should've left Trey the first time he hit me."

Maggie got another tissue and gave it to Corey. "It's not your fault, Corey. You did nothing to endanger your son."

"It *is* my fault. I stayed with him."

"Because you felt like you had nowhere else to go."

"I'd still be with him if that ER doctor hadn't told me about Matthews House."

"You got out as soon as you could. You took care of yourself and your child by leaving when you did."

Corey broke down into heartbroken sobs. "It was too late. The baby... He's so small."

"He's in the best possible place, and I'm sure they're doing everything they can for him. Are you sure there isn't anyone else I can call for you? What about your parents?"

"It's just my mom, and she told me to stay away from Trey. I didn't listen to her. I can't call her and tell her she was right."

"She might be happy to hear from you."

"I'm not calling her." She looked up at Maggie. "How will I care for a premature baby when I can't even take care of myself?"

Maggie held her hand and thought long and hard about what to say to that. "Have you spoken with the hospital's social workers?"

"Someone came in earlier, but I didn't talk to her about this."

"Why not?"

"I was afraid to say it out loud."

"Well, now you have, and that's okay. If you don't feel capable of caring for your baby, you have options."

Corey's chin quivered violently as tears rained down her face. "I love him so much. I've only had a few seconds with him, and I already love him."

"You've had months with him."

She nodded.

"No one can tell you what the right thing to do is, Corey. Only you can know what's best for you."

She buried her face in her hands and sobbed.

Maggie got up, sat on the edge of the bed and held Corey's trembling body. "Nothing needs to be decided today. He's going to be here for a while, so you've got time to think about it—"

"No."

"No?"

"H-he needs parents who can step up for him r-right now, and I... I can't do that."

Maggie smoothed the matted blonde hair back from Corey's face. "What do you want to do?"

"I... I think I'd like to talk to the social worker again."

"Do you want me to ask the nurses to call her?"

"Yes, please," Corey said softly.

MAGGIE CRIED ALL the way home. Corey's heartbreak had been so deep and so profound that Maggie had felt as if she were taking steps to give up her own child for adoption. Things had happened quickly after the social worker arrived, along with a member of the hospital's counseling team, who'd ensured that Corey was fully aware of what she was doing before allowing her to sign the forms necessary to give up her parental rights. When the social worker asked about the baby's father, Corey had shaken her head and refused to say another word. The social worker hadn't pushed her, but Maggie wondered if or when Trey would have to give up his rights.

Maggie had promised to provide shelter to Corey for as long as she needed it during her recovery, had stayed with her throughout the entire process and for two hours after the others left, rubbing the young woman's back until she fell asleep, her shoulders still heaving from hours of sobbing.

Feeling shredded, Maggie drove up the driveway to Matthews House and around the stables, where she encountered a shirtless Brayden hammering nails into a wooden platform and discovered that under those Western shirts he favored, he had muscles on top of muscles. She watched him move, mesmerized by the play of those muscles and the snug fit of faded denim over his ass and legs. She propped her sunglasses on top of her head to get a better look.

Dear God, the man was absolute perfection.

She blinked several times, trying to remember what she'd been doing before she came upon him. Oh, right, parking her car, getting out, going back to work. After pulling into her space, she shut off the engine, grabbed her purse and got out of the car to find that Brayden had turned around, giving her the full-on view of his chest and abdomen. Holy moly… The front was even better than the back. His chest was covered with dark hair—not too much. Just enough. His abdomen was cut, and his jeans hung low and—

"You've been crying."

When she snapped out of the lust-induced fugue state she'd slipped into, Maggie realized he was now standing right in front of her, half-naked, sweat making his golden skin gleam in the early afternoon sun.

"Maggie?"

"What?"

"I said you've been crying. Why?"

"I was with Corey at the hospital. She made the difficult decision to give her son up for adoption."

"Oh damn. That's a tough one."

"It was brutal, but she really feels like it's the right thing to do. She said she can't take care of herself, let alone a child with special needs."

"What will she do now?"

"We'll bring her back here to recover from the birth, and then I guess we'll see. She's welcome to stay here as long as she needs to."

"She's so lucky to have you and everyone here. This place will save her."

His kind words put a lump in Maggie's throat, and fearing she would break down in front of him—again—she shifted her gaze to the platform he'd built. "You got a lot done."

He glanced at his work in progress. "It's pretty straightforward, and I'm under the gun to get it done before I leave tonight so we can start next Monday." After a pause, he added, "You remembered I mentioned an already-planned vacation, right?"

"Yes, I remember. Where're you going?"

"Key West with my college friends to do some fishing."

"That'll be fun."

"Yeah, it will. We go every year. Hit me up if you need anything while I'm gone."

Maggie, who had started to walk away, turned back to him. "What would I need?"

He shrugged as his lips curved into a small smile. "Someone to talk to? Someone to vent to? Someone to listen? Whatever the need, I'm around."

He'd rendered her speechless with his kindness as much as his sexiness. "I'll, ah, keep that in mind. Thanks."

"Have a good week with your family."

Maggie had almost forgotten that her parents were arriving in a few hours. "Thanks. Enjoy the time away."

"Oh, I will. It's nonstop laughs, hijinks, beer, fish and sun."

"A winning combination for sure."

"You ought to try it sometime. I bet you'd like it."

"I know I would. I used to fish off my dad's boat all the time. I was the only one of the kids who ever caught anything."

"What kind of boat does your dad have?"

"A sailboat named *Blueprint* that he and his business partner brother-in-law own together. They're architects."

"Clever."

"They think they are."

"Wait. I've heard about your dad and his firm. They're kind of well known, right?"

"I guess. They've done well for themselves."

"It was an article about Kate that mentioned him and his firm. I read about their work."

"My aunt Frannie, who's my dad's sister, and my uncle Jamie, the partner brother-in-law, are also coming with their kids to meet Poppy." Why was she telling him all this, anyway?

"You guys will be overrun with guests. Where will they all stay?"

"The bunkhouse I told you about at Kate's. Reid built it before their wedding last Christmas. The whole family came for that."

"Smart idea."

"It's necessary since our family arrives in groups of ten or more."

"I can't imagine that."

Maggie told herself to walk away, to get back to work, to let him get back to work. "You don't have a lot of family?"

"Nah, it was just me and my mom after my grandfather died. We have a lot of good friends who are like family, though. Is it just you and your sisters?"

"We have five younger brothers, too."

"Holy crap!"

"We didn't all grow up together. It was me, Jill and Kate until Andi and Eric joined our family. She's my stepmother. She and my dad had twins, John and Rob. My mom and stepfather, Aidan, adopted Nick and Max. It's a big blended family."

"They all get along?"

"They do."

"So your parents had a friendly split, then?"

Maggie smiled. "That's a story for when we both have much more time than we do now."

"Can't wait to hear it."

"I'll, ah, let you get back to work. Safe travels."

"Thanks. Have a good week."

"You, too. Enjoy the fun in the sun." Maggie went inside the kitchen, where she found several female members of her staff gathered at the kitchen window. "What's up, ladies?"

Tonya, one of the program assistants, was standing with LeAnn, who cleaned the common areas, and Cathleen, who helped Mitch in the kitchen.

"He's lifting one of the big pieces of plywood," Tonya said.

"Look at those fine, fine muscles," Cathleen said with a dreamy sigh.

The three of them had their noses pressed to the windows.

Amused, Maggie said, "All right, that's enough."

Tonya looked over her shoulder at Maggie. "Are you going to tell me you weren't drooling when you were out there talking to him?"

"Nope, no drool."

"And you didn't happen to notice that he's the *sexiest man since Chris Hemsworth*?" LeAnn asked, her voice rising with every syllable.

"Is he? I hadn't noticed."

"Girl," Tonya said, "you're a damned liar."

Maggie laughed. "Back to work everyone. Show's over."

"I *love* working here," LeAnn said as she left the kitchen. "The view is *outstanding*."

Amused, Maggie went into her office and sat at her desk, spinning with thoughts and emotions after the difficult morning with Corey and her reaction to half-naked Brayden Thomas. The other women were right—he was the sexiest man since Chris Hemsworth—and in just a few days' time, he'd begun to feel like a friend.

Hit me up if you need anything.

It occurred to her in a moment of startling clarity that she would miss having him around for the next week, which was ridiculous. He'd been there a few days so far. How was it possible that she would *miss* him?

"You're so stupid," she muttered to herself as she fired up her computer to do some of the administrative work that never ended. Reports, statistics, data, updating the website, coordinating the open house Reid suggested they have to show off their new facility to the larger community and starting a newsletter to communicate with donors and other stakeholders.

When Reid and Kate had announced the formation of Matthews House and detailed its mission, they'd been inundated with donations from other music business luminaries as well as former colleagues of Reid's in the local contractor community who wanted to support the program.

Managing the donations was one of the many hats Maggie wore. She checked her voicemail and found a message from local law enforcement, updating her on the case pending against Corey's boyfriend, Trey. The man had been held without bail on outstanding warrants and felony assault charges after the incident that had brought her to Matthews House.

Maggie was relieved to learn he was still being held, so even if Corey gave in to temptation and reached out to him about the baby, he wouldn't be able to take the call. Corey was better off with him out of the picture.

LeAnn came to Maggie's door. "There's a Ruth Samuelson here from the Department of Children's Services. She'd like to see Trish Lawson."

CHAPTER 12

hat the hell is this about? Maggie struggled to remain calm so she could fully support Trish. "Will you please go up and ask Trish to come to my office and ask Tonya to watch Chloe while Trish and I meet with DCS?"

"You got it."

While she waited, Maggie wondered what DCS wanted.

Trish came to her door a couple of minutes later. "You wanted to see me?"

"Come in. Shut the door."

When Trish was in the office with the door closed, Maggie sat next to her. "DCS is here, asking to see you."

Trish recoiled. *"What? Why?"*

"I don't know. Do you have any idea why they'd want to talk to you?"

"None whatsoever."

"Then let's go find out."

Maggie stood and started for the door.

Trish grabbed her arm and held on tight. "Maggie, please. No matter what, you can't let them take my kids."

"I can't see any reason why they would. Try to remain calm. That's the best thing you can do."

Trish swallowed hard and nodded.

Maggie gave Trish a minute to get herself together before she opened the door and led the way to the conference room, where a woman was seated at the table waiting for them. Maggie estimated her to be in her late forties with dark-brown skin and kind brown eyes. She wore a sharp gray suit and projected an aura of professionalism and compassion, which was comforting.

"Hi there, I'm Maggie Harrington, Matthews House director, and this is Trish Lawson."

She stood to shake hands with them. "Ruth Stapleton. Nice to meet you both. I've heard wonderful things about your program, Ms. Harrington."

"Thank you. Feel free to call me Maggie."

"Wonderful, and I'm Ruth. Ms. Lawson, I understand you've been quite ill."

Trish glanced at Maggie before she nodded hesitantly. "I'm being treated for ovarian cancer."

"That's what I was told."

"By whom?" Maggie asked.

"I'm not at liberty to share that information."

"Someone has reported me to you! How is it fair that I'm not allowed to know who?"

Under the table, Maggie put her hand over Trish's and gave a gentle squeeze. "Ms. Lawson has struggled during her illness to maintain employment, and that's what ultimately brought her to us. Her children are well cared for. They're clean, well dressed, well nourished, bright, articulate, happy children. Their medical and shot records are up-to-date, and the older two have perfect attendance at school. Ms. Lawson made us aware that the eldest child, Lily, suffers from anxiety due to her mother's illness. She's old enough to understand the battle her mother is waging. The anxiety is managed with medication. You're more than welcome to visit with the children and see for yourself that there's no need for your agency's services."

"I would like to see them."

Trish trembled violently.

Maggie squeezed her hand again, trying to keep her calm. This was shaping up to be one hell of a day. "The older two children will be home in half an hour. In the meantime, you can meet Miss Chloe." She nodded to Trish, who got up and left the room to go get her daughter.

When they were alone, Maggie addressed Ruth directly. "Ms. Lawson is a wonderful mother."

"That's good to know."

"She's provided for her children admirably during her illness."

"And you know for certain that they have always been well cared for?"

"No, I don't. I only know what I and my team have observed since they arrived here, and we've seen nothing concerning."

"Then there shouldn't be anything to worry about. I'm sure you're aware that when we receive a report, we're obligated to follow up on it."

"I am aware of that, and I'm aware that Ms. Lawson and her children have rights, too, and among them would be information about the source of the complaint as well as the opportunity to respond to it."

"If we determine there's an issue, she'll be given every opportunity to respond."

Maggie's stomach ached. She could only imagine how Trish must feel. The poor woman had been through enough.

Trish came into the room carrying Chloe. "She was napping, so she may be a little out of sorts."

The child's cheeks were rosy from sleep, and her thumb was in her mouth.

"Chloe, honey, this is Ms. Stapleton. Can you say hello?"

Chloe shook her head and burrowed more deeply into her mother's embrace.

"She's always slow to wake up after a nap, especially when she's disturbed."

Maggie hid a grin behind her hand. Good for Trish for pointing out the disruption the other woman had caused in the child's schedule.

"How did she get the bump on her head?" Ms. Stapleton asked.

"She tripped over one of her brother's trucks and bounced off a table."

"Do the children get along well with each other?"

"They do. Before I was ill, they used to fight a lot. But now they're better about working things out and playing nicely together. They've been troupers through all of this, Ms. Stapleton."

The next half hour passed slowly while Ms. Stapleton observed Trish and Chloe and waited for Lily and Jimmy to come home. Maggie helped by going to get a snack and a drink for Chloe, who became more animated as the time went on and she fully awakened from her nap.

Right at three twenty, the van deposited the school-age children at the kitchen door, and they came in with the usual clatter of voices and backpacks hitting the floor. Mitch's voice was low as he greeted them with after-school snacks and orders to put their backpacks where they belonged.

The children loved Mitch and his snacks, so they happily complied with his instructions. After-school supervision wasn't in his job description, but after he mentioned to Maggie how much he loved being the one to greet the kids, she'd turned the role over to him.

"I'll go get Lily and Jimmy," Maggie said.

She went into the kitchen, where the kids were enjoying cheese sticks, carrots, grapes and one cookie each. "Did everyone have a good day?"

They responded with, "Yes, Ms. Maggie," along with reports of everything that'd happened since they left the house that morning.

"I need Lily and Jimmy for a minute."

Maggie hated the wary look that Lily gave her, as if anticipating disaster had become the child's default. "Nothing's wrong." At least she hoped that was the case.

Mitch handed each of the two children a baggie with their snacks and winked at them.

"Thank you, Mr. Mitch," Jimmy said.

They followed Maggie obediently to the conference room and rushed to give their mother and sister hugs.

"Guys," Trish said, "this is Ms. Stapleton. She came by to say hello to us and to see how we're doing in our new home."

"We *love* it here," Jimmy said. "There's horses! Mr. Derek and Mr. Brayden said we can learn how to take care of them, and yesterday, I got to help fill their water. They drink a *lot* of water! We're even going to learn how to *ride* them!"

Ms. Stapleton smiled at the boy's enthusiasm. "And you, Lily? Do you like it here at Matthews House?"

"It's very nice," Lily said softly.

"The children have made a great adjustment to their new surroundings," Trish said. "It's a relief to all of us to have the support of Matthews House and their wonderful staff during this difficult time."

"Trish and the children are welcome to stay with us for as long as they need to."

Ms. Stapleton spent another thirty minutes with Trish and the kids before asking for a minute alone with Trish and Maggie, who asked Mitch to watch the kids for a couple of minutes. "I'm very glad you're settled at Matthews and have the support you need during your illness."

Trish stared at her. "So that's it?"

"That's it."

"You can't tell me who reported me?"

"I can only say the report came from the children's school and was related to your daughter's anxiety. There was concern about whether she's being properly supported."

Maggie could tell that information didn't sit well with Trish, but she refrained from saying so.

"You can assure the concerned party that Lily is being fully supported with medication and regular visits to the counselor, who's helping her develop coping skills. She's always been perceptive, and she understands the implications of her only parent fighting a serious illness."

"Understood. I'll pray for your return to full health." Ms. Stapleton stood, collected her belongings and shook hands with both of them. "I'll see myself out."

After her footsteps faded, Trish turned to Maggie. "Why would the school report me to DCS before they asked *me* about Lily's care?"

"I don't know, but I suspect as mandatory reporters, they felt it was something they needed to do to protect Lily. I know it's hard not to take it personally."

"You're damned right it is. Like we're not dealing with enough already."

"The good news is that people at her school care, and Ms. Stapleton found nothing of concern. It's over."

"No, it isn't. Now we're on the DCS radar, and if anything goes wrong, they'll be back."

"Try not to worry. For right now, everything is good. You and the kids are safe and supported. You can focus on your treatment and not have to worry about rent or anything else for as long as necessary."

"I'll never have the words to thank you and your sister for what you're doing here. You're saving my life in so many ways."

"We're happy to help."

They left the conference room, and Trish went to check on the kids in the playroom.

Maggie ducked into her office and closed the door, taking a much-needed minute to regroup. Her phone chimed with a text from Brayden.

I'm at the airport. How was the rest of your day?

Stressful. She filled him in on the DCS visit, without giving specifics he didn't need to know.

Go enjoy your family. Have a drink. You've earned it.

Thanks. Safe travels.

He replied with the thumbs-up emoji.

Maggie appreciated him checking in and that he already seemed to care about what went on with her and their clientele. Compassion was such an important quality in their field, and to realize he had it in spades was reassuring.

She spent another two hours dealing with emails and phone messages and then met with Arnelle to go over several health-related items. Corey and Trish were at the top of her list for Arnelle.

"Trish has given me permission to confer with her medical team, which is very helpful," Arnelle reported. "I've got a good handle on what's going on and how we can support her."

Maggie told her about the visit from DCS. "I want to make sure we're doing everything we can for Lily, too."

"I'll consult with Trish and see what I can do there."

"We need to arrange for transportation to counseling appointments so Lily can continue her therapy."

"I'll take care of that."

They often sent residents to appointments via Lyft or Uber, and the fees came out of the program budget.

"Now about Corey," Arnelle said. "We'll need to get her into counseling as soon as possible."

"Agreed." Maggie handed her a list the hospital social worker had provided. "Here're some resources."

"We may want to look into hiring a part-time counselor so we can offer that service right here rather than sending people into town for it. It's a safe bet that most of our residents would benefit from regular therapy."

"I'll talk to the bosses about that. I'm sure they won't have a problem with it." Reid and Kate had basically written a blank check to give the residents everything they needed. Although Maggie had created a budget for the program, they were willing to make additional funds available as needs arose. They had figured there would be extras, especially in the first year.

"Corey will be discharged tomorrow or the day after," Maggie said. "I gave them my number to call when she's ready for a ride. I'll keep you posted."

"Sounds good. Congrats on the new niece, by the way."

"Thank you." Maggie showed her some new pictures Kate had sent earlier.

"She's a beauty."

"Yes, she is. The grandparents are arriving as we speak to meet her."

"You should get out of here and go be with your family."

"That's the plan. See you tomorrow." Maggie locked up her office and went to her apartment to shower and change clothes before she left for Kate's. She stood under the hot water for a long time, letting it wash away the stress of the day so she could focus on her sister and the rest of the family.

Maggie wanted to show them a strong, competent woman who was adjusting well to her new life, not an emotional basket case who was forever bordering on the verge of breakdown.

She brushed her hair, put on enough makeup to conceal the dark circles under her eyes and got dressed in jeans, boots and a lightweight sweater. With her purse, keys and phone in hand, she left her apartment and encountered the chatter and voices of residents having dinner in the conference room, which once again became a dining room at dinnertime.

Her inclination was to check in with everyone before she left, but tonight, she left things in the hands of her capable staff and got out of there while she could. The next crisis, she had discovered, was always imminent.

She'd received a text from Jill two hours ago, letting her know the family had landed at Nashville International Airport. They would be settling in at Kate's by now. When she'd asked, Reid had told her the runway at Matthews House was too short to accommodate the private jet her dad chartered to bring the whole crew.

As she drove the short distance to her sister's place, Maggie kept the window down and the music loud, hoping to reset from the difficult day so she could enjoy the time with her family. In the driveway at Kate's were two large black SUVs that'd been rented to transport the family from the airport. Knowing their dad, he'd gone to enormous lengths to make sure their visit wouldn't be a burden to the new parents.

Maggie went in through the mudroom and dropped her bag and keys on a bench before continuing into the kitchen, where Buddy's mother, Miss Martha, was stirring a big pot on the stove.

"*Now* the gang's all here," Martha said, opening her arms to hug Maggie.

Martha, who had white hair and wise brown eyes, was one of the sweetest ladies Maggie had ever met. She'd immediately made Maggie feel like a beloved granddaughter and was an extra mother to Reid, after having worked as his family's housekeeper. She had to be eighty-five by now, but you'd never know it to look at her.

"What're you making? Smells delicious."

"I whipped up a big pot of chili and cornbread to feed the troops tonight so no one would have to cook after traveling."

"That was awfully nice of you."

"Truth be told, I also wanted to get a look at my new grandbaby. She's a stunner."

"She certainly is."

"Your first niece or nephew, right?"

"That's right."

"Such a special time for all of you. How's it going at the house?"

"It's great. Something different every day."

"It's such a wonderful thing y'all are doing there. I couldn't think of a better way to make that old house come alive again."

"It's definitely alive."

Martha smiled. "Go on in and see your folks. They were asking about you."

Maggie gave Martha's arm an affectionate squeeze. "Always good to see you, Miss Martha."

"Likewise, sweetheart."

As she followed the roar of voices into the great room, she was nearly mowed over by four young brothers who rushed toward her as a group.

"*Whoa*, Nelly." Maggie laughed as she wrapped her arms around them.

They all talked at once, bombarding her with news and laughter and boyish exuberance.

Her dad rescued her. "Boys. Give your sister room to breathe."

The boys backed off, and Maggie stepped into the outstretched arms of her dad. He smelled like home to her and held her close for a long, perfect moment.

"Hi, Daddy."

"Hi, Mags. So good to see you."

"You, too." She pulled back to look up at him. Other than a few more gray hairs around the edges of his dark hair, he looked the same. Growing up, her friends had always commented on how handsome her dad was, and at the time, Maggie had been revolted by that. But now she got it. He was a good-looking man who seemed to get only more so as he aged.

Andi came over to join them, hugging Maggie. Her mom and Aidan came next, followed by Frannie, Jamie, Owen and Olivia.

"Where's Eric?" Maggie asked.

"He couldn't miss school, unfortunately," Jack said. "He was super bummed, but it was the right thing with finals next week."

"Aw, I'm so sad I won't get to see him."

"We are, too," Andi said as she secured long dark curly hair into a messy bun, "but you'll see him for graduation and then again for the wedding."

"You look good, Mags," Clare said. "How's life in Tennessee treating you?"

"Very well, as you know, because I talk to you every day."

Clare laughed. "You can't blame a mom for asking."

"Today was a bitch. I need a drink. Anyone else want one?"

"Sign me up," Jack said. "Lead the way."

He and Maggie went into the kitchen, where she poured herself a glass of wine from one of the bottles that'd been put on the counter and Jack got beers for himself and Jamie.

"How's it going being a grandfather?" Maggie asked him.

Martha snickered under her breath.

"I'm adjusting," Jack said. "Slowly."

"Comes at you outta nowhere," Martha said. "One minute you're minding your own business, raising your family. Next minute, bam. You're a grandparent."

"That's exactly how it happened for me, only I've got ten-year-old boys still at home."

"Well, that's your fault, my friend," Martha said.

Jack laughed. "Indeed it is. They're keeping me young, though, so there is that."

"*That*," Martha said, "is everything."

CHAPTER 13

The family passed a delightful evening of food, drinks and laughter. Everyone took turns holding Poppy, the star of the day, who slept through most of the action. When she was awake, she seemed to take it all in with wise gray eyes. Kate said she couldn't really see anything yet, but Maggie wanted to dispute that. Clearly, the child was going to be exceptional based on the way she rolled with her boisterous family with a minimum of fuss.

Maggie helped her mom, Andi and Jill clean up the kitchen after dinner. Being with them helped to settle her after the rough day, but her emotions continued to churn, especially after she checked her phone and saw a text from Corey that she would be released in the morning.

I'll be there to pick you up, Maggie replied.

"Everything all right, Mags?" Clare asked.

"Today was a rough one at the office. I had one mom, a domestic assault victim, decide to give up her premature baby for adoption, and another mom, who's battling ovarian cancer, visited by the Department of Children's Services."

"Oh wow, that's a lot."

"Is it always like that?" Andi asked as she refilled her wineglass and

Clare's. Jill had gone to find Ashton, and Martha was sitting with her feet up at Kate's directive. Reid would drive the older woman back to her home on Buddy's property when she was ready to go.

Maggie declined another glass since she had to drive. "Thankfully, no. Today was an unusually crazy day. And very emotional. Seeing Corey through the process with the social workers was brutal."

"I can only imagine." Clare put an arm around Maggie. "She's lucky to have you and the team at Matthews."

Maggie leaned into her mom's embrace. "We'll get her through it. I hope."

"You will," Andi said. "For sure."

"So we hear there's a horse whisperer," Clare said.

"And that he's hot AF," Andi added, her expression full of mirth.

Maggie rolled her eyes. "What else did they tell you?"

"That you brought him here last night to meet your sisters and the baby," Clare said.

"Which has them wondering what's up with you two," Andi said.

It was interesting to note how her mother and stepmother finished each other's sentences these days. There'd been a time when Maggie had wondered if their family would ever recover from the way her parents' marriage had ended. Now they were all friends and had put the past where it belonged so they could fully support all their children.

Clare waved a hand in front of Maggie's face. "Hello? Maggie?"

"Just making sure you guys were done before I respond."

"Spill it," Clare said.

"He works with me at Matthews. He's a nice guy and a big fan of Kate's. I thought he might like to meet her. That he got to meet Buddy and Taylor and everyone else was an added extra."

"That's nice of you, but you brought him here the night your sister had a baby, which tells me he might mean more to you than you're letting on." Clare O'Malley, shrewd as always. Other than a slight limp when she overdid it, she had no lingering effects from the accident and long coma.

"I met him three days ago when he came to work for me. He's a nice guy who I'll be working closely with in the equine therapy program. That's all there is to it. Nothing to see here."

Clare glanced at Andi, skepticism in her expression and tone of voice. "As an experienced mother, I tend to find that when I'm told there's 'nothing to see here,' there's almost always something to be seen."

Andi covered her mouth to smother a laugh.

"She's not funny," Maggie said.

"She's kind of funny," Andi said.

"Not even kinda."

"I'm well known for being funny, so give it up."

"What's my lovely wife telling you?" Aidan asked as he came into the kitchen. Tall and handsome with wavy brown hair and hazel eyes, Aidan had about three gray hairs, which drove Clare crazy, as she was seven years older than Aidan and relying on her stylist to keep her blonde these days.

"She's trying to convince me she's funny."

Aidan glanced at Clare, smiling warmly the way he always did around her. "She is pretty funny."

"Not you, too!"

Clare gave Maggie a smug smile. "Told ya. I won't pile on about the sexy horse whisperer—"

"His name is *Brayden*, and he's my *employee*."

"As I was saying, I won't pile on, but I will say I'm glad you're making new *friends* here."

"Did it hurt you to show that kind of restraint?" Maggie asked her mother.

"Deeply."

"Don't let her fool you," Aidan said. "She figures she'll get any and all dirt from Kate and Jill, so she's letting you off the hook easily."

Clare gave her husband an outraged look. "Will you please shut your mouth?"

Andi laughed helplessly.

"You're all insane," Maggie said, but she loved them unreasonably, and having them in town made her realize how much she'd missed them.

"You say that like it's news to us that we're unhinged," Aidan said.

Her stepfather was one of Maggie's favorite people in the world. He was the first to treat her like an actual adult, and she'd never forget that. When the rest of the family had been melting down about Kate's relationship with Reid, Aidan had been the one to tell Maggie that sometimes she was better off not knowing the adult details. She'd learned since then, many times over, how right he'd been about that.

"In other news, how's Grammy doing?" Maggie asked Aidan. His mother was another of Maggie's favorite people. She treated Maggie and her sisters like grandchildren, and they adored her.

"She's hanging in there. The arthritis is a bitch. Wouldn't wish it on my worst enemy, but she doesn't let it get her down. She is counting the days until the wedding and is very determined to be there."

"I can't wait to see her and all the O'Malleys."

"You'll get to see the whole mob. Everyone is coming."

"That's what Jill wanted—the entire family."

"She'll get more than she bargained for with the O'Malleys," Aidan said.

Maggie stayed until everyone started to pack it in for the night. "I'll see you tomorrow after work."

"Would you mind if we came by to check out Matthews House?" Jack asked. "I'd love to see where you're living and working."

"Of course. Just shoot me a text to let me know what time." Thinking of bringing Corey home and getting her settled, Maggie added, "Afternoon would be better."

"Sounds good. We'll see you then." He hugged her and kissed her cheek. "Drive carefully."

"Always do. My dad taught me."

His smile lit up his handsome face. "That's right. Some of the most spectacular fights I ever had with my children involved teaching them to drive. Ah, good times."

Maggie laughed at the face he made. "The best of times."

"For you, maybe. I lived in mortal fear of imminent death."

"Such a drama queen."

Andi curled her hands around Jack's arm. "That's my husband. The ultimate drama queen. But that's why we love him."

"I'm standing right here," Jack said dryly.

Maggie drove home with a smile on her face, thinking of each of her family members and the enjoyable evening they'd spent together. In the midst of it all, Kate had reigned from her spot on the sofa, sharing her baby with the family and glowing with hard-won happiness. She'd worked her ass off to earn this well-deserved break. Maggie couldn't be happier to know that she'd have her sisters around for the next year before they possibly headed back out on the road to tour.

She pulled into her spot behind the stables, feeling an odd sense of sadness at knowing Brayden wasn't there. *For fuck's sake*, she thought as she walked across the driveway to the kitchen door. *Knock it off, Maggie.*

Matthews House was blessedly quiet when she stepped into the kitchen. She went into her apartment and shut the door, feeling wrung out after the long day. After changing into her pajamas, brushing her teeth and getting into bed, she looked at her phone for the first time since she got Corey's text earlier.

A flutter of elation went through her when she saw that Brayden had sent her a picture of the Florida sunset. *Greetings from sunny Florida. Hope you had a nice time with your folks.*

It was a great time. Nice to see them all.

He wrote right back. *Glad to hear it. You needed that after the day you had.*

She sighed with the pleasure that came from knowing he understood that a day like today had kicked her ass. It was so comforting to have someone around who *saw* her struggling to juggle the many competing needs that arose in a day and got how challenging it could be. She didn't have to pretend to be super competent around him, which was a huge relief. *Yeah, this was one for the record books, for sure. Thankfully they aren't all like that.*

One of my grandfather's favorite sayings after a hard day was you got 'rode hard and put up wet.' Applicable for a number of scenarios. Brayden added the laughing emoji.

The suggestive phrase mingled with images of Brayden's bare chest and handsome face. Thank goodness he wasn't here to see how flustered he'd made her with his innuendo. The thought of being rode hard by him and put up wet... *Stop it, Maggie!* She forced herself to come up with a reply that gave nothing away. *That's a good summary of my day. Corey is getting released in the morning.*

Are you picking her up?

Ya.

Ugh, I hope that goes ok. She's so lucky to have you and the team at Matthews. You'll get her through it.

We'll do our best for her. Are you in Key West?

Driving through Alligator Alley as we speak. We'll get there around midnight.

You aren't texting and driving, are you?

No, ma'am, my buddy Josh is driving.

Don't ma'am me.

Yes, ma'am. He added a row of laughing emojis.

Maggie replied with a scowl emoji.

He sent back more laughing emojis. *Text me tomorrow and let me know how it goes with Corey.*

She sent a thumbs-up, touched that he cared enough to want to know how it went when he hadn't even met Corey yet. He'd started to feel like a "partner in crime" to her, and it was kind of nice to have someone to talk to about everything that was going on. While she continued to tell herself that developing feelings for a man she worked with was inadvisable, the feelings were happening regardless of those inner warnings.

He was a nice guy, a decent guy, someone who understood the world in which she lived and worked, and who'd offered support on multiple occasions in the short time she'd known him. Sure, she had Teresa and Arnelle and the rest of the staff as well as her sisters and family to rely on, but for some reason, talking about it with Brayden made her feel like she had her very own confidant.

It was all so confusing. On the one hand, she wanted to be as professional as possible. On the other hand, she was struggling with life-and-death issues on a daily basis, and having someone like him around to lean on made the burden feel lighter than it had been before he came along.

She went to bed feeling conflicted about the clash of personal versus professional and hoping she wasn't creating a disaster for herself—and the program—by relying on the very sexy Brayden Thomas.

MAGGIE WOKE to a sunrise photo from Key West and a text that said, *Wasting away in Margaritaville.* He'd included sun, sunglasses, palm tree, beach ball and cocktail emojis.

She smiled and typed her reply. *It's a tough life, but someone's gotta do it.*

The reply bubbles appeared immediately, and she waited, breathless, to see what he would say. *You know it! Good luck with everything today. I'll be thinking of you while I'm fishing, soaking up the sun and drinking beer.*

Now you're just being mean. Haha! But thanks for the good luck. I need it today.

You got this. Let me know how it goes.

I will. Have fun fishing. Send pics. I'm living vicariously!

Will do.

Maggie appreciated the boost the exchange with him had given to what would be a tough morning. Looking forward to sharing the details with him later made it seem more bearable. She got dressed in comfortable jeans and a lightweight top as the temperature was set to top seventy-five. She'd been warned to expect a humid summer that would make the humidity at home in Rhode Island seem tame by comparison.

Until then, she was enjoying the warmth and the sunshine and the occasional rainy day that kept the grass green and lush. While she missed living at the coast, she'd come to appreciate views of a different sort since she'd moved to Tennessee.

After checking in with everyone at Matthews and helping to see the children off to school, Maggie headed out to the hospital to pick up Corey. On the way, she prepared herself for the emotional battering she was about to endure so she could be ready to support Corey in any way necessary.

When Maggie got to Corey's room shortly after ten, she found the young woman almost exactly where she'd left her the day before —on her side in bed, facing away from the door—but she was dressed in street clothes, and her bag was sitting on the bedside table.

"Hi, Corey."

"Hey."

"Are you ready to go?"

Corey didn't answer, so Maggie walked around the bed and sat in the visitor chair, which put her at the other woman's eye level. "You want to talk about it?"

"Nothing to say."

"Is there anything I can do for you?"

Corey gave a subtle shake of her head.

They sat together in silence until a nurse named Eleanor came in with discharge paperwork and a wheelchair. The woman was in her fifties, with dark hair and kind eyes. "You're all set to go, Ms. Corey. Can I help you up?"

Corey fisted the blanket and began to cry. "I don't want to leave him."

Maggie felt helpless in the face of the other woman's heartbreak. She wished there was something she could do for her.

"Would you like to visit him before you leave?" Eleanor asked.

Corey visibly brightened at the prospect of seeing her baby. "I can do that?"

"I'm sure we can arrange it."

Corey looked to Maggie. "Do you think I should?"

123

Oh God, what to say? "If you see him, will that make it harder to leave?"

"I don't know." Corey sat up, moving carefully and slowly. She glanced at Eleanor. "What do people usually do?"

"Some want to see the babies while others prefer not to." Eleanor sat next to Corey and took hold of her hand. "Personally, I think it might help you to see him once, so you have an image of him to take with you when you leave."

Maggie wasn't sure she agreed with that, but it wasn't up to her.

"I… I think I'd like to do that. T-to see him. Just once." To Maggie, she said, "Will you come with me?"

"Of course." Maggie told herself she could handle this, but in fact, she wasn't at all sure she could. Nowhere in the job description Kate and Reid had given her was the sentence "go with heartbroken mom to see child being given up for adoption for the last time." She grabbed Corey's bag and discharge paperwork and followed them out of the room.

Thank goodness for Eleanor, who had obviously done this before and pushed Corey in the wheelchair to the NICU. Bringing the chair to a stop outside the door, Eleanor went around to squat in front of Corey, laying her hand over the young woman's. "He's going to be attached to a lot of tubes and machines. It'll be frightening to look at, but he's stable and doing as well as can be expected."

Corey stared at the double doors to the NICU, her expression unreadable.

"Are you sure you want to do this, honey?" Eleanor asked.

Corey nodded.

Eleanor stood and pressed a button on the wall that brought another nurse to the door. The two women conferred before the one inside the NICU stepped aside to hold the door to admit the wheelchair.

Maggie brought up the rear, her heart in her throat as she took in the bright lights, the tiny incubators, the machines, the tubes, the quiet urgency of life-and-death struggles. She swallowed hard, fighting to keep it together for Corey, to get her through this. That was Maggie's only goal.

Eleanor parked the wheelchair next to one of the incubators.

Maggie noted the label: Baby Boy Gellar.

Corey had told Maggie the day before that she hadn't given him a name, choosing to allow his adoptive parents to name him.

Raising her hand, Corey touched the outside of the incubator and leaned in for a closer look at the baby.

His chest rose and fell in rapid succession.

Maggie had never seen a premature baby, except for on television, and was unprepared for the sight of such a tiny human. She blinked back tears as she watched Corey stare at the baby.

"Do you have any questions?" the NICU nurse asked.

"Is he going to make it?"

"I can't say for sure yet, but he's stable, which is a very good sign."

Corey seemed satisfied with that response. "Someone will want him, right?"

"Absolutely," Eleanor said. "The social workers have already reached out to several agencies. I expect they'll have someone in the next day or two."

"Will I be notified?"

"If you'd like to be."

"I would. I want to know he has someone."

"I'll make sure you're told."

That seemed to pacify Corey. "I think I'm ready to go now." She kept her gaze fixed on the baby until Eleanor moved the chair toward the door and she had no choice but to look away.

In the elevator, Maggie noticed tears rolling down Corey's cheeks, but the young woman didn't make a sound as she stared straight ahead. Eleanor waited with Corey while Maggie went to get the car.

With Corey loaded into the passenger seat, Eleanor leaned in to grasp the young woman's hand. "I'll pray for you and for your baby."

"Thank you for everything."

"You're a great mom to do what's best for him, even if it's breaking your heart."

Corey nodded. "Thank you," she whispered.

Eleanor stepped back and closed the door. She handed a business card to Maggie. "Call me if you need anything."

"Thank you, Eleanor. You're very good at your job."

"Some cases are more difficult than others, which I'm sure you're learning in your job."

"For sure."

"She'll be all right. It'll take some time, but she'll bounce back."

"We'll take good care of her."

"She's lucky to have y'all at Matthews. I'm sure I'll see you around before much longer."

"No doubt. See you."

CHAPTER 14

*M*aggie got into the driver's seat and put the car into gear, heading for home with the window open to let in the warm spring air. She kept the radio turned down low so as not to disturb Corey, who didn't say a word on the thirty-minute ride. Only the sound of an occasional sniffle came from her.

Maggie left her alone, deciding to take her lead from Corey. Back at the house, Arnelle was waiting to greet them and whisked Corey upstairs to her room to get her settled in bed. Maggie headed for her office and sat in her desk chair, releasing a deep breath.

Teresa came in a minute later. "How'd it go?"

"What're you still doing here?"

"I hung out until you guys got back to see how you made out."

"She asked to see the baby before we left."

"Ugh." Teresa sat in the other chair. "How was that?"

"Brutal, but she held up better than I would have."

"She knows she's doing the right thing. That helps."

"I guess. Who knows what the right thing is in this situation?"

"She knows. She knows she isn't equipped to deal with a baby with the health problems he's going to have for quite some time. It was the right thing for both of them under the circumstances."

"I suppose so."

"Are you okay?"

"Yes, of course. It's not about me."

"Maggie... This is tough stuff. It's okay to feel undone by it."

"That's good to know, because it was rough, and I just tried to hold it together for her."

"You're doing great. She needed someone there with her, and you provided that shoulder for her to lean on. You did your job and then some."

"Thanks for the support. I appreciate it. Now go home and get some sleep."

"I'll see you tonight."

"I may not be here. Got the family in town to meet Poppy."

"Oh, that's right. Enjoy that."

"I will. Thanks for sticking around."

"No problem."

A few minutes after Teresa left, Mitch came to the door with a bowl and a glass that he put on Maggie's desk. "Greek yogurt with homemade granola and locally grown blueberries and sweet tea."

"Thank you, Mitch."

"Figured you could use a snack."

"You figured right."

He glanced toward the stairs and then back at Maggie. "Is she all right?"

"Not at the moment, but I hope she will be. In time."

"Would it be all right to take a snack up to her?"

"That'd be lovely, Mitch. I'm sure she'd appreciate it."

"Great." He seemed relieved to be able to do something for the young woman. "We'll get her through this, Maggie. One day at a time."

Maggie was moved nearly to tears by the sentiment coming from the usually brusque man. "Yes, we will. Thank you."

He nodded and left the room.

Maggie ate the yogurt and delicious granola and then let her hair down from the ponytail, running her fingers through the long strands and massaging her scalp as she tried to process the overabundance of emotions. She had to keep telling herself that *she* hadn't given up a baby. Corey had done that, not her. As a bystander, she'd absorbed Corey's grief so fully that it felt like she'd lost something dear to her. She needed to shake off those feelings so she could get back to work on behalf of the other residents, who were counting on her to keep her shit together so she could help them do the same.

This was no time for a meltdown.

She could tell herself that a hundred times, but fearing the meltdown would materialize anyway, she left the office and went out the kitchen door to the stables to see Thunder.

As always, Thunder was happy to see her and nuzzled her neck as she shed some tears into his coat. "Tough day, buddy."

He nickered in response, which made her smile.

"Morning, Ms. Maggie," Derek said from behind her.

"Morning." Maggie hastily wiped away her tears before she turned to the older man. "Are you feeling better?"

"Much better, thank you."

"Glad to hear it."

"Is everything all right?" Derek asked.

Maggie thought about that for a second. "It will be. Eventually."

"Let me know if I can do anything for you."

"That's very sweet of you. Thank you."

He went on his way, tending to the horses while Maggie spent another few minutes with Thunder while giving thanks for the great people who were supporting her on this journey. "I'll try to get back for a ride later."

The horse nuzzled her, giving her exactly what she needed to continue her day.

She kissed his nose and walked back to the house, feeling fortified by the time with him. Horses had always done that for her, had calmed and sustained her through the most difficult times in her life. After her mother's accident, riding had given her an outlet to deal with the pain.

Arnelle was in the kitchen getting a cup of coffee when Maggie came in.

"How is she?" Maggie asked.

"She's resting."

"That's good. She has to be exhausted."

"We've got another situation."

Maggie steeled herself for the next challenge. "What's that?"

"Debbie McBride sent the kids out this morning but didn't come down to breakfast with them or see them off to school, which she always does. I knocked on her door earlier and again just now. She didn't answer either time. I know the policy is to respect their privacy, but we've done that. It might be time to take it to the next level."

Maggie processed the information before going to her office to retrieve the pass key from a locked drawer in her desk. Upon arrival, each of the residents signed a form acknowledging that Matthews House staff could enter their rooms at any time, for any reason, without prior notice. However, this was the first time she'd had to use that key.

She followed Arnelle upstairs to the second floor, where they knocked on Debbie's door again.

When there was no answer, Maggie inserted her key into the lock and opened the door.

The room consisted of four twin-size beds, a large wardrobe closet and a tub full of toys in the corner. Debbie appeared to be asleep on one of the twin beds.

Arnelle approached her and tried to wake the woman, who didn't stir. She placed her fingers on Debbie's neck and then looked at Maggie, shaking her head.

Maggie's heart dropped. *Dear God.* The woman was *dead*? She took a deep breath and let it out. "I'll call the coroner." She went into the hallway, ducked into the bathroom, closed the door and pulled her cell phone from her back pocket. She googled the number for the Davidson County Coroner and put through the call.

"I need to report a death at Matthews House," she said, giving the address.

"Was there an accident?"

"Not that we're aware of. One of our residents was found deceased in her bed just now."

"We'll send someone right away. Please don't touch the body and leave everything just as it was when you found her."

"Will do. Thank you." Maggie left the bathroom and went back to the room. "Arnelle, come out, please."

Arnelle joined her in the hallway.

Maggie shut the door. "We have to leave her and everything in the room just as we found it."

Trish Lawson came down the hallway, carrying a glass of Mitch's iced tea in one hand and holding Chloe in her other arm. "What's wrong?"

Maggie hesitated, but only for a second. "Debbie McBride has passed away."

Trish's face went flat with shock. "*What?* What happened?"

"We don't know. After the kids came down alone this morning, Arnelle checked on her. When she didn't answer her door, we entered the room and found her deceased."

"My God," Trish whispered. "That poor woman. And her babies..."

"What do we know about the extended family?" Arnelle asked Maggie.

"She has family in Arizona."

"You should call them. If we can get them here to care for the kids, DCS might not take them."

Maggie nodded. "I'll go do that now." She raced down the stairs and into her office, closed the door, booted up her computer, typed in her access code and called up her file on the McBride family. She found the next-of-kin contact for Debbie McBride listed as her mother, Karen Truver, in Phoenix. Before she could give herself a chance to freak out about what she had to do, she put through the call on the desktop phone.

"Hello?"

"Is this Mrs. Truver?"

"It is. Who's calling?"

"This is Maggie Harrington at Matthews House in Nashville, Tennessee."

The other woman gasped. "What is it? What's wrong?"

Maggie closed her eyes and forced herself to say the words. "I'm sorry to have to tell you that Debbie has passed away."

A loud scream came from the other woman. "Oh God, no! Oh Lord." Karen broke down. "What happened?"

"We aren't sure yet. The coroner is on the way."

"And the children? Are they there?"

"They're at school right now but will be home about three thirty."

"I'll come for them. I have documents to prove that Debbie designated me as their emergency guardian should the need arise. I'll see about a flight and get there as soon as I can. May I call you back on this number?"

"Of course." Maggie also gave the woman her cell number. "Whatever we can do for you."

"Thank you so much. Debbie was so happy since she'd been at your facility. She said she could breathe for the first time in years."

"We've enjoyed having them."

"If you would... Wait for me to get there before you tell Mandy and Patrick."

Maggie tried to figure out what they would tell the children in the meantime. "We'll do our best."

They ended the call, and Maggie took a second to glance at her texts, noting a new one from Brayden that she would read later and another from her dad asking when would be a good time to come by to visit.

It's going to have to be tomorrow, Maggie replied. *Sorry.*

He wrote right back. *No problem.*

Maggie put through a call to Kate, who answered on the second ring. "Sorry to bother you."

"No bother. I was just doing some baby gazing."

"How is she?"

"Delightful and perfect."

"So, Kate, I'm calling you as my boss and the owner of Matthews

House to tell you that Debbie McBride, one of the mothers, passed away in her room."

"Oh my God. Maggie!"

"I don't know what happened or anything more than that the children came down alone this morning, had breakfast and went to school. When Arnelle checked on Debbie, she didn't answer the door, so I used my pass key to gain access. That's when we found her. The coroner has been called, and I've contacted Debbie's mother in Arizona. She's on her way to be with the kids. I'm also required to report Debbie's death to the Department of Children's Services."

"Are you all right?" Kate asked softly.

"I've had better days."

"I can ask Reid to come over to help."

"I appreciate that, but I don't think there's anything he can do."

"He could be there for you."

"I'm all right. The staff is here, and we're doing what needs to be done."

"Will you please call me back when you can and let me know how it's going?"

"I will."

"Sending you a big hug and so much love. This is above and beyond."

"Whatever it takes. I'll call you in a bit."

"I'll be waiting to hear from you."

Maggie ended the call, and since she couldn't do anything else until the coroner arrived, she took a second to glance at Brayden's text. It was a picture of him holding a big fish and grinning widely.

She sent back a thumbs-up and then went into the kitchen to tell Mitch what'd happened.

"That poor woman," Mitch said. "She tried so hard. She talked to me some about her struggles with drugs. I wonder if she was using again."

"I'm sure her family will request an autopsy."

"I think it might be required any time there's an unexplained death."

"I'm learning a lot of things I never expected I'd have to know."

"Such is life in the social services business, or so I'm told. I have friends who've been in this field for years, and the stories they could tell…"

"I'm sure."

"That's going to be us now. We'll be the ones with stories to tell."

"I guess so."

Mitch and the rest of the staff were well aware of the need to protect the privacy and dignity of their clients. Each of them had signed robust nondisclosure agreements before starting their jobs.

A short time later, the sound of sirens in the distance alerted Maggie to the arrival of the police and coroner. The next few hours passed in a blur of conversation, details and heartbreak. Maggie conferred with Ruth Stapleton at DCS and let her know that the children's grandmother was on her way with documentation to prove her daughter had made her the emergency guardian for the children should the need arise.

When the children came home, they were told their mother wasn't there and that the police were doing an inspection. The other moms stepped up to help supervise Mandy and Patrick in the playroom and through homework and dinner until their grandmother arrived at eight o'clock.

Maggie made the conference room available to Karen and the children so she could have privacy to tell the children the dreadful news. Maggie was thankful that she wasn't asked to be in the room for that.

In the meantime, she helped the staff prepare a different room for Karen and the children to sleep in that night, since the McBrides' room hadn't been released yet by the police, who were still working the scene.

It was well after ten before Karen had the distraught children settled in their new room.

Maggie went upstairs to check on them and met up with Karen coming out of the bathroom. She was petite but had a stocky build, short dark hair and a round, pretty face. "Do you have everything you need?"

"We do. Thank you so much for everything you and your team have done today and over the last couple of months. You helped to make Debbie's final weeks so much more peaceful than they would've been otherwise."

"She was a lovely person. We were happy to have her and the kids. I'm so sorry for your loss."

"Thank you."

"I'll let you try to get some rest. You have my number if you need anything during the night."

"You're a godsend, Maggie. Thank you again for everything."

"You're very welcome." As Maggie headed for the stairs, she heard voices coming from the residents' lounge and went to check on them. All the other mothers were there, and Maggie was happy to see that Corey was among them. "How're you all doing?"

"We're shocked," Niki Ross said. "Debbie was right here with us last night."

"I know. It's hard to wrap your head around it when something happens suddenly like this."

Zara, another of the younger moms, cradled a baby monitor between her hands. "I just think about how her mom came and what would happen to Marcus if I died. My mom wouldn't come."

"I'd take him," Trish said.

Zara stared at her in disbelief. "You *would*?"

"Of course I would."

"I would, too," Kelsey said. At thirty-six, she was the oldest of the mothers in residence.

After the day she'd had, Maggie had needed this, to see the mothers supporting one another, forming a community they'd have to lean on long after they left Matthews House. That was one of the central goals of the program, and to see it happening before her eyes was indeed validating. "I hope you ladies are able to get some rest."

"You, too, Maggie," Trish said. "Good night."

As Maggie went downstairs, she took a call from Jill. "Hey, what's up?"

"Ashton and I are outside. Can we come in for a minute?"

135

Maggie wasn't at all surprised that they'd come to check on her. "Sure. Come to the kitchen door." She turned the light on and met them there a minute later.

Jill came through the door and wrapped her arms around Maggie in a fierce hug.

"Um, is it okay if I come in, too?" Ashton asked.

Keeping Maggie in her tight embrace, Jill shuffled them into the kitchen.

Ashton followed, closing the door behind him.

"Are you okay?" Jill asked.

Maggie closed her eyes and gave in to her sister's comfort when she might normally chafe at the thought of one of them thinking she needed babying. "I'm hanging in there. It's been quite a day."

"Dude, you're the master of the understatement."

"What can we do for you?" Ashton asked.

"It's nice of you guys to come by. Did Kate send you?"

"She might've asked us to check on you since she's stuck at home."

"And I haven't had a chance to call her with an update."

Ashton squeezed Maggie's shoulder. "My dad wanted to come running when he first heard the news, but Poppy was fussy, and Kate's been in a lot of pain today."

Jill finally let go of Maggie and took a step back to lean against the massive island in the middle of the kitchen.

"Is Kate okay?"

"She's fine, just sore."

Maggie's phone rang, and she declined the call from Brayden, even though she very much wanted to talk to him. She'd call him back after Jill and Ashton left.

"I can't stop thinking about that poor woman and her sweet kids," Jill said. "They must've been so shocked."

"It was awful."

"Does anyone have any idea what might've happened?"

"Nothing definite. She's had drug issues in the past. We're not sure if she was using again. The cops didn't find any sign of drugs in her room. We'll have to wait and see what the autopsy uncovers."

"Thank God their grandmother was able to get here quickly," Ashton said.

"I know. It was so hard to keep them busy until she arrived. Mandy knew something was going on and was asking a lot of questions."

Jill sighed. "Those poor babies. Life as they know it will never be the same."

After having their own mother suddenly wrenched from their lives, Maggie and her sisters certainly understood how Debbie's children were feeling. While Clare didn't die, she might as well have for the three years she was lost to them.

"We'll go and let you get some sleep," Jill said. "You must be exhausted."

"I'm pretty tired."

"Mags, is it too much? Seriously, you'd say so if it was, wouldn't you? We all worry about you."

"I'm really okay, rattled after today, but overall, I'm good. I love the job and helping people and learning so much every day. I'll let you know if you need to worry. I promise."

Jill hugged her again, as long and as hard as she had when she first arrived. "We're here if you need us."

"I know, and that helps."

Ashton kissed her forehead. "Hang in there, kiddo. You're doing a great job."

Maggie appreciated him saying that. Someone dying on her watch had shaken her confidence. She saw them out, shut off the light and activated the alarm before going into her apartment, closing the door and releasing a deep breath. If she'd survived this day, she was fairly confident she could get through just about anything.

CHAPTER 15

*A*fter changing into pajamas, brushing her teeth and falling into bed, Maggie remembered the call she'd missed from Brayden.

He'd left a voicemail. "Hey, it's me. I heard from Mitch about what happened today, and I wanted to check on you. I wish I was there to help. Call me when you can."

It was so sweet of him to reach out when he was supposed to be on vacation. Maggie didn't hesitate to return the call, because she knew he'd be anxious to hear from her.

"Hey, I'm so glad you called. Jesus, Maggie. Are you okay?"

"Yes, I'm fine—now. But it's been one heck of a day."

"If you don't want to talk about it, I'd totally understand."

"I don't mind." She retold the story—again—beginning with Arnelle alerting her to Debbie's absence at breakfast.

"Did the kids say if she was up with them?"

"Mandy said they tried to wake her, but figured she was sleeping in. They got themselves ready for school and came down for breakfast."

"God, so she was probably already gone."

"I think so."

"Do you want me to come home?"

"Brayden! No, of course not. You're on vacation."

"I wish I was there to help you."

She wanted to ask him why he wished that, but couldn't find the courage to pose the question. "It's really nice of you to call when you should be relaxing and having fun."

"Hard to do that in light of what's happening there. The other guys went out to the bars tonight, but I didn't feel like it."

"You're very sweet."

"Shut up. I am not."

Maggie cracked up laughing. "You are, too."

"Knock it off."

She realized that for the first time since she and Arnelle found Debbie dead in her bed, she could breathe normally again. He had done that for her just by caring. Her sisters cared, too, but for some reason, he was the one who'd made her feel better. "This helps. Thanks."

"Whatever I can do."

"How many fish did you catch today?"

"Like thirty altogether. There's a restaurant down here that we give them to. They cook them for us and their other customers. We do that every year."

"That's awesome. How many years have you guys been going there?"

"Since our freshman year of college, so like twelve, I think?"

"What a fun tradition."

"They're my very best friends."

"I'm glad you have them."

"Me, too. They came from everywhere to be with me when my mom died. They're very curious about this woman in Nashville that I've been texting."

"Oh. They are? Did you tell them it was just a work thing?"

After a long pause, he said, "Is that all it is, Maggie? Just a work thing?"

As his meaning registered with her, Maggie tried to formulate a response that would at least *attempt* to maintain a professional distance. But she found she couldn't lie to him, especially when he'd been so sweet to check on her. "No, that's not all it is."

"Phew. That was an awfully long pause."

"You know I'm conflicted."

"I do, and I get why, but I promise I'm not going to cause you any trouble at work."

"What if…"

"What if what?"

"Say that something happens between us and then it ends." She couldn't believe she was actually having this conversation with him. Chalk it up to the emotions of the day. Her defenses had been demolished. "We'd still have to live and work in the same place, and…"

"If that happens, I'll leave."

"That doesn't seem fair."

"Why not? You were there first. It's your program."

"I want you to feel at home here, not on the verge of being evicted and exiled."

"Sweetheart, you're already evicting me, and I haven't even taken you on a proper date yet."

It was a good thing she was reclined on the bed, because that sentence knocked the wind out of her, which he knew, judging by the low rumble of laughter that came from him.

Maggie turned onto her side, snuggling the torn, tattered remains of her beloved stuffed Froggie. They'd been through everything together.

"You still there?" Brayden asked.

"I'm here."

"Are you going to let me take you on that proper date when I get back to town?"

"I'm not sure that's a good idea."

"I think it's a great idea, perhaps the greatest idea in the history of good ideas."

Maggie smiled. "You might be overselling yourself, cowboy."

"No, I'm not. I'll make you so glad you said yes to me, you won't know what hit you."

"That's what I'm afraid of."

"You aren't seriously afraid of me, are you?"

"Not you so much as all members of the male species."

"Maggie, what happened to you was horrible, but I swear on the memory of my mother that you have nothing like that to fear from me. I'd treat you like a queen."

"I know."

"Do you? Really?"

"Yes, I do. You already have."

He moaned. "This vacation is the worst-timed trip I've ever taken."

Maggie laughed. "Maybe it's the best-timed trip."

"No, it isn't."

"Yes, it is."

"No."

"*Yes!*"

His low rumble of laughter had her thinking of his handsome face and the way he looked when he smiled. "I should let you get some sleep. You've got to be exhausted."

"Don't go yet."

"I'm here for as long as you want me."

"Tell me a story."

"What kind of story?"

"Something about you."

"Hmmm… let me think about what I can tell you that won't put you to sleep. Have I told you about how I rode a horse before I could walk?"

"Why am I not surprised?"

"My grandfather had me on his horse when I was three months old. He even had a special helmet made for me because my mom said I couldn't go without one, and they don't make riding helmets that small."

"I love that. I can totally picture it."

"I was hooked from the first time. From what I was told, I would have a complete meltdown every day around four o'clock until he got me on that horse. That was the only thing that calmed me. He took me every day until I was three, when he let me ride by myself for the first time."

"That's a great story."

"Horses have always been my thing. I'd run home from the bus stop, drop all my crap outside the back door and head for the stables. My mom would yell at me to come back and hang up my backpack and *then* I could go to see the horses."

"I bet you were so cute."

"I was a huge pain in the ass. I had a one-track mind. Every picture I drew in school was of horses, every story I wrote was about horses. My second-grade teacher suggested to my mom that I might want to write about something else. She said, 'Good luck with that.'"

Maggie laughed. "So the battle was already lost, and she knew it."

"Correct."

"You were lucky, though. How many people know exactly what they want to do with their lives from the time they're three months old?"

"Not many. My mother absolutely insisted I go to college, which I absolutely did *not* want to do. But once I got there and started getting into the program, I came around to liking it."

"She must've been very pleased."

"She was smug and vindicated."

"With good reason."

"She was right, and I told her so. I'm glad to have both degrees and to have them to fall back on if need be. You want to hear a true confession?"

"Absolutely."

"If this job with you hadn't worked out, I was going to have to look into something different or move out of state, which I also didn't want to do."

"How is that possible when everyone I talked to about equine therapy recommended you?"

"I have a very good reputation, but there aren't tons of jobs in the field. Or I should say not tons of jobs that pay enough for someone to actually live on their earnings. The fact that you provide housing and boarding for Sunday was a huge score."

"I'm really glad it worked out for both of us."

"So am I."

"Are you trying to sleep over there?"

"Nope."

"You should be. The kids will have you up early."

"What about you? Don't you need to rest up for another taxing day of fish, sun and beer?"

"It is quite taxing to fish and drink beer in the sun all day."

"I am *so* not a day drinker. It puts me to sleep for twelve hours and gives me the most massive headache the next day."

"I can teach you some work-arounds."

"Thanks, but I'm good."

He laughed. "How's Poppy today?"

"I heard she was a little fussy earlier and her mama was feeling sore, but otherwise, all is well."

"And Corey? How is she?"

Maggie couldn't believe the way Corey's story had been pushed off the front page by much bigger news. "She seems to be holding up. She wanted to see the baby before she left the hospital and asked me to go with her."

"Damn. What was that like?"

"As you can imagine. Sad and a little bit frightening. The baby is so small and attached to so many tubes and wires. It was overwhelming for me. I can't imagine how she must've felt. She told me her boyfriend pushed her down the stairs."

"He needs to be strung up by his balls."

Maggie sputtered with laughter. "Tell me how you really feel."

"I just did, and I mean it. Any guy who'd push a pregnant woman down the stairs deserves to be strung up."

"I happen to agree with you. I think she's going to be okay, though. She was with the other moms in the upstairs lounge when I went to check on them earlier."

"It's good that they have each other."

"That's one of the central goals of our program—to give the mothers a network they can rely on when they leave here. One of them was saying how lucky Debbie's kids are to have a grandmother to come running and how she didn't have anyone like that. Two of them said they'd take in her child if anything ever happened to her."

"That's so awesome. I'm so impressed by what you're doing there."

"It takes a village, that's for sure."

"And you're the boss of the village."

"Sometimes I feel like the village idiot."

"Stop," he said, laughing. "You're way too hard on yourself. You're doing a great job. Every day you're giving them things they haven't had in a long time, if ever. Safety, security, a sense of place, a home, a community of support. To them, you're a miracle worker."

"My sister and brother-in-law are the miracle workers."

"The three of you are."

"If you say so."

"I do and so do a lot of other people. The job is still somewhat new to you. It'll take some time for you to feel truly confident."

"If people are going to die here, that might never happen."

"You're going to find out that she either had some sort of medical condition, or she took something she shouldn't have. Her death was not your fault. If anything, give thanks for the fact she was there when it happened so her children would be well supported."

"You're kind of a glass-half-full sorta guy, aren't you?"

"I try to find the positive in any situation."

"Thanks for the support and the encouragement. It helps a lot."

"I wish there was more I could do."

"This was just what I needed."

CHAPTER 16

$\mathcal{M}$aggie's four parents, aunt and uncle came to visit Matthews House the next day at lunchtime. They greeted her with hugs and condolences over the loss of Debbie as well as concern for her children. The McBride children had gone with Karen to their school to collect their belongings and transcripts and to say their goodbyes. They'd be leaving to fly to Arizona that afternoon.

Mitch had prepared a feast for Maggie's special guests, who had a million questions about the facility, the services and Maggie's daily routine, such as it was.

"It's different every day," she told them as they enjoyed lunch in the conference room after she'd introduced them to the staff and showed them around. "Just depends on what the residents need."

"You're doing such important work here, honey," Clare said. "I couldn't be prouder."

"Me, too," Jack added. "You're making such a difference for the people you serve."

"We're trying," Maggie said. "Some days, I feel like we're spinning our wheels, but then something wonderful happens, like last night, when the other moms came together to support each other. That was really special. I like knowing they'll have each other after they leave here."

"I don't know about you guys," Andi said, "but my job feels rather superficial in light of what our girl is doing here."

"Agreed," Aidan said. "I love what I do, but this… This is so meaningful. Good for you, Mags." A gifted carpenter who specialized in historical restoration, Aidan was also a cardiologist but had stopped practicing after the loss of his first wife to cancer and their son to stillbirth.

Maggie basked in the parental praise. "You guys are good for a girl's fragile ego."

"How many families can you host at one time?" Jamie asked.

"We have rooms set up for ten families, but we could squeeze in a few mothers with one child or a baby in addition to that. We haven't had to do that yet."

"When does your equine therapy program begin?" Jack helped himself to another half sandwich from the platter Mitch had put together. Maggie had invited him to join them for lunch, but he'd told her to enjoy the time with her folks.

"Monday, when Brayden gets back from a vacation he already had planned before he was hired. He'll start with getting the kids acclimated to the stables and the horses and how to care for them, with an emphasis on safety, of course. This week, I'm meeting with the mothers to create a profile for each child so we can work to address their various needs."

"So you're very much involved, then?" Andi asked.

"Brayden is required to work in concert with a qualified counselor to tailor the program to the individual needs of the children. I'm the so-called qualified counselor in this case."

"Kate and Jill said he seems really great," Clare said.

"He is. He came highly recommended, and he's already built the platform we need to help the children mount the horses." Maggie tried not to think about him shirtless, swinging a hammer in the bright sunshine, but the image was indelibly etched upon her memory. She'd probably recall that image of him in her last moments of life.

"Working on that program is a perfect fit for you, too," Frannie said.

"How many horseback riding lessons did you drive me to?" Maggie smiled at her beloved aunt. Frannie had come to live with them after Clare's accident and had been so essential to Maggie and her sisters as they coped with life without their mother.

"Too many to count. Those were good times. Olivia is starting to make noise about taking lessons."

"She'll love it. It was the best part of childhood for me. So what else is new at home?"

"For us, baseball, baseball and *more* baseball," Jack said. "Which will stretch into summer again because both boys are probably going to make All-Stars."

"They love it so much," Andi said, "but it's still *freezing* in Rhode Island this time of year, especially at the ball field—or so it seems."

"You should see her in a winter down coat, wrapped in two blankets," Jack said.

Andi laughed. "And I'm still cold!"

"I can't wait to see them play," Maggie said.

"They're really good," Clare said. "We went to one of their games last week, and they were easily the best players on both teams."

Maggie loved that her mom and Aidan went to the games of her dad's sons, and knew the opposite was true, too. Jack, Andi and the boys went to Max and Nick's hockey games. The four boys referred to each other as cousins. They had no idea there was anything different about that arrangement. Once upon a time, Maggie would've bet her life none of that would've ever happened, but look at them now. They were the poster couples for how to do divorce the right way for their children.

They left a short time later to go back to Kate's to relieve Reid from Rob, John, Owen and Olivia, all of whom they'd left with him for a nature hike on Kate's property.

"They've probably got him tied to a tree by now," Jack had quipped.

Each of them had hugged Maggie and told her again how proud they were of her. They would be heading home early the next morning so the kids could get back to school.

"Nice people," Mitch said after Maggie came in from seeing them off.

"They're the best."

"So the dark-haired guy, Jack, is your dad, and the blonde lady, Clare, is your mom, right?"

"That's right. Jack is married to Andi with the dark hair and Clare to Aidan. The blond guy, Jamie, is married to my aunt Frannie with the red hair."

"And your folks, they hang out together regularly with their new spouses?"

Maggie nodded. "They're all friends."

"Wow, you don't hear that every day."

"They've worked hard at it for our sakes, but it wasn't always this way."

"It's a pretty cool thing."

"Yes, it is. Thanks for making lunch. They loved it."

"My pleasure. Glad you got to show them what we're doing here."

"They were very impressed."

"As they should be. We're doing God's work."

Maggie hadn't thought of it that way, but she supposed that was true. The rest of her day was spent helping to pack up the McBride children and making sure they had everything they needed to make the move to their grandmother's home in Arizona. The children hugged her and thanked her, bringing Maggie to tears with their composure in the face of such a tremendous loss.

"I'll be thinking of you, so please make sure you write to me," she said to Mandy and Patrick.

"We will," Mandy said.

Derek had offered to drive them to the airport in the van before picking up the other children at the bus stop.

Maggie helped Karen get the children loaded in and seat belted before she hugged the other woman. "Take good care, and let us know if we can do anything for you and the kids."

"We'll get through this together," Karen said. "Thank you again for all you did for Debbie and the children."

"It was a pleasure knowing them."

"She spoke so highly of you and everyone here. You made her final days very special, and I'll never forget that."

"Thank you for telling me that," Maggie said, moved to tears that she fought to hold back while she waved them off.

After they left, she walked over to see Thunder, and as always, he seemed to know just what she needed. "I'll be back in a bit for a ride."

He nickered in response, making her smile.

She kept her promise later that afternoon with an hour-long ride on Thunder that helped to calm and center her after the emotional couple of days. When they returned to the stables, she spent an extra hour brushing and grooming him before heading inside to see what Mitch had made for dinner.

Maggie fell into bed at ten and checked her phone for the first time in hours, looking for a text from Brayden.

He didn't disappoint. He'd sent more fish pictures, a few goofy selfies from the boat and another Key West sunset.

I'm green with envy, she replied, thrilled to see him responding right away.

Have you been here?

Nope.

Oh, we gotta get you here. It's like Disney World for adults. Beaches, bars, boats and ballads.

That's a Jimmy Buffett rip-off.

Guilty as charged.

It sounds delightful.

The phone rang with a FaceTime call from him.

Maggie panicked for a second, because a girl needed a minute to prepare for a call like this, but she told herself to stop being stupid and took the call. "Hi there."

"Hey. I thought you were gonna shoot me down for a second there."

"I was considering the disheveled state of my hair."

"Your hair looks great, and so does the rest of you."

"You give good compliment."

"I only speak the truth."

"Why're you FaceTiming with me when there're bars to be visited?"

"I'd rather FaceTime with you."

"That can't possibly be true."

"Well, it is. Truth speaker, remember?"

"Your friends will be merciless."

"Too late—they already are. I've taken a shitload of abuse over you the last few days. You're not going to let me down, are you?"

"What do you mean?"

"When I ask you out, which I will be doing very soon—like the second I get home—you're not going to say no, are you? Because that'd be a huge bummer after all the horseshit I had to shovel with your name on it with these guys."

Maggie couldn't contain the gurgle of laughter that erupted from her. "That has to be the most romantic request for a date I've ever received."

"It was the horseshit that put it over the top, right?"

"That was very special."

"In light of my very special, super romantic request, I do hope you won't let me down when I ask you out the second I get home."

"I'll have to think about that."

"Maggie! *Seriously?*"

She laughed again. She did that a lot when she talked to him. "Yes, seriously. You know I'm conflicted about the work situation."

"And you know I meant it when I said if you and I don't work out, I'll leave if that's what you want."

"I just… I don't know, Brayden."

"What don't you know, sweetheart?"

Oh damn, when he called her that, she melted inside. "If I'm ready to date anyone."

"I understand why you might feel that way, but I meant it when I said you have nothing to worry about where I'm concerned. You believe me, don't you?"

"I want to."

"But?"

"There're things you're not willing to talk about."

"My juvenile record, you mean."

"Yes."

"I don't talk about that with anyone."

"Which is your prerogative, just as it's my prerogative to be hesitant to date someone who doesn't want to talk about what got him into trouble back in the day."

"It was a one-time thing, something that happened that I don't regret because I was defending something that couldn't defend itself. Under the same circumstances, I'd do it all over again, even knowing the outcome."

Maggie was more intrigued than ever after hearing that much. His use of the word *something* that couldn't defend itself led her to believe that the incident had involved a horse.

"I think you probably would've done the same thing I did in that situation."

"Do you understand that I'm reluctant to get involved with you without knowing more about this?"

"Yes, I understand, but I hope you'll consider what I've done with my life since then and weigh that against one thing that happened when I was a kid that was well worth every bit of hell I went through afterward."

He was extremely convincing. She'd give him that.

"Will you think about it?"

"I'm not sure how I'll think about anything else."

"Maggie…"

"Brayden…"

151

He took a deep breath and released it slowly. "Let's change the subject. How was your day?"

"It was good. My parents, aunt and uncle came for lunch and a tour."

"How was that?"

"Great. They loved the place and everything we're doing here."

"You said your parents are divorced, right?"

"Yep, and both remarried to people we adore."

"That doesn't happen every day."

"We got very lucky—and we know it."

"You said you'd tell me about how your parents ended up divorced."

"I did say that, didn't I?"

"Uh-huh."

"And you really want to hear about that?"

"I want to hear about everything, Maggie Harrington. Every freaking thing."

No man had ever been more blatant about his interest in her. She'd gotten her share of attention from guys in high school and college, but this one was in a league all his own, and she rather liked his league. "I told you about my mom's accident, right?"

"You did."

"Well, after that, my dad... He was pretty much a mess for a long time, so much so that my aunt Frannie, who's his sister, moved in to help take care of us. He did everything he could for my mom, but after a while, we had to accept that she probably wasn't going to recover, and we had to get on with our lives. He moved her out of our dining room into a place of her own with round-the-clock nurses."

"That must've been a very difficult thing for you."

"Saying it was rough is putting it mildly. My mom... She was the glue who held us all together. We were a mess without her. So after a year had gone by and my mom was in the new place, my dad made a real effort to get things back on track with us and at work. He'd taken an entire year off, which was funny because before the accident, it was a big deal to get him to take a week off.

"He and Jamie had been hired to build an Infinity hotel in Newport, and that's when my dad met Andi, who was their director of interior design. She was headquartered in Chicago, but things between them got pretty intense. She and her son, Eric, eventually moved to Rhode Island to live with us."

"Was your dad still married to your mom?"

"Oh yeah, he was adamant about how he'd never leave her, but he was forty-four and had a lot of life left to live. Everyone was encouraging him to move on. Even my grandmother, my mom's mom, was supportive of him after the way he'd suffered after my mom's accident. Watching that was almost as hard as seeing my mom get hurt."

"You all went through so much."

"We did, but we were very well supported. In addition to my dad and Frannie and Jamie and our grandmother, we had my dad's parents and Jamie's parents, who're like extra grandparents to us. Everyone stepped up for us. We got through it, thanks to my dad and Frannie. And Andi... She was just... We love her very much. She somehow managed to get it mostly right coming into our mother's home and befriending us and supporting us as best she could without appearing to try to 'replace' our mother, which wasn't possible."

"Wow, what a challenge that must've been for her."

"It was, but she's just the nicest person you'll ever meet, and we *adored* Eric. I told you he was born deaf, right?"

"You did, and when he came into your life, that's when you learned sign language."

"That's right. He and I had an instant bond. I can't even explain it, but from the minute we met, we were just buddies. We still are. He's one of my closest friends, and vice versa."

"You've got me sitting on the edge of my seat here, because you told me your mom recovered, so now I'm wondering what that was like."

"It was amazing and insane at the same time. A lot happens in three years... You don't realize as life goes on its merry way, but Andi got pregnant."

"Oh my God. *Whoa.*"

"Yeah, it was pretty crazy. Then we found out she was expecting twins, which was super exciting. I couldn't believe there were going to be *six* of us. My dad was hilarious about it. I could tell his head was spinning, but he was thrilled. He and Andi were crazy about each other, and it was so nice to see him happy again after everything he'd been through. And Andi, too. Eric's father left them when they found out he was hearing-impaired."

"Shut up. Who does that?"

"I couldn't believe that, either. It's his loss. Eric is amazing."

"Wow, just when you think you've heard everything..."

"I know. So Andi is pregnant and due in September, and that April, my mom got really sick with a high fever that went on for days. She was in the hospital, and we really thought that was it, that we were going to lose her for good this time. My dad was there around the clock, and Jamie kept him fed while the rest of us tried to focus on school and stuff."

"That must've been hard."

"It was. All our grades suffered during that time. My dad was with her two weeks after she went into the hospital when she opened her eyes and looked at him."

"He must've freaked out."

"He did. We all did. It was unbelievable. A total miracle."

"What did he do? What did Andi do?"

"Andi moved out."

"Oh man. I'm heartbroken for people I've never met."

"It was brutal for all of us. When she moved to live with us, her company hired her to manage the Newport hotel, so she took Eric and moved into the manager's suite. She told Dad and us to focus on our mom and to not worry about them, but my poor dad was a wreck over it all."

"Who wouldn't be?"

"He's a good guy, always tries to do the right thing, and he'd promised Andi he'd never leave her alone with their babies, and now..."

"I can't even imagine that dilemma. And your mom! Waking up

after all that time to find out her husband had someone else and twins on the way. Christ have mercy. Someone should make this into a movie."

Maggie laughed. "Sometimes real life is too painful to be entertaining."

"True. So what happened?"

"My dad tried to tell my mom, as gently as possible, everything that'd happened. He started with us, how Jill had graduated and was at Brown and how Kate wanted to go to Nashville after she graduated and how I was almost thirteen. She couldn't believe that she'd been 'gone' for three years. And when he told her about Andi and the babies, she asked him to leave."

Brayden took a sip from a bottle of beer. "Did he go?"

"He did, but he kept going back, trying to get her to talk to him."

"And what about Andi? Did he see her?"

"No. She wouldn't see him, but she arranged for Eric to see him every week. He'd become like a dad to Eric, and she made sure they saw each other."

"He must've been dying over her being pregnant with twins and living apart from him."

"He was. It was so hard for him. Then my mom had a dream that brought back the memories of being attacked by a client she was showing a house to. She'd been a Realtor before all this happened, and the guy threatened to kill one of us if she ever told anyone. So she didn't tell anyone. When she saw that car coming at her that day, all she saw was a way out."

"Sweetheart... My God. I don't even know what to say."

It occurred to Maggie that she should've told her mom about Ethan, because she would've understood in a way that no one else ever could have.

"What're you thinking? Your expression totally changed."

She shared the thought with him. "Everything with my mom happened such a long time ago that I didn't even think to tell her. I haven't told anyone that story in years."

155

A warm smile lit up his sinfully handsome face. "I'm very honored that you're telling me. So what happened after she had the dream?"

"I'll tell you the rest the next time we talk. I have to get some sleep."

"Oh come on! You can't leave me hanging! I'll go crazy waiting to hear the rest."

"No, you won't. You've got fish to catch and beaches, boats, bars and ballads to keep you busy."

"I never would've suspected you were so mean to leave me on a cliffhanger this way."

Maggie laughed at the outraged expression on his face. "You're going to want to tune in for the next episode."

"Have no doubt I'll be there. Same time tomorrow?"

"Go out and get drunk, Brayden. You're on vacation."

"I'd much rather talk to you and hear the rest of this captivating story than get drunk. I can do that any time."

"If you say so."

"I say so. Same time tomorrow?"

"I'll be here."

CHAPTER 17

*B*rayden thought about Maggie and the story she'd told him all day while fishing with his friends, eating dinner and trying to pass the time until ten o'clock.

"You're not staying in again tonight, are you, dude?" Josh asked while he got ready to go out. The two of them had been roommates in college and always shared a room when they traveled with the guys.

"I'm afraid I am."

"I don't even know who you are anymore."

Brayden laughed. "Yes, you do. Who's the one who can never go out anymore at home because he's so *married*?"

"That's different! That's home. This is vacation."

"What can I say? I'd rather talk to her than go out drinking with you losers."

"That's hurtful, Brayden."

Josh's efforts to make a hurt face only further amused Brayden.

"Go have a good time. That's what this is all about, right? Everyone doing what they want."

"That's right, and what we all want is to go out and party—with you—like we always do."

"Remember how it was when you first met Ashley?"

Josh, who'd been using the mirror over the dresser to bring order to his wet blond hair, turned to face Brayden, his tanned face as serious as Brayden had seen it in a long time. "You're comparing this chick to *Ashley?*"

Josh and Ashley had been together since college and were crazy about each other, had been from the get-go.

"So what if I am?"

"You just met her a couple of weeks ago?"

Not even that long. "So what?"

"You're putting her on Ashley's level? This is more serious than I thought." He opened the bedroom door and summoned the other four guys, all of whom were dressed in shorts and T-shirts after having showered. "Boys, we have a situation."

Brayden rolled his eyes and flopped back on his bed like a fish landing on a deck, resigned to his fate.

"What's up?" Max asked. He still had the body of the linebacker he'd been at UT as well as the dark hair and blue eyes that'd made him the ultimate chick magnet in college.

Josh was more than happy to fill them in on what was happening. "Our boy Brayden just compared this chick he's been mooning over all week to *Ashley.*"

"Shut the fuck up." Taylor's face went blank with shock. "She's your *Ashley?*"

"I didn't say that. I simply asked Josh if he remembered what it was like when he first met Ashley."

"This is huge," Isaac said. Tall, with dark-brown skin and the same muscles he'd had when he too played football at UT, Isaac worked as an accountant these days. "We gotta meet this girl."

"*No,* you don't."

"Are you ashamed of us, bro?" Max asked.

"Fuck yes. You're to stay far, far, *far* away from her."

"I'm hurt," Taylor said. He'd been training to be a doctor for so long, he said he'd forgotten what it was like to not be in school of some kind. One more year, and he'd be done.

"You have to have feelings in order to be hurt," Brayden said. "Now all y'all need to fuck off and get out of here so I can call her."

"*So* whipped," Josh said.

That led to a cacophony of whip-cracking sounds being made by the lot of them. Thankfully, the siren call of the bars was more appealing to them than continuing to bust Brayden's balls. They weren't done with him. That much was certain. He'd made a critical error with the question about Ashley. She was the gold standard, and evoking her name had raised the stakes in his fledgling relationship with Maggie, at least in the feeble minds of his friends.

He waited for twenty minutes after they left to make sure they wouldn't be back before he FaceTimed Maggie, ten minutes later than scheduled.

She answered on the third ring and seemed out of breath. Her cheeks were rosy, her hair was up, and her eyes, as always, were gorgeous.

"Where'd I get you from?"

"I was in the kitchen, heard my phone ring and realized I'd forgotten it in my room."

"And here I thought you'd be counting the seconds until I called. After what I've just been through for you, that hurts me, Maggie."

Her brows furrowed with confusion. "What've you been through for me?"

"Another ass-kicking from my friends wondering who this chick is that has me skipping the bars so I can stay in and talk to her for hours."

"Oh. What did you tell them?"

"I said her name is Maggie, and she's the most gorgeous woman I've ever met and has a heart of gold, too."

"You did not tell them that!"

"No," he said, chuckling, "but every word of that is true."

"Stop it."

"Stop what?"

"I am not the most gorgeous woman you've ever met."

"Yeah, you are, and you love horses, too. Win-win, baby."

"Brayden..."

"Finish the story, Maggie. I've been dying to hear the rest all day."

"Where did we leave off?"

"You know exactly where we left off. Your mom woke up, Andi moved out, she's pregnant with twins, your dad is freaking, and your mom remembered what'd happened to her."

Maggie smiled at his rapid-fire review. "Right, so when my mom had that dream that brought back all those memories, she asked the nurses to call my dad. After he told her about Andi and the babies, she hadn't asked for him in weeks, even though he continued to go by the hospital to check on her and see if she needed anything."

"The poor guy was trapped in a nightmare."

"He kept saying how thankful he was that my mom had recovered, no matter what complications it caused for him and Andi. He was glad she was back, that we had our mother again. He never once said anything other than that, at least not to us."

"Do you think he meant it? That he was glad she'd come back?"

"Yes, I do believe he meant it. But it was a challenge for all of us to bring someone back into our lives who'd been absent for such a long time."

"I'm sure it was."

"You think, oh, my mom is back, and thank God for that, but do I have to ask her if I can go to Sophie's house like I used to, or do I still ask my dad that, or which end is up, you know?"

"Yeah, that's a little wild."

"It was, and I was anxious about what would become of Andi and Eric and the babies. By then, I loved them as much as I loved my mom, and I didn't want anyone to get hurt."

"That's totally understandable."

"It was all very confusing. I didn't hear the details of all this until years later, but when my mom told my dad what she'd remembered, they decided together to call the cops and report it."

"Good for her."

"They found out that the guy who attacked her had been convicted of almost the exact same crime in California, and it was his third offense. Since he was already in prison and would be staying there for a very long time, they decided not to file new charges. Shortly after that, my mom asked Andi to come see her in the hospital."

"No way."

"Yes! I couldn't believe it when I heard about it, but she wanted to meet the woman her husband had fallen in love with."

"Oh my God. Did Andi go?"

"She did."

"Wow. What happened?"

"From what I was told much later, they had a very nice conversation after which my mom asked to see my dad. She told him that she wanted what she'd had before, but after meeting Andi and hearing about her and how they were as a couple from us, she knew that she could never again have that, because he was in love with someone else. She said she was letting him go because she didn't want to have to always wonder if he'd rather be somewhere else."

"Holy crap, Maggie. Your mom is amazing."

"She really is. They'd been married more than twenty years, all of them good years, but she was so wise to see that everything had changed, and there was no going back to who they'd been before all this happened."

"It takes some kind of courage to be able to see that and do what's best for everyone else."

"I was too young to realize that at the time, but I've come to see what an enormous thing she did for my dad and our family."

"So he must've gone right to Andi."

"Not quite. He took the time to get divorced and went to her on the two-year anniversary of the day they met after he planned a wedding at the hotel that brought them together. She was told so many lies by everyone to keep it a secret from her. After all, she was the hotel manager and lived on the property. But he pulled it off. I'll never forget what she said."

"I'm dying to hear. This is better than any movie I've ever seen."

Maggie grinned at him, and he wanted to freeze that moment so he'd have that picture of her forever. "She said, 'I thought you weren't coming.'"

"Oh *damn!*"

"Kate was working at the hotel that summer, performing at the outdoor bar, and she'd told Andi what my mom had done weeks earlier."

"And then he never came for her! What she must've thought."

"I know, right?"

"What did your dad say to that?"

"He said, 'I wasn't coming until I could offer you everything.'"

"I'm dead." He placed a hand over his heart and fell back on the bed. "Your dad is the most romantic guy who ever lived."

"Ew, that's *gross.*"

"Maggie, that line is *epic.*"

"Maybe a little."

"Totally epic. He's the dude who ruins it for the rest of us mere mortals."

Maggie laughed. "I cannot think of my dad as a romantic or I'll vomit."

"So they got married?"

"They got married, and Andi went into labor *during* the reception. My identical twin brothers, John and Rob, were born an hour later at the hotel. They discovered later that she'd been in labor for two days, but it was all in her back, so she didn't realize it was labor until it was too late to get to a hospital."

"Best story ever. Thank you for sharing that with me."

"You're welcome, but there's more. I have to tell you about my mom going to Vermont to help with renovations to her brother's ski house and falling for the contractor who's now my wonderful stepfather, Aidan, and how Kate came to Nashville and fell for Reid and how Aidan's amazing O'Malley family became part of our family."

"I can't wait to hear all of it. You have the best stories."

"I guess they're pretty good. When you're living it, sometimes it doesn't seem so great, but in hindsight, I can see how someone else would find it pretty cool."

"You went through a lot in the midst of the best story ever."

"We did. My mom's accident and three years without her… Those were hard times, even if we got a lot of new people to love out of it. I can't imagine my life without Andi, her mom, Eric, John, Rob, Aidan, their sons Max and Nick and Aidan's amazing family."

"It's good that you can see it that way."

"My glass is way more than half full, for sure. That's one of my Grammy O'Malley's favorite sayings. She's been nearly incapacitated by arthritis, but her glass is always more than half full."

"I'd love to meet the stars of this amazing story someday."

"You would? Really?"

"Yes, Maggie, I would. Are you going to put me out of my misery and agree to go out with me?"

"You're in Key West basking in the sun. You're not in misery."

"I'm in total hell waiting to hear if you're going to shoot me down because you're worried about us working together or some other manufactured reason."

"That's not a manufactured reason! It's a real concern."

"That I told you won't be an issue. If we go out and it turns bad, I'll leave. I know Matthews House is your gig, not mine."

"The therapeutic riding program is important to me."

"To me as well."

"I'm also worried about the thing you won't talk about."

"I told you that's nothing to be concerned with. It happened a lifetime ago. It doesn't matter."

"Still… You want me to go out with you, but you won't tell me why you were in juvie."

"If I didn't work with you, you never would've known about that."

"If you didn't work with me, I never would've met you."

"I think we would've met anyway."

"Why do you say that?"

"Some things just feel fated, you know?"

"You think *this* feels fated?"

"Maybe."

"I don't even know what to say to that."

He'd flustered her, and as he watched her face portray an astonishing range of emotions, Brayden discovered he liked her flustered, especially when he was the one causing it. "I know that sounds like a line of bullshit, but all I can tell you is I've thought of you constantly since I last saw you, and I can't wait to get home. I've never once said that when I was here. Usually, I'm dreading going home because I know it'll be a year until we get back here again."

Maggie rolled her bottom lip between her teeth, which was incredibly sexy. Her stunning blue eyes were bigger and bluer than they'd ever been. He was getting to her, and getting had never felt so good. "Say something. You're leaving me out on the limb all alone over here."

"I don't know what to do about you."

"I can give you some pointers if that would help."

She let out an adorable snort of laughter. "Stop."

"Don't wanna."

"When do you get home?"

"Sunday."

"We'll talk then."

"You're not cutting me off until then, are you?"

"You should enjoy the time with your friends."

"I am enjoying the time with my friends. But I'm enjoying the time with you even more." He laughed at her perplexed expression. "You're very cute when you're flustered."

"I am not cute—and I'm not flustered."

"Oh, sweetheart, yes, you're both. You're beyond cute, and I've developed a very serious crush on you."

"You shouldn't do that. I'm your boss."

"Which is totally fine with me. You're the boss at work. I'll be the boss the rest of the time. You'll see. It'll work out great."

"Slow your roll, cowboy. I haven't even agreed to go out with you."

"I think you will, though."

CHAPTER 18

*M*aggie thought about Brayden and the things he'd said as she tossed and turned when she should've been sleeping and all the next day as she sleep-walked through work. Kate had invited her to dinner, but she declined because she was so tired. During the rough night, she'd relived the thing with Ethan and wondered if what was happening with Brayden had somehow triggered that memory.

She knew she ought to talk to a professional about the incident with Ethan, but the last thing in the world she wanted to do was relive it, even though talking about it might possibly help her get past it. She had gotten past it. Since it happened, she'd relocated to Tennessee, helped to start Matthews House and was doing her best to make a difference for the community she served every day.

Things had been going along just fine until Brayden Thomas had shown up and tipped her life upside down. Was it fair to blame him for her current state of unrest? Probably not, but he'd stirred things up between them, and she'd been out of sorts ever since.

When he called that night, she declined the FaceTime call and texted him. *Not feeling great. Going to bed early.*

He wrote back right away. *Feel better.*

The next night, he didn't call.

Maggie didn't hear from him again while he was away, and was infuriated with herself because she actually missed talking to him. How was that even possible?

She and Thunder went for a ride every afternoon, which was the only comfort she got from her racing mind. For whatever reason, her thoughts went quiet when she was riding. Thankfully, after the nightmare of Debbie's sudden death, things at the house had been relatively quiet for the rest of the week, as if the universe knew that Maggie needed a break.

She'd spent individual time with Corey as well as the other mothers, checking in with each of them as she did weekly about how they might transition to independent living over the next few months. Each of them had different needs and concerns, and Maggie did her best to provide support.

On Saturday night, she went to Kate's for dinner that Jill was cooking for the new parents. If she'd had her way, Maggie would've declined that invite, too, but they would come to her if she continued to hold her sisters at arm's length. So she showered, dried her hair, put on clean jeans and a lightweight top and went to Kate's.

Besides, she hadn't seen Poppy in days except for the pictures Kate sent daily to the family group chat, so she was in need of a baby fix.

As she drove, she hoped her sisters wouldn't immediately tune in to the turmoil that had wrecked her concentration the last few days. She didn't understand why she was so spun up. A nice, sexy guy had asked her out. Why the hell was she freaking out?

Maybe it was because she suspected this, with him, could be a big deal if she allowed it to be. With everything else she was juggling, did she have the emotional capacity for him, too? She wasn't sure, and because of that, she should probably tell him the time wasn't right for them. But then they'd have to work together, which would be awkward, and *ugh*.

"I'm a freaking mess and nothing has even happened." Hadn't it, though? Through texts and phone calls and FaceTime chats, not to mention the time she'd spent with him before he left, *something* had definitely happened. He'd made it clear he wanted it to be more. And therein lay her problem.

She was so freaking conflicted.

After parking next to Ashton's Jaguar, Maggie went in the mudroom door and kicked off her shoes. She walked into the kitchen, where Jill stood watch over the stove. Maggie looked to see what they were having. Spaghetti and meatballs. "Is there garlic bread?"

"Hi to you, too. And yes, of course there's garlic bread. What do you take me for? A rookie?"

"Sorry to question you. I should know better." After their mother's accident, Kate and Jill had helped out with the cooking and had learned to feed a family much earlier than they would have otherwise.

"How's it going at work?"

"A quiet few days, thankfully."

Jill reached for her glass of white wine and leaned back against the island that housed the stove. "I'm sure everyone is still trying to wrap their heads around what happened. Have you heard how the kids are doing in Arizona?"

"Karen emailed me yesterday to say they'd arrived and the kids are doing as well as can be expected. They're having a memorial service next week. Debbie was raised there and still has a lot of friends."

"I wonder why she didn't go home when things went south for her here."

"Karen said it was probably because she didn't want them to know that she was struggling. Debbie was always so proud, and after her husband left, things really unraveled for her."

"It's just so sad. I can't stop thinking of her and her kids."

"I know. Me, too. Karen said they got the preliminary results back from the autopsy, and Debbie had an enlarged heart. I guess it was undiagnosed. They're pretty sure that's what killed her."

"Wow, the poor thing." Jill released a deep sigh. "Are you doing okay through all this?"

"I'm good. The place keeps me so busy, I don't have much time to dwell on what happened."

"You look tired."

Maggie had known her sisters would take one look at her and know something was up. "Maybe a little."

"How's the horse whisperer?"

"Fine. He's still on vacation."

"When does he get back?"

Maggie helped herself to a carrot from the salad on the counter. "Tomorrow."

"Hmm."

"What?"

"I'm wondering if you're looking forward to him getting home."

"I can't wait to get the riding program started on Monday."

"Don't be obtuse, Maggie. I'm asking if *you*, Maggie, are looking forward to seeing *him*, Brayden."

Maggie had never felt so tortured by what she ought to do and what she *wanted* to do, which, of course, her sister tuned in to.

"What's going on, Mags?"

"Can I talk to you and Kate after dinner? Just us?"

"Of course."

Maggie swallowed around the lump in her throat and nodded. They'd know what she should do. They always did. "Where is everyone?"

"Kate's in the nursery with the baby. Reid took Ashton to the bunkhouse to look at something."

"I'm going to check on Poppy before dinner." Maggie was eager to escape Jill's knowing gaze and hoped she wasn't making a mistake by confiding in her sisters. But she needed to talk to *someone* about this situation, and there was no one she'd rather tell than them. She was going to have to tell them everything—about what happened in New York with Ethan and about Brayden's refusal to share what put him in juvie as a teenager. They needed all the facts before they could advise her properly.

"Knock, knock," Maggie whispered from the door to the adorable nursery Kate and Reid had put together for Poppy.

Not knowing the sex of the baby before her birth, they'd gone with earth tones and a warm shade of orange on one wall that also contained a mural with animals a friend of Kate's had done. Kate was seated in the rocker, holding the baby.

"Come in," she said. "We're awake, aren't we, angel?"

Poppy's foot, which had snuck free of the blanket she was wrapped in, reacted to the sound of her mother's voice with a dance kick.

Maggie came over for a closer look. "How's she doing?"

"She's amazing. Up all night and sleeping all day, but we hear that's perfectly normal at first."

"You must be beat."

"I'm doing all right. I try to sleep when she does. That's what the books say to do."

Poppy looked up at them with big gray eyes.

"Does it seem like she already knows everything, or am I reading too much into the way she looks at us?" Maggie asked.

"I think she's an old soul."

"I can see that. She looks wise somehow."

"I know! I said that to Reid last night, and he said, 'Darlin', all mamas think their babies are geniuses.'"

Kate's impression of her husband was so spot-on that Maggie cracked up. "Does he know you can do that?"

"Oh yeah. I do it to his face all the time."

"That's awesome."

"Not sure he agrees."

"Are you kidding? He thinks the sun rises and sets on you." Maggie had never seen a man look at a woman the way Reid looked at Kate. At first, Maggie hadn't understood how Kate could be attracted to a guy their dad's age. But after having spent so much time with them, she got it now. There was no doubt the two of them were madly in love. Jill and Ashton were the same.

"I'm a lucky girl for sure. Even more so now that my sweet Poppy is here."

"How're you feeling besides being sleep-deprived?"

"Okay. I'm sore and my boobs are killing me, but I'll be fine in a week or two. Every bit of it was worth having her."

Maggie's heart ached. She wanted what Kate had, what Jill had.

None of it had come easily to them. She knew that, but still… She wanted her own happy ending. Which made her think of Brayden asking her out. "I asked Jill if we can talk, just us, after dinner."

"What's going on?"

"I need some girl time."

"You got it. Is Poppy invited?"

"Of course. She's one of the girls now."

Jill came to get them for dinner, which was delicious, especially the garlic bread that Maggie had far too much of. She helped Jill clean up the kitchen while the guys took Poppy for a bath. Reid insisted he could handle bathing the baby on his own, and Ashton said he'd make sure his father didn't mess it up.

"I'm not sure how I feel about this," Kate said when the sisters were settled in the great room with glasses of wine for Maggie and Jill and iced tea for Kate, who wasn't drinking while breastfeeding.

Maggie sat next to Kate on the sofa, while Jill was in a chair next to the sofa.

"He raised Ashton alone from the time he was two," Jill reminded Kate.

"That was more than thirty years ago."

"Some things you never forget," Jill said.

"Your little girl will be fine," Maggie assured Kate. "The two of them are crazy about her."

"Yes, they are," Kate said. "They stare at her for hours."

"I expected that of Reid," Jill said. "I mean, he's her daddy. But Ashton is absolutely gone over her."

"He waited almost thirty-six years for a sibling," Maggie said.

"True."

"Enough about us," Jill said. "You wanted to talk. What's going on?"

Maggie's stomach hurt as she tried to find the words to tell her sisters about Ethan and what'd happened. "I have to tell you something that's going to make you mad."

"Is it about work?" Kate asked. "We think you're doing such an amazing job."

"That's nice to hear, but no, you're going to be mad because something happened in December that I should've told you about long before now."

Jill leaned toward Maggie and gave her hand a gentle squeeze. "Whatever it is, we're here for you always. You know that."

Jill's kind words reduced Maggie to tears. "I know, and I knew then I should've said something, but Kate was getting married, and you got engaged, and everyone was together for Christmas for the first time in years."

"I knew something was up with you," Kate said. "I told Mom you weren't yourself, but with the wedding and a houseful of guests, I dropped the ball."

"I wouldn't have wanted to talk about it then. I still don't, but I really need to." She took a deep breath to calm her emotions before diving in. "There was a guy at work, an attorney I saw all the time at the courthouse. Ethan." Saying his name made her sick, but she forced herself through the retelling of the story, and when she was finished, her sisters were in tears. "I'm not telling you this to upset you."

"You should've called me," Jill said softly. "I would've been on the first plane. We both would've been."

"I know that, and I knew it then. I didn't want to talk about it. It happened. I dealt with it."

"Did you report it?" Jill asked.

Maggie shook her head. "I figured it would be my word against that of a seasoned defense attorney. I wanted to put it behind me, and I couldn't do that if I reported it." She glanced at Jill. "I know what you're going to say."

"I actually get it. You figured he'd squash you even more than he'd already tried to."

"Yeah, exactly."

"I'm so, so sorry that happened to you," Kate said, "and that you felt you couldn't tell us in December. I know Jill would agree that nothing would've been more important to us than making sure you were okay. That's always been important to us."

"You guys were so happy. I just couldn't bring that into it."

171

"I'm really glad you're telling us now," Jill said. "But has something happened that made you feel the need to talk about it?"

"Brayden happened."

"I knew it," Kate said, smiling.

"I'm the worst boss in the history of bad bosses."

"Why in the world would you say that?" Jill asked. "Everyone at the house loves you."

"And PS," Kate added, "*your* bosses are thrilled with the job you're doing."

Maggie sent Kate a grateful smile. "After you had the baby, Ethan texted me."

Jill's eyes bugged. *"What?* How could he do that?"

"I thought I'd blocked him, but I found out the hard way that I hadn't. I was pretty upset to get that text, congratulating me on my new niece."

"That son of a bitch," Jill said. "He knew that would upset you and did it anyway. Fucker."

"Brayden came into the office right after that happened, realized something was up and asked me if I wanted to ride. I did, so we went, and while we were out, I spilled the whole thing to him. He was the first person I'd told."

"I'm so glad you told someone," Kate said.

"My brand-new employee?" Maggie dropped her face into her hands, still mortified that she'd unloaded on him, of all people.

"There must've been something about him that made you feel comfortable telling him," Kate said.

"That's the problem. *Everything* about him makes me feel comfortable. Too comfortable. We work together. I keep telling myself to keep my distance, and then I end up inviting him here and talking to him for hours on FaceTime while he's been away with his friends in Key West."

Maggie caught her sisters exchanging glances and smug smiles. "What?"

"We had a bet," Kate said sheepishly.

"What kind of bet?" Maggie asked, annoyed.

"The kind of bet where we take wages on how long it'll take you two to end up together," Jill said. "By the way, I win. I said less than a month. Kate thought it would take at least two."

"In case I forget to tell you later, you guys suck."

They cracked up laughing.

"We're very sorry," Kate said.

"Shut up. You're not sorry."

"We're not sorry you might've found someone special, Mags," Jill said. "We really liked him, and we could tell you do, too."

"I do like him. As an employee. And maybe a friend. But that's all it can be."

"Why?" Kate asked, her brows furrowed.

"Because! If I date him and it turns into a mess, he said he would leave, and I don't want him to leave. He's the best at what he does, and I was so lucky to get him."

"Wait a minute," Jill said. "Back it up. He said he would leave if it doesn't work out? Does that mean you've talked about it being more than just coworkers?"

"Maybe," Maggie said.

"Tell us everything," Kate said. "What did he say? What did *you* say?"

Maggie rolled her eyes and sighed. Too late to turn back now. "He asked me to go out with him when he gets back."

"What'd you say?" Jill asked.

"I haven't given him an answer."

"Why?" Kate asked. "You said you liked him. You've spent hours talking to him while he's been away. And don't say it's because you work together. You're both adults and professionals, and he already said he'd leave if things don't work out. What's the problem?"

"When Ashton did the background check, he discovered that Brayden has a sealed juvenile record."

"What?" Jill's mouth fell open in shock. "And *he encouraged you to hire him and work with kids* and—"

"Easy, Counselor." Maggie held up a hand to stop her sister's tirade. "We discussed it and agreed that the twelve years he's been an adult mattered more than whatever happened when he was a kid. His reputation, credentials, education and references are all impeccable."

Jill sat back, still seeming incredulous. "I want to know what he did. Does he know that *you* know about his record?"

Maggie nodded. "I asked him about it before I hired him. He won't talk about it. He said he never talks about it."

"That's a deal breaker for me," Jill said, looking to Kate for agreement.

Kate appeared to be wavering.

"Kate! Come on. She can't take up with a guy with a record!"

"His adult criminal record is clean?" Kate asked.

"Completely, or I wouldn't have hired him. The testimonials on his website from grateful parents are incredible. They say he changed their children's lives with his skill, passion and dedication. I called all his references, and they said the same, that he was magic with the kids. I've seen that for myself in just a few days. He was only available because his previous employer lost funding for their program, and he was holding out for something around here so he could move back home to the Nashville area. He has friends here."

Jill and Kate were quiet as they absorbed the info.

"I say it's not a deal breaker," Kate said.

"Kate! Be serious! It *is* a deal breaker, especially because he won't tell her what he did."

"We all made mistakes when we were kids. I made them, you made them, Maggie made them. No one is perfect."

"None of us ended up in juvie!"

"What was it that Gram used to say? 'There but for the grace of God go I'? We got lucky. We never got caught."

"I never did anything that could've landed me in juvie," Jill said.

"I did," Kate said.

Maggie raised her hand. "Me, too."

Jill eyed them skeptically. "What did you guys do?"

"I'm gonna take the Fifth on that, Counselor," Kate said.

Maggie gave her a high five. "With you there, sister. The statute of limitations hasn't fully expired."

"Joke all you want," Jill said. "I don't like it, and I *cannot believe* Ashton didn't tell me this."

"I'm his client, not you," Maggie said. "He was under no obligation to tell you."

"You're my baby sister."

Maggie scowled at her. "I'm not a baby anymore, in case you hadn't noticed."

Jill scoffed. "You'll *always* be my baby sister. He should've told me you had a criminal living in your midst over there."

Maggie bristled at that, feeling oddly defensive of him. "He's not a criminal, Jill. Don't say that."

"What do you think Dad would say if he knew about this?"

Maggie gave her a pointed look. "He's not going to know about it, do you hear me?"

"He won't hear it from me, but I can't promise he won't hear it from someone else."

"How would he hear it? No one else he knows is aware of it."

"Ashton is."

"And he's got a bit of a reputation for tattling," Kate said.

Jill turned on Kate. "Are you seriously holding that against him? Of course he was going to tell Dad that you were dating his father! Dad asked him to *keep an eye on you*."

"I'm not holding it against him," Kate said. "I'm merely pointing out that he has a track record."

"He would tell you he learned a lot from that incident and would never interfere in someone's relationship like that again. Be fair, Kate. That was more than ten years ago."

"This trip down memory lane is great fun," Maggie said sarcastically, "but it does nothing to help with my dilemma."

"I say you don't go out with him until he tells you what he did," Jill said. "That'd be a hard stop for me."

Maggie looked to Kate. "What do you think?"

"I think it matters that he's not willing to tell you what happened, but I don't think you have anything to fear from him. If you felt concerned about that, you never would've hired him to work with the kids."

"Right."

"So go out with him and put him on notice that if it seems like this thing between you is going to be something significant, he's going to have to tell you everything."

"I, um, I think it might already be something significant, and I'm just not sure *I'm* ready for that." She wrapped her arms around her legs, curling into the corner of Kate's comfy sofa. "We've had these incredible conversations while he was away. We talk for hours about so many things. I told him about our family, what happened after Mom's accident and all that."

"Wow, you don't like to talk about that stuff," Kate said.

"I know. It was weird. I just found myself telling him like it's no big deal when I've hardly told anyone about it."

"You feel a connection to him," Kate said.

"I do. I have from the beginning, from even before I met him, if I'm being completely honest."

"How do you mean?" Jill asked.

"I felt it the first time I talked to him on the phone, this odd sense of familiarity with someone I'd never even met."

"Go out with him, spend time with him, get to know him," Kate said. "Follow your gut."

"My gut let me down big-time with Ethan," Maggie reminded her.

"There was a reason why you hadn't invited him into your apartment," Kate said. "That was your gut telling you not to. You *were* following your gut. What he did has nothing at all to do with that."

"You really think so?"

Kate nodded. "I do, Maggie. You're a savvy, street-smart woman after living in New York City for six years. You can't let what one guy did undermine your self-confidence. Look at the way you fought him off and left him in a heap on the floor."

"I agree with that," Jill said. "You shouldn't let what happened with that asshole ruin your self-esteem. You survived that, and he was the one who got injured."

"It scared me to realize how quickly it happened."

"Of course it did." Kate reached for Maggie and embraced her. "It had to be completely terrifying. But instead of focusing on how it happened, think about how it *ended*."

"I did put a wicked hurt on him."

Kate laughed. "Yes, you did."

Maggie continued to lean against Kate. "You really think I ought to say yes to Brayden?"

"I do," Kate said.

"Jill?"

"I want to know what he did—and I want to know sooner rather than later. I think you need to make that nonnegotiable."

"I hear you, and I agree that he's going to have to tell me at some point."

"Do you feel any better, Mags?" Kate asked.

"I do. Thanks for listening, you guys."

"We're always here for you, no matter what," Jill said. "Don't ever feel like we're too busy for you. The three of us have been a team for a long time. No matter what else changes, that never will."

Kate kissed the top of Maggie's head. "Love you."

Maggie smiled. "Love you, too."

CHAPTER 19

"Jcan't believe you didn't tell me he has a freaking *record*," Jill said to Ashton the second the car doors slammed shut for the ride home. They'd been out doing errands before dinner, or they would've walked to Kate's.

"Who has a record?"

"Brayden! You knew this and didn't tell me!"

"It's a juvie record. His adult record is clean."

"Still, you should've told me! He's working and living right near my sister, not to mention the residents. I can't believe she actually *hired* him knowing this about him."

Ashton started the car but let it idle as he turned to face her. "First of all, Maggie was my client, and as such, I was under no obligation to share the results of his background check with you." When she started to object, he held up a hand to stop her. "Second of all, Maggie and I discussed it in depth, and she made a reasonable decision based on the information we had about his adult record, which showed twelve years of impeccable credentials. There's no story here, Jill."

"Yes, there is. She asked him about what he did, and he refused to tell her."

"Which is entirely his right. Juvie records are sealed for a reason.

You know that. How thankful am I, are all of us, that all our bone-headed mistakes as teenagers aren't being held against us now?"

"You never did anything to end up in juvie."

"Come on, Jill. I never got caught. That's the only difference between me and him."

"You don't know that, because we have no idea what he did."

"I know what he's done as an adult. He's gotten undergraduate and graduate degrees in animal science. Look up what's involved with that major. I wouldn't have lasted a semester before flunking out. His employment history is solid, as are his references, all of which Maggie and I checked before hiring him. People raved about his work with horses and kids. There's nothing to worry about where he's concerned."

"She's interested in him. Romantically."

"Oh."

"And you're okay with my baby sister potentially dating a man who's keeping a former criminal record hidden from her?"

Ashton thought about that for a second. "I would say that Maggie is a fully grown adult who can decide for herself if she's willing to date him while knowing he's keeping that info private."

"What if he killed someone?"

"He'd probably still be in lockup or, at the very least, on probation. They don't just let juvenile murderers run free after they become adults."

"I'm going to google him and find out what he did."

"I already did a full search. There's no record of it anywhere. I had to really dig to find the juvenile record even existed."

Jill blew out a deep breath. "I don't like this."

"Yes, I can see that." Ashton put the car into Drive and headed for home.

On the short ride, Jill thought about what Ashton had said about Brayden's impeccable adult record and tried to settle the nagging feeling she had that he was keeping it hidden for more reasons than just privacy.

"You should've told me about this."

"No, I shouldn't have. Maggie is going to be my sister-in-law. She asked me to do a job for her, and I did it. If I go running to you with every little thing that comes up between us, she'll never trust me to have her best interests at heart when I do work for her."

"Once upon a time, you wouldn't have kept something like this to yourself."

He pulled up to their house, cut the engine and looked over at her. "What the hell does that mean?"

"Kate reminded me of your role in breaking up her and Reid the first time around."

"That's kind of a low blow, Jill. That happened more than a decade ago, and I've said more than once that I wouldn't do it again if I had it to do over. Not sure how long I'm going to have to pay for that mistake."

He got out of the car, slammed the door and walked toward the house, not waiting for her the way he usually did.

Jill followed him inside, locked the door, shut off the porch light and went into the master bedroom. She changed into a nightgown and robe, slid her feet into slippers and went to find him.

He was in the living room watching *SportsCenter*, which was a deviation from their usual routine of going straight to bed when they got home at night. He always said he couldn't wait to be in bed with her, but apparently, that wasn't the case tonight.

Jill sat next to him on the sofa, for once uncertain of what to say to him.

He stared straight ahead at the TV.

"I shouldn't have brought up what happened in the past. I'm sorry about that."

"It's okay. It happened. I own that I was wrong to call your dad about Kate being with my dad. I fucked up their lives for years. I get it."

"They would tell you a number of things screwed them up, not just you."

"What I did was the worst."

Jill moved closer to him, put an arm across his middle and rested her head on his chest. She was relieved when he wrapped his arm around her. "I'm sorry I brought that up. I know it's a sore spot, and I shouldn't have said that."

"It's really okay."

"I'm worried about Maggie."

"I don't think you need to be. She's a very capable woman who survived on her own in New York City for years."

"She told us tonight that a guy she dated there attacked her last December. She fought him off, but the whole thing was deeply upsetting."

"Damn. She just told you this now?"

"Yeah, it happened right before she came here for the wedding and Christmas, and she didn't want to upset everyone's good time."

"Poor Maggie. That's awful." He ran his hand up and down Jill's arm. "For what it's worth, I don't think you need to worry about Brayden. Whatever happened was years ago, and his life since then has been about horses and kids. People like him, they trust him with their kids, and more important, horses like him. Animals are the best judge of character. They run on pure instinct."

"That's true."

"I know you think I should've told you about his juvie record, but I still don't agree. I was in a tough spot on this, since Maggie was my client. His adult record was clean. That's what mattered to me—and her."

"I understand why you didn't tell me, I guess."

"I talked to him the other night. I let him know I knew about his past and that I'd be watching him."

"You did that? Really?"

"I did. I get what Maggie means to you, to all of you. I put him on notice that someone else knows about his record. I thought it might help."

Jill raised her head and kissed his cheek. "Thank you for doing that."

"Are you still pissed with me?"

"No. Are you still pissed with me?"

"Kinda," he said, flashing the sexy grin that made her melt. "But I can think of a number of ways you can make it up to me, Counselor."

When he leaned in to kiss her, Jill met him halfway, relieved to be back to normal with him, even if she was still concerned about what Maggie might be getting into with Brayden Thomas.

MAGGIE HADN'T HEARD from Brayden in a few days, so she had no idea what time on Sunday he was due home. She kept herself busy all day with laundry and returning emails from friends and catching up on magazines. Late in the afternoon, she took off for a ride on Thunder, which was a welcome relief from waiting and wondering if she would see Brayden when he returned, or if she'd ruined things with him before they ever got started.

For the first time since she'd lived on the Matthews estate, she ventured into the thicket of trees on the south end of the property, following a well-worn trail through towering oak and pine trees. Sunbeams came through the trees, creating a magical sight as she rode slowly to take it all in.

Why hadn't she come this way sooner? she wondered.

She followed the path for more than a mile, breathing in the fragrance of pine and dirt and decomposing vegetation. After another bend in the trail, she gasped at the sight of a huge meadow full of wildflowers with a pond in the middle of it. Thunder seemed to know where he was going, so she let him take her where he wanted to go, which was straight to the pond for a sip of water.

Maggie dismounted and waited with him while he drank. After he was done, she tied his lead to a nearby shade tree. She stretched out on the grass and lifted her face to the warm sunshine, feeling more relaxed and at peace than she had in months. She actually dozed off and awakened when she heard hooves coming toward her. Immediately on alert, she jumped to her feet and turned toward the tree line in time to see Brayden on Sunday as they emerged from the trees.

He brought the gorgeous palomino to a stop a couple of feet from

Maggie. "Fancy meeting you here. Thought you didn't do the forest."
He wore a denim Western-style shirt, old boots and dark jeans.

Maggie immediately noticed how tanned he was. "I haven't before, but Thunder and I were feeling adventurous today."

"Derek told me you were riding, and I looked all over for you. I was starting to get a little worried."

"Sorry. Didn't mean to worry you. I let Thunder go where he wanted today, and he brought me here."

Brayden dismounted and took Sunday for a drink before securing her to a tree in the shade near Thunder. "This is quite a spot."

"It's great." Maggie's nerves went batshit crazy now that he was off the horse and standing before her, looking even better than he had before he spent a week in the sun. "How was the trip home?"

"Long." He took his hat off and stepped closer to her. "Felt like it took forever to get back here. Was it only a week I was gone? Felt like a month."

She swallowed hard when he came even closer.

"I want to hug you, but only if you say it's okay."

As if she were a bystander watching this moment unfold for two other people, Maggie was acutely aware that if she allowed him to touch her, she'd be taking a step that could never be undone. Even knowing that, she wanted to hug him. "It's okay."

He took two steps to close the distance between them and put his arms around her.

The second she was engulfed in the scent of soap and laundry detergent and horse and leather, she was a goner. He held her just right, making her feel as if she'd suddenly come home after a long, perilous journey. Her hands found his back, and they stood like that for a long time. Days or weeks might've passed for all she knew.

"I'm so sorry I wasn't here to help when you lost Debbie."

"You did help."

"I wish I'd been here with you."

Maggie pulled back a little only because she wanted to see his face. "Brayden..." She forgot what she'd been about to say when she noticed the hungry, almost desperate way he was looking at her mouth, as if he was thinking of a thousand different ways to kiss her and trying to figure out which one to go with. She licked her lips.

He must've made his decision, because he raised his hands to her face and went easy at first, waiting for her to catch up.

At first, Maggie was too stunned by the way her legs nearly gave out under her to properly respond, but then she pressed herself against him and opened her mouth to his tongue. Of course the man could kiss like nobody's business. Somehow she'd already known it would be this way with him, unlike it'd ever been before. Maybe that was why she'd been so hesitant to let this happen, because she'd known instinctively that he'd change her life if she let him.

He kissed her senseless. There was simply no other word for it.

Maggie clung to him so she wouldn't embarrass herself by falling to the ground in a boneless pile.

When he backed off from the kiss, she went up on tiptoes to keep him from getting away.

"Easy, sweetheart. Hold that thought for just a second." He let her go in increments, while Maggie blinked a couple of times to clear her brain and recover herself.

She'd been kissed plenty of times, but never before had a kiss left her feeling like she'd just survived an earthquake. While taking a deep breath and releasing it, she watched his impatient stride eat up the ground between her and Sunday.

Brayden pulled the sheet from the saddle bag, and as he returned to her, Maggie noticed the way the denim of his jeans hugged the distinctive bulge that told her their kiss had affected him the same way it had her. He spread the sheet on the ground and held out a hand, inviting her to join him.

Maggie took his hand and sat with him.

He put his arm around her and kissed the top of her head. "I couldn't wait to get home to see you. Longest vacation ever."

"You're silly. You were in Key West with your boys."

"And all I wanted was to be here with you."

Her heart beat so fast, she could hear it and feel it in all her pulse points. Every part of her was tuned in to him and the way he made her feel. "Brayden..."

"Hmm?" He nuzzled her hair until he gained access to her neck.

Before she had time to prepare, she was falling backward as he hovered above her, looking down at her with intense brown eyes that seemed to see right through to the heart of her.

"Is this okay?" he asked.

She nodded and reached for him, taking advantage of the opportunity to run her fingers through silky strands of thick hair.

A groan came from deep inside him. "I knew it would be like this with you."

"Like what?"

He ran his lips lightly over hers. "Like a wildfire burning out of control."

"How did you know that?"

"Because I've never wanted to leave Key West before I even got there."

"I missed you."

His brows lifted. "Did you?"

"I did. And I kept asking myself how that was possible when you'd only been here a couple of days before you left."

"I know what you mean." He ran a finger over her cheek to her mouth, where he outlined the shape of her lips. "My attraction to you was instant. Even as I was thinking it wasn't a smart idea to be attracted to my potential boss, I couldn't seem to help it. My new boss is just so incredibly smart and competent and devoted to her job and beautiful. So, *so* beautiful. And sexy."

Maggie felt the creep of heat in her cheeks. She'd never been with any guy who was so blunt about how he felt. Most of the time, she'd had to drag information out of the guys she'd dated. With Brayden, there would never be any doubt, which was rather refreshing.

His fingers slid lightly over her throat and down her chest.

She realized he was unbuttoning her shirt, and while she knew she ought to stop him, she couldn't bring herself to actually do it.

The brush of his fingertips against her sensitive skin set off a wave of reactions she felt everywhere, especially in the tight points of her nipples and in the throbbing heartbeat between her legs.

"Breathe, sweetheart. Just breathe."

He kissed her neck and throat, laying a path to her chest, where he kissed the plump tops of her breasts that spilled out of the cups of her bra. His finger touched the front clasp. "Yes or no?"

She should say no and put a stop to this before it went any further. They were out in the open where anyone could see them, even though she was certain no one else was around for miles.

While he waited for her to reply, he dragged his fingertips lightly over her belly while continuing to leave damp kisses on the tops of her breasts. He nudged at her nipple through her bra, and Maggie nearly levitated off the ground, so he did it again and again until she said, "Yes, Brayden. *Yes.*"

He twisted his fingers and had her bra open within seconds. "Fuck me, you're so, so pretty." And then he dropped his head to take her nipple into the heat of his mouth, licking, sucking and generally making her crazy.

Her hips came up off the ground, looking for more.

Brayden shifted so he was fully on top of her, pressing his hard cock into the V of her legs as he moved from one nipple to the other while holding her breasts in callused hands that added to the tsunami of sensation coursing through her.

God, she'd had full-on sex with other guys and not felt anything even close to what he was making her feel simply by touching her breasts. This was too much and not enough at the same time.

She yanked on the front of his shirt until the snaps gave way to reveal his beautiful chest, which he brought down on hers, rocking back and forth, feeding the fire that blazed so hot between them.

When she felt the tug of his fingers on the button to her jeans, Maggie came out of the lust-induced fog to realize what was going to happen unless one of them found some sense.

"Brayden." She covered his hand with hers. "Not here."

He exhaled roughly and sagged into her.

Maggie put her arms around him and caressed his back under his shirt.

"Didn't mean to get carried away," he said after a long silence.

"We both did."

He raised his head to look down at her, his sexy lips curling into a smug smile. "Does this mean you'll go out with me?"

"I'm still not sure."

His lips parted, and his eyes went wide with surprise.

Maggie laughed. "Close your mouth before flies get in there."

Brayden closed his mouth and moved so he was on his side next to her, his head propped on an upturned hand. "Are you planning to torture me? Is that the plan?"

Maggie pulled her shirt closed and fiddled with the two sides of her bra until they were clasped together. She sat up and ran her fingers through her hair. "I'd like to spend time with you."

"But?"

"Despite the kissing and stuff, which was very nice, by the way, I continue to be concerned about the thing you won't talk about."

His expression immediately hardened. He didn't like that.

Maggie buttoned her shirt, stood and brushed grass off her pants.

Brayden stood, snapped his shirt and grabbed the sheet, shaking it out before folding it and tucking it under his arm.

She looked up at him and forced herself to say the things that had to be said. "I shared things with you that I hadn't told anyone else. I told you the thing about Ethan before I told my *sisters*. I *never* talk about what happened to my family. Friends I've known for years haven't heard that story. I trusted you, Brayden. All I'm asking is for you to do the same. After what happened to me in New York, I'm more cautious than I used to be. I hope you understand."

When he had nothing to say to that, Maggie forced herself to walk away. She mounted Thunder and headed for the path in the trees, keeping her gaze fixed on the way forward. If she looked back at him, she might remember what it'd been like to be held and kissed by him and waver in her determination to get to the truth before this went any further.

CHAPTER 20

*B*rayden managed to avoid running into Maggie until noon on Monday, when they were scheduled to meet about the therapeutic riding program and the unique needs of each child. He'd spent a sleepless night staring up at the ceiling, tortured from wanting more of her and trying to decide if he could trust her with something he'd told no one since leaving juvenile detention.

He entered the house through the kitchen and stopped to talk to Mitch, who was stirring a pot on the stove. "Something smells good."

"Pasta sauce for spaghetti night. The kids' favorite after tacos and pizza."

"They'll be excited for dinner."

"That's the goal. How was your trip?"

"Good time with the boys. Key West is always fantastic."

"Looks like you got some sun, too."

"Yep. Is Maggie around?"

"In her office, I believe."

"Okay, thanks."

Brayden tried to brace himself to see her, but nothing could've prepared him for the gut punch that happened every time she turned those startling blue eyes on him. And when she smiled... God, she was gorgeous. While she looked as great as she always did, with her long dark hair pulled into a ponytail, he could see the hint of reserve coming from her that hadn't been there before their encounter yesterday. He hated having given her reason to pull back from him, but he certainly understood why she felt it was necessary.

"Hey, are we still on to meet about the kids?"

"Sure. Come in."

He sat in the seat across from her desk, pulled a pen from his shirt pocket and settled a notepad on his lap while trying not to think about her gorgeous breasts. As if he would ever forget that or what it had been like to kiss her sweet lips and mold her sexy body to his.

Feeling a stirring in his groin, he crossed his legs and tamped down those thoughts to focus on business.

Over the next hour, they discussed each child, what had brought their family to the shelter, what particular issues and needs their mothers had identified at intake and what Maggie had observed during their stay.

"Last but not least is Travis, who you've met. He and his mother came to us after a domestic situation in their home. Travis intervened when his mother's boyfriend was assaulting her and ended up being assaulted himself."

Brayden took notes while seething on the inside at the thought of a grown man raising his fists to a four-year-old child.

"When we first met him, his face, arms and torso were covered in bruises. His mother suffered a shattered eardrum and a concussion in the altercation."

"Tell me the guy is in jail."

"He is—for now, but only because of outstanding warrants. Otherwise, he would've been released on bail by now."

Brayden shook his head with disgust.

"Believe me, I know," Maggie said. "I'm in an online support group with other shelter directors, and the lack of justice in our criminal justice system is a frequent topic of discussion. It's not just an issue here. It's everywhere."

"I agree. What else can you tell me about Travis?"

"I believe you'll find him to be the most excited to work with the horses. It's all he talks about since he arrived and realized he could see the horses every day. His mother is a little hesitant about the program because she's afraid he'll get addicted and she won't be able to afford riding lessons after they leave us."

"I'd do it for free afterward if that puts her mind at ease."

Maggie stared at him for a long moment before blinking. She looked down at her notes before glancing back at him. "That's very nice of you."

"I'm not going to abandon these kids just because they don't live here anymore. I'll see them on my own time afterward."

"It doesn't have to be on your own time. Kate and Reid believe in making an indefinite commitment to provide support to our families for as long as they need us."

"My program could do that as well."

"I'd hoped so, but I wasn't sure how you'd feel about that."

"Well, now you know. I'm in it for the long haul with these kids, for as long as they want to be part of it."

"I really appreciate that."

He shrugged. "I know what horses and riding meant to me as a kid. I'd never take that away from any kid who was loving it." Clicking the pen closed, he returned it to his shirt pocket. "Where are we with hiring additional support staff?"

She handed him two pieces of paper. "I hired two local high school kids last week, and they'll be here by three. Both come highly recommended by local stables. They're interested in studying therapeutic riding and family counseling in college."

"Excellent. I guess I'll see you out there when the kids get home."

After hesitating for a second, as if she had something else she wanted to say, she only nodded. "See you then."

Brayden walked out, feeling like he was leaving something important behind as he went to the stables to prepare for the first lesson with the kids. All he wanted to do was go back in there, find Maggie and tell her everything she wanted to know if that would mean she'd give him a chance to be something more to her than a friendly colleague she kept at arm's length.

He already knew he wouldn't be able to stand having her so close but eternally out of reach, especially after having held and kissed her. She wanted him to tell her something that even his closest friends didn't know.

On the advice of his attorney at the time, he'd told no one in his adult life about the things that'd happened before his eighteenth birthday. "If no one knows," the attorney had said, "the information can never be used against you. If you tell even one person, you're risking everything we've worked so hard to protect."

Brayden had religiously followed the attorney's advice for twelve years. His sealed juvenile record as well as the GED he'd received in lockup had come up at other job interviews, but he'd always declined to discuss it. His boilerplate response was, "Juvenile records are sealed for a reason." Fortunately, his professional skills had been in enough demand that the information hadn't kept him from enjoying a fulfilling career.

It'd never been an issue with the women he dated because they didn't know. When they asked him where he went to high school, he'd say a private school in Nashville. No one had ever asked him to elaborate on that, and he'd told himself that it didn't count as a lie if he was following his attorney's advice to be vague about his childhood and the fact that he'd received a GED while in juvenile lockup.

His conscience had never been bothered by the lie because none of the other women he'd dated had really mattered to him. Those relationships—if you could call them that—had been about fun and sex and lighthearted entertainment. He'd never come close to having anything serious, and he'd liked it that way. Until he met Maggie and knew almost right away that she could be different.

She could change everything.

He was seriously torn by this dilemma, and more than at any time since he'd lost his mom, he yearned to talk to her about it. She'd been the only person from his childhood he'd stayed in contact with and thus had been the only one who'd known his full story. She'd have known what he should do about Maggie.

Brayden went through the motions preparing for the day's lesson on the basics of the stables, how to care for the horses, the parts and pieces of the tack. Tomorrow, they would learn how to saddle a horse and how to lead a horse around the paddock. He'd asked Derek to leave two stalls for the children to work on cleaning, and he would use Sunday to teach them how to groom and care for a horse after riding.

Usually, he felt pumped to introduce a new group of kids to the joy of interacting with and caring for horses, but today, he couldn't seem to find anything approaching joy due to the ongoing torment over Maggie.

After what she'd been through with that douchebag Ethan, he didn't blame her for drawing her line in the sand with him. She had every right to feel the way she did, even if her line in the sand had him tied up in knots of uncertainty. He wanted so badly to trust her the way she'd trusted him, but the attorney had put the fear of God into him. The thought of spilling his guts to anyone, even Maggie, made him feel sick.

Brayden knew he'd gotten lucky to have a skill that made him highly employable despite the black mark he carried on his record. He'd spent his entire adult life working hard to overcome his past, to create an unimpeachable reputation for professionalism and results for the kids he worked with. There'd been so many success stories, far more successes than failures. But none of that mattered to Maggie when it came to pursuing a relationship with him.

His mind spun in circles that went from understanding where she was coming from to anger that she'd put him in this untenable position and back to understanding without finding a solution he could live with that would satisfy her need to know his secrets.

He was no closer to finding a solution to his dilemma when the kids got home and came out to the stables, full of pent-up energy and excitement to get started on their riding lessons, which was how the program had been billed to them.

There were ten kids in all, ranging in age from four to eleven. They came from a variety of backgrounds, and all had experienced some form of trauma.

Brayden had them sit in a circle with him on clean straw inside a stall he'd prepared for their opening session. He sat in the circle with them, his back to the open gate to the stall, aware of Maggie behind him. He kept his focus on the children where it belonged.

"Hi, everyone, I'm Brayden, and I'll be teaching your horseback riding class every day after school. I want to go around the circle and have everyone introduce themselves by telling me your name, age and grade in school."

As the children complied with his request, he committed the information to memory. He made it a point to call the kids by name, to make eye contact with them, to treat them with the same respect he hoped to get back from them.

"The first lesson to being around horses is about safety. Horses are usually friendly animals, but like people, they don't like to be startled. They don't like loud noises or flashes on cameras or any sudden movements. It's very important that you always approach them slowly and respectfully. Extend a hand to let them sniff you so they can decide if they want to be friends with you."

"Like dogs?" eight-year-old Maisy asked.

"Just like dogs, only horses are much bigger. The height of horses is measured in hands, with each hand being four inches, but you can see they're pretty tall and often weigh around a thousand pounds. They can hurt you very badly without meaning to if you aren't careful around them. Another rule is to never approach a horse from behind. When they feel threatened, they lash out by kicking their hind legs, and trust me, you don't want to be kicked by a horse." He pointed to a white line on his forehead. "See this scar?"

The kids leaned in for a closer look, each of them nodding.

"This happened because I didn't listen to my grandpa when he told me not to go near the back of a horse unless he was with me. I didn't want to wait for him and ended up with a hoof to the forehead. It took fifteen stitches to close the wound, and because I had a concussion, I couldn't ride for weeks, which was much worse than the stitches for me. I was really lucky that the horse didn't kick me hard enough to kill me. He definitely taught me a lesson about listening and doing what I was told."

The children hung on his every word. He always told the story of how he'd gotten hurt to let them know he'd once been right where they were now, eager to learn and eager to ride. Impressing upon them the potential for grave injury was the most important part of this first day.

"You may have seen me or Ms. Maggie or Mr. Derek feed the horses carrots or apples from our hands. But I don't want you guys to do that because you can get nipped by their teeth even when they don't mean to. They get excited about snacks just like you do, and sometimes they accidentally get a piece of hand with the snack, which doesn't feel good. Each of them has their own bucket of feed, and they should only be fed with permission and supervision by me or Mr. Derek or Ms. Maggie and only from their own bucket of feed. Am I clear on that?"

"Yes, sir."

"Yes, Mr. Brayden."

"It's very important to follow the rules in the stables, not only for your safety, but for the safety of the horses, too."

"Because we want them to like us," Jimmy said.

"That's right," Brayden said. "And we want them to feel safe with you and you to feel safe with them. Horses are very smart animals. If you're nervous, they can tell, so it's really important for you to stay calm and quiet and respectful around them so they'll do the same for you."

Thunder let out a loud whinny that made the children laugh.

"Are they listening?" Lily asked.

"Thunder is always listening. He's Ms. Kate's horse."

"She's the famous singer," Travis said.

"That's right. The next thing is you never duck under a horse's leads when they're at what's called cross ties." Brayden used two leads to show them what he meant. He'd learned to speak in simple terms the children would easily understand. "Stand back from a horse that's tied until one of the adults is with you."

Brayden reached for a helmet from the items he'd stashed in the stall earlier. "This is a helmet, and each of you is required to wear one when you ride the horses. Ms. Maggie has purchased helmets for each of you. When we're done here, I'll show you where you can find them."

A nine-year-old boy named Dante raised his hand.

"Yes, Dante?"

"I saw you and Ms. Maggie riding the other day without helmets. You had your cowboy hat on. How come you don't have to wear a helmet?"

Brayden smiled at the cheeky question. "That's a really good question. Ms. Maggie and I have been riding for years, and we know what we're doing with the horses. When we were youngsters like you guys, we had to wear helmets, too. When you get older, you can decide for yourselves if you'd like to wear them or not. But while you're in my class, helmets are nonnegotiable."

Travis raised his hand.

"Yes, Travis?"

"What does that mean? Nonneg... nego..."

Brayden smiled at the adorable child. "Nonnegotiable means it's a rule, and we aren't going to debate whether or not it should be."

"Like bedtime?" Travis asked.

"Just like bedtime." Brayden talked to them about the riding boots Maggie had purchased for each of them and how important they were to protecting their feet while around the horses and for keeping their feet in the stirrups. He held up a boot and a stirrup to show them what he meant. "Your feet go in the stirrups while you're riding, and the boots keep your feet from sliding all around. Boots are also nonnegotiable, as are long pants."

That met with loud groans.

"Even when it's hot?" Lily asked.

"Even when it's hot. Sorry. Pants protect your legs from sores, rub rash and scratches and wounds from brush while you're on the trail. That's why we say no shorts."

He talked to them about the importance of putting things where they belonged in the stables and doing exactly what they were told at all times. "I want you guys to enjoy this and have a lot of fun, but anyone who can't follow the rules won't be allowed near the horses until they're able to behave properly. Okay?"

They nodded in agreement.

"Great, now let's get up and have a tour of the stables." Over the next half hour, he showed them the tack room and how each horse had their own equipment that was labeled with their names above their hooks. Similarly, each horse had their own bin of food, also with their names on them. He familiarized them with the various pieces of tack, from reins to leads to saddles to stirrups. "We'll get into the tack more when we start to ride next week."

"We hafta wait a whole week?" Jimmy asked mournfully.

"It'll take that long to get you ready." Brayden led them out to the paddock where he'd left Sunday earlier. He whistled, and she came to him, nuzzling his side with her nose the way she always did. "This is my horse, Sunday Morning."

"She's so pretty," Lily said.

"Yes, she is, and she loves children. I want each of you to take a turn saying hello to Sunday and stroking her muzzle."

"Will she bite?" Travis asked.

"Nope. She's sweet and gentle as long as you're sweet and gentle to her. When you're done, step back over to the fence by Ms. Maggie." Brayden held Sunday's lead while each of the children took turns greeting and touching the horse. He corrected a few of them on the proper way to place their hand on the horse's muzzle.

Accustomed to being around kids, Sunday stood by his side and allowed each of the children to approach and touch her.

When they were done, he gave Sunday a kiss and sent her on her way. "You guys did great," Brayden told the children. "Sunday thinks you're all going to be very good at riding."

"How do you know that?" seven-year-old Jayden asked. He had

olive-toned skin, big dark eyes and curly brown hair.

"I've had Sunday for a long time. I know what she likes and doesn't like, and she liked you guys a lot. Tomorrow, we'll go over how to groom her and work on getting her ready to ride."

He led them out of the paddock and back into the stables, where they returned to their original seats. "Who can tell me what we learned today about safety around horses?"

Every hand went up.

"Let's take turns going around, and everyone can say one thing we learned." He dismissed them ten minutes later, feeling confident they had absorbed the day's lessons and understood the rules.

He'd been so caught up in the kids that he hadn't noticed that their mothers had been watching the class along with Maggie and two young people named Wyatt and Jessica, whom she introduced to him and the children.

"Sorry we were late." Wyatt shook hands with Brayden as the kids headed inside with their mothers. "There was an accident that shut down one of the roads from town."

"No worries. Good to meet you. Just give me a second, and we'll talk." He walked over to speak to Maggie. "That seemed to go well."

"You were great with them. They loved it."

Her praise meant everything to him. He wanted her to be happy she'd decided to take a chance on him. "Nice bunch of kids."

"Thank you, Brayden." She seemed almost emotional, which he chalked up to seeing the program she'd envisioned coming to life.

"My pleasure."

She started to walk away, and his gaze was drawn immediately to the snug fit of her jeans. "Hey, Maggie?"

She turned back to him, brow raised in inquiry.

"Can we talk later?"

She studied him for what felt like a full minute before she gave a swift nod and then headed for the house.

Elated to know he'd get to see her later, he watched her walk away and then went to find Wyatt and Jessica to get them up to speed on what he needed from them.

CHAPTER 21

$\mathcal{M}$aggie had been off-kilter for hours, ever since she'd watched Brayden spin his magic with the children. Of course she'd known he would be great with them, but to actually see him in action was something she wouldn't soon forget. For so long, she'd dreamed of being part of an equine therapy program, and now that hers was up and running, she felt a tremendous sense of accomplishment. And the only person she wanted to share that with was the man who was making it happen.

After dinner, she went upstairs to check in with Corey, who hadn't come down to eat with the others. She knocked gently on Corey's door and listened for sounds from within. "Corey?"

The door opened, and Maggie was taken aback by the young woman's ravaged face. Her eyes were red and swollen and full of heartbreak.

"May I come in for a minute?"

Corey nodded and stepped back to admit Maggie, who had brought a covered plate of Mitch's lasagna with her.

"I thought you might be hungry."

Corey shrugged and returned to her rumpled bed. "Not really."

Maggie set the plate on a table and pulled a chair over to Corey's bedside. "You need to eat to keep up your strength."

"Why? What's the point? The baby's gone, Trey's gone... What does it matter if I keep up my strength?"

"You matter, Corey. I know everything seems so awful right now, but it won't always be this way."

"How do you know that?"

Maggie recalled how Brayden had told the kids how he'd gotten the scar on his forehead and decided to follow his example. "I once went through a really difficult time when my mom was in a bad accident that left her in a coma." Corey seemed interested, so Maggie pressed on. "The doctors told us she would never recover."

"How old were you?"

"Almost ten."

"That's really young to lose your mom."

"It was pretty rough for a long time, even though my sisters and I had a lot of people supporting us."

"No one can take the place of your mom."

"Exactly. As bad as I felt, though, it did get better in time. I missed my mom all the time, but it wasn't as painful as it had been at first. You get used to the new normal. Somehow. That's what this is for you, Corey. Your new normal, and as painful as it is right now, in time, it'll get easier to cope with what's happened. You'll always miss the baby, and maybe you'll always miss Trey, but you have a big, long life ahead of you, and anything is possible."

"It's hard to believe that. How can I still want Trey when he caused all this?" Tears spilled down her cheeks. "He's the reason our baby was born too soon and why I had to give him up. It's all his fault, and I still want him anyway. I hate myself for that."

"Dr. Wright is coming out from town tomorrow," Maggie said, referring to the counselor she'd asked to meet with Corey. "I'd like you to see her and talk to her about how you're feeling. Will you do that?"

"I guess." She glanced at Maggie. "They found parents for him. A couple who've been trying to have their own children for years. The social worker told me they're elated and haven't left his side for a minute."

"It's good news that he'll have loving parents. Does that make you feel any better?"

Corey nodded. "It does. I'm happy for them—and him."

"Will you have some dinner?"

"It does smell good."

"Mitch's lasagna is the best." Maggie got up to get the plate and silverware she'd brought and delivered the meal to Corey.

She sat in the chair to keep Corey company while she ate.

"You don't have to stay if you have stuff to do. It was nice of you to check on me."

"I don't mind staying." Maggie vastly preferred sitting with Corey to staring at her phone wondering if or when Brayden was going to text her.

She spent half an hour with Corey and stopped to talk to the other moms in the lounge before she headed downstairs.

"The kids couldn't stop talking about Brayden and the horses," Trish said. "Thank you so much for making that possible for them."

"I'm so glad they loved it."

"They did," Kelsey said. "Brayden was amazing with them. I feel very good about Travis taking lessons from him."

"That's great to hear," Maggie said. "He's very excited to work with them."

"Did you talk to Corey?" Niki asked.

"I did and got her to eat some dinner."

"Oh good," Trish said. "We were worried about her."

"I'll see you all in the morning. Sleep well."

"Night, Maggie."

She went downstairs, put Corey's dish in the dishwasher and went into her apartment to check her phone. Her heart leaped when she saw a new text from Kate with the day's photos of Poppy, which she scrolled through before replying. *She's getting so big!*

I know! Kate replied. *I'll be shopping for college before I know it.*

Maggie sent the laughing emoji and put her phone down, feeling out of sorts and uncertain about whether she ought to reach out to him or let him make the next move. She would wait on him since he was the one who had asked if they could talk, and he was the one who had to decide whether he was going to trust her.

She changed into pajamas and brushed her teeth, exhausted after another challenging day that'd been made more so by the uncertainty with him. Resigned to not hearing from him, Maggie got into bed with a book on her reading app and tried to focus on the story. She read the same line three times before realizing she lacked the concentration to read. So she switched on the TV and tried to find something to watch until she felt sleepy.

When her phone rang an hour later, it startled her out of a doze. She found the phone wrapped up in her blanket and took the call from Brayden.

"Did I wake you?"

"No, I was watching TV." And sleeping, not that he needed to know that.

"Could I come over?"

"Sure. Meet you at the kitchen door?"

"Be there in a minute."

Maggie got up, put on a robe, ran her fingers through her hair and went to deactivate the alarm and turn on the light over the kitchen door.

Brayden jogged across the yard and up the stairs to the kitchen door.

Maggie opened the door for him and then shut and locked it behind him. She'd reactivate the alarm when he left. "Come on in." She led him to her apartment.

He shut the door and followed her to the small sitting room that adjoined the tiny kitchen that she rarely used thanks to Mitch.

"You want something to drink?"

Brayden shook his head and sat in the other chair rather than joining her on the sofa. With his elbows on his legs and his head down, he seemed distraught.

"Are you okay?"

"I'm deeply conflicted."

"Do you want to talk about it?"

"No, I really don't." He glanced up at her, his eyes conveying more emotion than she'd ever seen from him. "But I will. For you."

Maggie held out her hand to him. "Come here."

He stared at her hand for a long moment before he reached out to grasp it and joined her on the sofa.

Maggie turned toward him and put her arms around him.

Brayden rested his head against her.

"You don't have to do this. I totally understand the need to keep some things private, and I'd never want you to feel like you *have* to share something with me that you don't want to. We can go forward as good friends and colleagues."

"I've been telling myself that same thing all day, that I could not tell you, and we'd just not do this. But then I thought about the things you shared with me, how courageous you were, and I feel like I owe you the same in return."

"You don't owe me anything, Brayden. I told you the things I did because I wanted to, not because I expected anything in return."

"I know, but the thing is…" He raised his head so he could see her face and lifted his left hand to cup her cheek. "I want to be more than friends with you, Maggie. I look at you, and I just want… well… everything with you. I've never wanted to go all in with anyone else, so I'm willing to take the risk, to trust you."

Maggie leaned in to kiss him. "Thank you."

"But it's super important to me that this stay between us. You can't even tell your sisters."

"I understand, and you have my word that it'll go no further."

"When I left lockup, my lawyer was very clear with me. If you don't talk about it, your past can't be weaponized against you. I took that advice very seriously, and I haven't told *anyone*. When I went to college, I left everything else behind, made new friends and had a fresh start that I've been living off of ever since. Only my mom knew about my life before college."

"And then you lost her."

"Yeah. I really wanted to talk to her the last few days."

"I'm so sorry you couldn't and that you've been so tortured over this. Maybe I shouldn't have made such a thing of it..."

"No, you were right to look out for yourself, especially after what happened to you."

"I'm well aware that if you weren't working with me, I'd never have known there was something I should be asking about."

"Yeah, and I want to be clear, if you hadn't found out I had a juvie record from the background check, I never would've told you, no matter what happened between us. I drew a line in the sand years ago that divides my life into before and after, and I never, ever cross that line."

Maggie took a deep breath and released it slowly. "My stomach hurts."

"Mine, too." He took her hand and brought it to his lips. "I have this feeling that you're going to be worth crossing the line for."

"You have my absolute word that no matter what happens between us, I'll never repeat what you tell me. Ever. I'll take it to my grave."

His sinfully sexy lips curved into a small smile, but she still saw torment in his warm brown eyes. "I never knew my dad. My mom said it was a short-lived thing, and he wasn't worth knowing. For most of my childhood, it was just me, my mom and my grandpa. He ran a small ranch about fifty miles from here, and my mom helped him with the books, the housekeeping and chores. When I was old enough, I was expected to help out, too, which was fine with me. I loved being with my grandfather. I followed him around like a pesky little dog, and he was always endlessly patient with me. He's the one who taught me everything I know about horses. People tell me I have a gift with them. If that's true, it came right from him."

His eyes went soft with affection when he talked about his grandfather. "He died suddenly when I was thirteen. We found him in the barn where he'd collapsed. They said it was probably a massive heart attack and that he hadn't suffered. But I suffered over losing him. Oh, how I suffered. In some ways, I was never the same."

"I can totally relate to that. It's the most incredibly difficult thing to discover the people you love best can be taken from you with no warning."

"Yes, exactly."

"I'm sorry that happened to you."

"Thanks. I still miss him every day. I think all the time about what would've been different if he'd lived."

"It's amazing how one incident can set off a chain of events that changes everything."

He glanced at her, seeming less tortured than he had just a short time ago. "That is so, so true. About a year after my grandfather died, my mom decided to start dating for the first time in years. What a shit show that turned out to be. She quickly learned not to tell them about the ranch she'd inherited or her teenage son, both of which became either pros or cons, depending on the guy. Then she met Clive."

His entire body tightened with tension that radiated off him. "He was a retired rodeo star. Had made his name as a bull rider. Won a lot of awards and money and acclaim. All the money was gone by the time he met my mom, and he saw dollar signs when he eventually found out about the ranch. My mom was crazy about him for reasons that I never quite understood. He wanted nothing at all to do with the teenage son, but he put up with me to get his hands on her land. I hated him the first time I met him, and my opinion of him never changed."

"God, Brayden. That's so awful." All Maggie could think about was how lucky she and her sisters had gotten when Andi and Aidan came into their lives. Brayden had had the opposite experience.

"It was. He knew I hated him, and he sort of got off on pushing my buttons."

"What did your mom say?"

"She pleaded with me to help her make it work because we needed help running the place, and she fancied herself in love with him for a while. That didn't last long, but by the time she woke up to who he really was, she'd married him, he was in charge of my grandfather's ranch and wanted nothing to do with me. And vice versa. I started getting into a lot of trouble around that time. Skipping school, drinking, smoking pot, basically acting out in every way I could, which I can see now only justified his dislike of me."

He cradled her hand between both of his, caressing her skin with callused, scarred hands from a lifetime of hard work. "I only came home to take care of the horses and see my mom. Otherwise, I crashed with my friends and generally stayed away. I was fifteen and getting around on a motorbike that had belonged to my grandfather. The bike made it so I could get out to the ranch to tend the horses. I tried to time my comings and goings for when I knew he wouldn't be there. But this one day, I went home after school. He... he had all the horses in the paddock and..."

Maggie cradled his head against her chest the way she might a child who'd had a bad dream. But this was no bad dream. It was Brayden's life, and her heart broke for him as she waited to hear the rest of his story.

"He had a bullwhip and was beating them."

Maggie gasped. "Oh my God."

"They had nowhere to go." He spoke in a flat-sounding tone, devoid of inflection. "They couldn't get away from him, and obviously, it'd been going on for a while, because all of them were bleeding, especially Dancer, my grandfather's horse, the one I'd learned to ride on. He'd focused on him because he knew I loved him the best."

Maggie sniffed as tears ran unchecked down her face. "Brayden..."

"I don't really remember a lot about what happened next. But I vividly recall climbing the paddock fence and going after him and the whip. From what I was told, I beat him until he was unrecognizable. My mom came home in the middle of it, pulled me out of there, called 911 for him and the emergency vet for the horses. Everything after that was a blur. The cops came, they took me in. Later, I heard Clive was on life support. I didn't care."

Brayden looked up at her, his gaze fierce. "I want you to know if I had it to do over again, even knowing how it would fuck up my life, I wouldn't change a thing."

"I wouldn't want you to. Those poor horses. Were they okay?"

"They recovered from their wounds, but I'm sure they were never the same."

"You don't know?"

He shook his head. "My mom rehomed the horses and sold the ranch to pay for my attorneys."

"Oh, Brayden... God, I'm so sorry."

"She did the right thing. She couldn't handle it all on her own anyway, and the horses needed care we couldn't give them."

"But still... It must've broken your heart to lose your home and the horses."

"It did, but I had bigger problems by then. I was charged with attempted murder, and there was talk of trying me as an adult. My mom got me the best lawyers money could buy, and they eventually got the charges reduced to felony assault and kept the case in juvenile court, which was a huge break. I spent three years in juvie and five years on probation after I was released and have been trying ever since to get my record expunged, but it hasn't happened yet. My mom managed to keep the story locked down. She told people I went to live with my uncle in Colorado, and no one questioned her story because my friends knew how much I hated Clive."

"And what about him?"

"He survived. I was told I should be thankful for that. If he'd died, I probably would've been charged as an adult and would still be in prison."

"Tell me he was charged with something."

"Misdemeanor animal cruelty with a provision that he sign the divorce papers, relocate and never speak of or to me or my mother again."

She wiped the tears from her face. "I'm so, so sorry, Brayden. I'm sorry that happened, that I forced you to talk about something so painful, that—"

"Hey." Brayden tipped her chin up to meet his gaze. "It's okay. I'm glad you know. It feels right to talk about it to you." He held her gaze for a long, charged moment before he leaned in to kiss the tears off her cheeks.

Maggie tipped her face ever so slightly, her lips meeting his in a soft, sweet kiss that quickly became heated and desperate. After hearing his story, she no longer feared falling for him, as it was far too late for such concerns. The fall had already happened.

His arms encircled her, his tongue rubbed against hers, and Maggie moaned as she tried to get closer to him. "Brayden," she said, gasping as she broke the kiss. "Wait."

He dropped his head to her chest as he fought to catch his breath. "Let me up."

Brayden pulled back, running his hands through his hair as he seemed to search for composure.

Maggie stood and held out her hand to him.

Seeming surprised, he looked up at her as he took her hand.

She gave a gentle tug that brought him to his feet.

"What're you up to?" he asked, smiling.

"Moving this somewhere more comfortable."

CHAPTER 22

$\mathcal{M}$aggie led him into her bedroom, feeling completely
confident that she was doing the right thing, regardless of their professional situation, which she had to believe would
work out even if they didn't. As she watched him untie the belt of her
robe, work was the last thing on her mind.

"Are you sure about this, Maggie?"

She smiled up at him. "Yes, Brayden. I'm sure. Are you?"

"Oh hell yeah. I was sure about ten minutes after I met you, and
when I caught you sleeping on the job…"

"I wasn't sleeping!"

His low chuckle rumbled through him. "If you say so."

"I say so."

He cradled her face in his hands and stared down at her. "You are
so, so pretty. I couldn't stop thinking about you while I was away. I
wished I'd had a photo of you because I missed you so much."

"I missed you, too, and it felt silly to miss someone I'd only just met."

"It's not silly."

There was nothing silly about the way she felt as she unsnapped
his shirt and pushed it off his shoulders. "The day you built the plat-

form in the yard..." She ran her hands over his muscled shoulders, arms and chest.

"What about it?"

"All the women on the staff were watching you through the kitchen window."

"No way."

"*Way.*" Maggie stepped forward to kiss well-defined pectoral muscles, his dark chest hair tickling her nose. "You put on quite a show that day."

"Sorry," he said, sounding embarrassed.

"Don't be. I haven't been able to get the picture of you, shirtless and sweaty, out of my mind ever since."

"Is that so?"

"Mmm." She continued to pepper his chest with kisses and little nibbles that had him gasping. "How lucky am I to get to be able to do this?" She licked his nipple, and he startled, burying his hands in her hair to anchor her to him. Maggie fiddled with his belt, trying to figure out how to release it.

Thankfully, he helped her, and when the two halves fell apart, she batted his hands away so she could release the button and zipper herself.

He groaned when her hand brushed against the head of his cock, which had breached the waistband of his boxer briefs. "Maggie..."

"Yes, Brayden?"

His grunt of laughter made her smile.

He pushed the robe off and found the hem of her T-shirt, whipping it up and over her head so quickly, she had no time to prepare herself to be completely bare except for bikini panties.

Brayden looked at her with sexy brown eyes that heated as he took her in. "So fucking beautiful." With his arms around her, he backed up to the bed and brought her down on top of him and then quickly turned them so he was on top, looking down at her. His gaze shifted to Froggie.

"Who do we have here?"

Maggie glanced at her beloved stuffed animal. "My oldest and dearest friend. Froggie, meet Brayden."

Brayden charmed her forever when he reached out to shake Froggie's shabby hand or fin or whatever it was. "Pleased to meet you, Froggie."

Maggie reached out to turn Froggie so he couldn't see what was about to transpire. "Now, where were we?"

Smiling down at her, Brayden pushed his hard cock into the sensitive notch between her legs. "Right about here."

"I remember now."

"Tell me if anything is too much?"

She appreciated his respect for what she'd been through, but that was the last thing on her mind with sexy Brayden Thomas in her bed. "I'm okay, but thanks for checking."

"Always." He touched his lips to hers in a teasing caress that had her arching into him, looking for more. "Easy, sweetheart. We've got all night, and I'm in no rush. We'll never again get to do this for the first time, and I plan to fully enjoy it."

Maggie exhaled and tried to relax as he kissed her neck and chest while cupping her breasts and running his thumbs back and forth over tingling nipples.

"I've been thinking about these beauties constantly since the other day." He dipped his head and took her left nipple into his mouth. "I wanted another taste so bad when we were in your office. So, so bad."

She felt like she was floating outside herself, watching someone else be kissed and caressed and utterly transported by desire for the first time in her life. Nothing had ever been like this, like him. He covered her abdomen with kisses as he moved down until his face was pressed to her core, the heat of his mouth scorching her sensitive flesh.

He reached under her with both hands and lifted her closer as her legs fell open in welcome.

Dear God...

Then he was tugging at her panties, trying to get them off, and Maggie could barely move to help him. Turns out he didn't need the help, and when he returned to his place between her legs, he set out to absolutely destroy her with his lips, tongue and fingers. She came twice in rapid succession, which had never happened. Before she could begin to come down from the incredible high, he was pushing into her, stretching and filling her.

"Brayden...

He nuzzled her neck and kissed her lips. "What, honey?"

"Condom."

"All set."

Somehow she'd missed that in the orgasmic frenzy he'd worked her into, and now she needed all her wits about her to deal with the hot, full press of him inside her. The man was big all over. She raised her knees snug against his hips and flattened her hands on his back, her fingers digging into the dense muscles that flexed as he moved in her. Maggie couldn't get close enough, couldn't take him deep enough...

Propping himself on his elbows, he pressed inside her and held still as he gazed down at her. "Hey," he whispered, his lips glancing over hers in a light caress.

Maggie opened her eyes and looked up to find him staring down at her intently.

"Hi."

She smiled. "Hi yourself."

"You okay?"

"Uh, yeah. You?"

"Never been better." He flexed his hips, perhaps to remind her of what they'd been doing before he called a time-out—as if she needed the reminder.

Maggie reached down to cup his ass, to keep him buried deep inside her as she rubbed shamelessly against him.

He groaned and began to move, picking up the pace until they were both straining against each other in a race to the peak. Brayden went still above her, his fingers digging into her shoulders until he collapsed on top of her, breathing hard as tremors of sensation rocked them both.

He was quiet for a long time, so long that Maggie wondered if he'd dozed off. It didn't matter if he had. She loved the weight of him on her as well as the scent of warm male skin, soap and spicy deodorant.

She found out he wasn't asleep when his tongue nudged her nipple, which caused her to jolt as if he'd struck a match against her sensitive flesh.

Laughter rumbled through him and into her. "Is someone a little sensitive?"

"More than a little."

He looked up at her, brows furrowed in concern. "You're good, though?"

"Better than good. Way better than good."

"That's what I want to hear." Propping his chin on her chest, he studied her face. "Am I crushing you?"

"No." She tightened her arms around him to keep him right where he was for a little while longer. As he'd said, they'd never again do this for the first time, and she wasn't ready to let him go yet.

He settled his head on her shoulder.

Maggie floated and dozed and luxuriated in a complete sense of relaxation that had been so rare lately.

Eventually, Brayden withdrew from her, got up to use the bathroom and then came back to stretch out next to her in bed.

Maggie looked over at him, propped up on an upturned hand, looking ridiculously sexy and confident while completely naked. Although, anyone who looked like him had every reason for ridiculous confidence. The thought made her giggle.

"What?" he asked, sounding indignant.

"I was just thinking you're rather confident in your birthday suit, but with good reason." She dragged a finger over the hills and valleys of his well-defined abdomen, her lips quivering with amusement as she watched his cock come back to life.

"My mom tells stories about how I ran around buck naked until I was five, and she made me put pants on before I went out to see the horses."

Maggie's heart ached when she realized he'd spoken of his mother in the present tense. "So you've always been a shameless exhibitionist, then."

"Pretty much. My grandpa used to say I was feral."

Maggie laughed. "Let me guess—you took that as a compliment, right?"

"Is there any other way to take it?"

"For you, probably not."

"I've always been happiest outside with the horses."

"It must've been torture for you to be locked up."

"It was. I almost lost my mind the first year. My mom came every week and pleaded with me not to give up, that she was working on her end to get me out of there."

"I was wondering…" Maggie thought better of what she was going to say. She'd already asked him to open an old wound. She didn't want to make the recent loss of his mother even worse than it already was.

"What are you wondering? You can ask me anything you want."

She turned on her side so she could see him better. "About your mom and how things were between you after what happened."

"It took a while for us to get back on track. I was very angry with her for a long time, because she knew he was no good and didn't do something about it sooner."

"What did she say to that?"

"That I was a hundred percent right, and that she should've picked me over him, even when he was charming and romancing her. She said my immediate and visceral dislike of him—and his dislike of me —should've been a warning, because I liked everyone and everyone liked me. It helped that she completely owned her role in what happened. No one was more heartbroken to see me locked up than she was, especially knowing she'd brought him into our lives and kept him there when she shouldn't have. She always owned that, and that's how we were able to put things back together between us. It also helped that she never stopped fighting for me the whole time I was in there."

Maggie ran her hand up and down his arm. "You worked hard to put things back together with her, which must've made losing her that much more excruciating."

"It did," he said on a long sigh. "The shit that happened years ago didn't break me, but losing her was almost too much." He brushed the hair back from her face and ran his fingertips lightly over her cheek. "I should get out of here before we get caught."

With the night staff working upstairs where the residents were, the risk of having him in her apartment was minimal. "Not yet. Mitch doesn't get here until six. But I do need to reset the alarm." She got up, found her robe on the floor, put it on, used the bathroom and went out to tend to the alarm before getting back in bed with him.

"Um, you forgot something."

"What did I forget?"

"To take the robe off." He tugged at it impatiently, like a child trying to get at a coveted Christmas gift.

Maggie laughed at his impatience and helped to remove the robe.

He brought her into his warm embrace, with one big hand completely cupping her ass to arrange her where he wanted her. "There. Much better."

"Been a long time since I had a sleepover."

"How is that possible? You must've had all the boyfriends."

"Not all. A couple. One in high school, two in college. Nothing much since then."

"It's my good luck that all those other guys missed out. What happened with them?"

"The high school one ended when I went to college in New York and he went to California. We made it to Christmas of freshman year before we both admitted we had no interest in a long-distance relationship."

"Were you heartbroken?"

"For a few days."

Brayden laughed. "Heartless."

"I know it sounds that way, but I met someone else a couple of months later, and that lasted awhile. Until he cheated on me with one of my friends."

"Ugh. That's awful."

"It was pretty bad. I didn't date anyone for a long time after that. Senior year, I dated someone I really liked, but we were both so busy with school and work, it just kind of burned out after a while."

"He was a fool to let you go."

"I know! That's what I said, too." Maggie loved the rich, deep sound of his laugh. "What about you and all the girlfriends?"

"There's only been one that really mattered, a hundred years ago before the trouble. That was another thing that got lost in the madness."

"Did you ever try to find her after you got out?"

"I looked her up on Facebook and saw that she was seeing someone. She looked happy, so I left it alone."

"I'm really sorry."

"It's okay. Wasn't meant to be. Since I got out, I've been focused on school, my career and rebuilding my life. I've dated here and there, but it never amounted to anything lasting."

"How are you still so amazing after everything you've been through? You should be bitter and resentful, and you're just... You're not like that at all."

"That's due to a lot of therapy that my mom made sure I got while I was inside and after. She was relentless in her effort to repair the damage in any way she could."

"Thank God for that."

His hand moved lazily over her back. "She also became a tireless advocate for other kids who got in trouble. In fact, while I was in Key West, I got an email from one of the groups she worked with. They're planning to honor her as their volunteer of the year at their annual fundraiser, and they want me to come."

"Are you going to?"

"I haven't responded yet. It's not until next week."

"You should go."

"Would you go with me?"

"If you wanted me to."

"I do. I want you to."

215

"Okay."

"Really?"

She nodded. "I'll trade you—one fundraiser for another. Jill and I are representing Kate at Buddy's annual Little Buddy fundraiser the week after next."

"That's sort of an unfair trade. I'll get to hobnob with celebrities at your thing."

"I get the better end of the deal. I'll get to hobnob with you at yours."

CHAPTER 23

The next morning, Maggie sent a text to her sisters. *I talked to Brayden, and he told me the whole story. I am 1000 percent comfortable with continuing to employ him and see him outside of work. In fact, I think I shall do that as much as I possibly can going forward. All is well. No need to worry, but thanks for caring.*

Jill responded first: *Sounds like there might be more to the story than just talking!*

Kate said: *I was going to say the same thing! Details! I need details!*

Maggie responded with the hear-no-evil emoji.

She and Brayden fell into a routine that included afternoons with the kids, regular consultations on the progress of each child, late-afternoon rides on Sunday and Thunder, dinner with the residents and hot, sexy nights in Maggie's bed. They'd gotten lucky so far and didn't think anyone else was wise to the fact that he spent every night with her.

If she'd ever been happier, Maggie couldn't remember when. Working with Brayden, talking to Brayden, riding with Brayden, laughing with Brayden, loving with Brayden... Her world revolved around him and his around her, and she wouldn't have it any other way.

She rushed through a shower on the night of the fundraiser at which his mother would be honored and dressed in a sleek black jumpsuit that Andi had sent after seeing it in a store and thinking of her. Thank goodness for relatives with fashion sense, because Maggie's idea of fashion—especially lately—was denim, flannel and T-shirts.

The jumpsuit fit like it'd been made for her, Maggie thought as she studied her reflection in a full-length mirror after stepping into the one pair of strappy black heels she'd brought from her life in the city. She'd used the curling iron Kate had lent her to put spiral curls in her long hair and had covered her freckles with enough makeup to make herself presentable.

A squirt of the Dolce & Gabbana Light Blue perfume Jill had given her for Christmas finished off the look. She grabbed a black purse she'd also borrowed from Kate, who'd said to feel free to raid her massive closet for whatever she needed, and a sweater before heading out to meet Brayden.

Mitch let out a low whistle when she stepped into the kitchen. "You look gorgeous, Maggie."

"Aw, thanks. I am capable of dressing up once in a while."

"Have a great time tonight. I'm glad you're going with him."

Maggie knew Mitch and Brayden had become friendly, but she wasn't aware that Mitch had been told where they were going or why. "Me, too." She walked outside to the parking area behind the stables, where Brayden had asked her to meet him. When she approached his truck, she saw him half in and half out of the passenger seat and walked up behind him, molding her body to his.

"Maggie?"

"Who else would it be?" She gave him a light spank on the backside and stepped back to let him out of the truck.

He stood and turned, starting to say something that died on his lips when he saw her. "Whoa... You look... *Wow.*"

Maggie loved the hungry way he looked at her. "So we like the jumpsuit my stepmother sent me?"

"We like it." He put an arm around her waist and kissed her. "We like you."

"We like you, too," she said, taking an appreciative look at the tweed blazer he wore with a dress shirt and khakis. "You look very handsome."

"I debated the tie."

"You're fine without it."

"Oh good. I hate them." He held out a hand to help her into the passenger side of his truck. "I think it might be clean enough for you. Just barely."

"It's fine. It even smells good."

Brayden pointed to the air freshener propped on the dash. "Gas station purchase in honor of our first real date."

Giddy with excitement for their first real date, Maggie put on her seat belt and waited for him to get in.

As he drove the truck around the stable to the driveway, he said, "Um, well…"

Maggie looked away from him to see what had drawn his attention.

The residents and staff were gathered in the driveway, waiting to wave them off. Even Derek, the stable manager, was there.

"Okay, well, this is rather mortifying."

Brayden laughed, tooted the horn and waved as he drove past the gathered group.

"So much for thinking we were getting away with it."

"Safe to say the cat's out of the bag, sweetheart. I think it's cool they all came out to see us off."

"I'm going to stick with mortifying."

He reached for her hand and held on as he drove them into town.

"How're you feeling about tonight?" Maggie asked as the Nashville skyline came into view.

"I feel better than I would have if you weren't with me. We'll stay for the thing about my mom and then go find something more fun to do."

"Please don't feel like you have to entertain me. This is your mom's night, and you should take all the time you need there. It's so great they're recognizing her this way." Maggie had read up on the organization online. "And besides, I'm looking forward to meeting the people behind the group and expanding my professional network."

"I see how it is," he said in a teasing tone. "You're just using me to get in the door."

"Exactly."

He laughed and brought her hand to his lips. "Thanks again for coming."

"It's my pleasure."

"It will be later." He waggled his brows at her. "You brought a toothbrush, right?"

"I did. But you're still not going to tell me why I'm going to need it?"

"All will be revealed in due time."

"I didn't figure you to be a man of mystery."

His sexy smile made her want to release her seat belt and crawl into his lap, regardless of the fact that he was driving. "You ain't seen nothing yet, baby."

This kind of happiness, Maggie was discovering, kept her on edge, wanting more of it while also dreading the possibility of losing what'd taken forever to find. She tightened her hand around his, wanting to hold on to him and everything that came with him.

He glanced over at her. "You okay?"

"I'm good."

They listened to one of the local country music stations, and when Kate's number-one hit "I Thought I Knew" came on, Maggie reached over to turn it up.

"I love this song."

"I do, too. She wrote it for Reid the first time they were together."

"I can't believe I've actually met her, that I'm dating her sister."

"Tell me the truth, is that really why you're dating me?"

"You found me out. It's all about access to your famous sister and her famous friends."

"I knew it."

He grinned at her, and they sang along to words Maggie had known by heart for years. They took on new meaning now that she'd met Brayden, which made her feel both scared and elated.

I thought I knew
what love was,
but then there was you...
I thought I knew
how it would be,
but now I see,
And now it's true...
I didn't know
until there was you...
Until there was you...
Until there was you...
I thought I knew
And now it's true...
I thought I knew
what peace was,
then there was you...
I thought I knew
what dreams were,
then there was you...
I thought I knew
how it would be,
but now I see...
I thought I knew
what love was,
but then there was you
Then there was you...

"Her voice is just magic," Brayden said. "I've always thought so, from the time she first appeared on the scene. I don't even like country all that much, but I make an exception for her, Buddy and Taylor. They just do it for me."

"Agreed. Country isn't usually my thing, either, but I do like some of it. I love Martina McBride and Faith Hill, too."

"They're both great, and so is Rascal Flatts and Tim McGraw."

"I like them, but I'm more of a Coldplay kinda girl at the end of the day."

"I saw them in concert a few years ago."

"Shut up! I'd love to see them."

"They come here every so often. You'll probably get your chance. What's your favorite song by them?"

"It's a tossup between *Fix You, Yellow* and *Viva La Vida*. I love them all."

"Those would be my top three, too."

After a forty-minute ride into town, made longer by rush-hour traffic, Brayden pulled up to the Hermitage Hotel on 6th Avenue North.

"I read about this place online," Maggie said. "Everyone who's anyone has stayed here—Patsy Cline, President Kennedy, Johnny Cash, Babe Ruth—and it played a big role in the women's suffrage movement. My sisters love this hotel."

"I can't wait to check it out."

A valet parking attendant greeted them, handing Brayden a ticket. Brayden gave him a five-dollar bill. "Thanks."

"Give a call to the bell stand thirty minutes before you need it back."

"Will do."

"Have a nice evening."

Brayden took Maggie's hand and walked inside, where they stopped to admire the gorgeous lobby.

As she gazed up at the stunning high ceiling with mosaics and glass details, she said, "I've got to bring my dad and stepmom here. They'd go crazy over this."

"It's like stepping back in time."

"It really is."

Maggie took another look around, wanting to commit the details to memory. At the entrance to the ballroom, Brayden gave his name at the reception table set up outside.

"Oh, Brayden! I'm Justine. We spoke on the phone." The young woman reached across the table to shake his hand, her gaze traveling the length of him in a way that had Maggie wanting to remind her that he was *holding hands* with another woman while she checked him out. Fortunately, Justine recovered quickly. "We're so honored to have you with us tonight." She handed him badges that had his name and Maggie's on them. "Your mom was an angel. We all loved her so much."

"Thank you."

"You're seated at the head table at the front. There's a reserved sign on the table and seating cards for both of you. Do you need help finding it?"

"I think we can figure it out," Brayden said. "Thanks again for having us."

She gave him a flirty smile. "It's a pleasure."

Maggie wanted to ask if she was for real, but she held her tongue until they were far enough away from the check-in table. "She wanted to come across the table and jump your bones."

"I sorta picked up a vibe..."

Maggie laughed. "It was a vibe, all right. She'll probably slip you her room key before the night is out."

"Not interested."

"Good answer."

He smiled down at her. In a massive room full of people, he let her know with just a look that she was the only one who mattered. Every time she was with him, she experienced something all new, and now was no different. He held the chair for her and waited until she was settled before sitting next to her. "You want a drink?" He eyed the bar set up on the far side of the room.

"Maybe later." Under the table, she noticed his leg bouncing and placed her hand flat on his thigh.

"Sorry."

"Are you nervous about this?"

"A little."

"You know they're going to sing her praises."

"Yeah." He glanced at the stage and then back at her. "I came with her last year. It's just weird to be here without her."

"I'm sure it is."

"Have I said thanks for coming?"

Maggie smiled. "I'm really happy to be here."

CHAPTER 24

*B*rayden put his arm around her, kissed her temple and removed his arm only when the waitstaff began serving dinner.

"This is really fancy for a benefit," Maggie said as she cut into delicious steak and asparagus.

"Apparently, the Hermitage donates the space and gives them a huge deal on the food and beverages. They also donate weekend packages to the silent auction. My mom used to talk all the time about how great they are."

After dinner and chocolate cheesecake for dessert, the program began with a welcome from the chairwoman of the board, who discussed accomplishments over the last year. They included sponsoring after-school programs that kept kids busy in what she referred to as the "at-risk hours" and matching young people recently "graduated" from the foster care system with adult mentors.

"My mom had something like ten kids she mentored and kept in touch with every one of them," Brayden whispered. "They came to our house for holidays and stuff."

"I wish I could've met her."

"Me, too. She would've liked you."

Maggie smiled at him and wished she could kiss him.

"At this time, we'd like to honor our volunteer of the year, Kathy Thomas. As all of you know, we recently lost Kathy in a tragic accident. I'm sure I speak for so many people in this room when I say the loss of this great lady can't be measured in mere words. I'd like to share this slide presentation that provides just a small glimpse into the impact Kathy had on our organization."

While holding his hand, Maggie kept one eye on the slide show and the other on him, noting the way his jaw had tightened with tension as the images of his mother with a wide variety of young people and other adults were displayed on the huge screen. In every one of them, Kathy was smiling, laughing, fully engaged in giving back to kids in need. It was obvious to Maggie that Kathy had sought to redeem the mistakes she'd made with her own son by helping other kids. Maggie found herself forgiving a woman she'd never met for having failed to protect Brayden.

The slide show ended with a warm round of applause.

A video played then in which several of the children and young adults Kathy had worked with talked about what she'd meant to them and the difference she'd made in their lives.

"We're honored to have Kathy's son, Brayden, with us tonight to accept the Volunteer of the Year award on behalf of his mother, the indefatigable, irreplaceable Kathy Thomas."

Brayden squeezed Maggie's hand and headed for the stage as the entire room stood to applaud his mother.

Maggie had a huge lump in her throat as she stood with the others to watch him take the stage, shake hands with the program chair and take a long look at the crystal award he'd been given.

The applause went on for minutes.

"Thank you all so much," Brayden said. "It's an honor to be here with you tonight and to accept this award on my mother's behalf. She had tremendous affection for this organization and for the amazing people she met through her work with y'all. If she were here, she would tell you she doesn't need awards.

"In fact, she declined this one many times over because she said the kids gave her the only reward she needed when they finished college or got a great job or started families of their own. She was so proud of every one of the young people she worked with, and I gratefully accept this award on her behalf. Thank you for remembering her this way. I appreciate it so much."

Maggie's heart swelled with pride along with a surge of affection and love for him that caught her off guard. It was too soon to love him. She couldn't... Not yet... But as he came toward her, stopping to accept condolences from numerous people, her heart hammered, and the feeling that overwhelmed her could only be love.

She loved him.

How was that possible?

Clearly, she was being ridiculous, caught up in the emotion of the moment and not thinking clearly. But then his gaze met hers, and...

Everything else fell away. In a room full of people, she saw only him.

She loved him.

He finally made his way back to the table and immediately reached for her.

Maggie closed her eyes and hugged him back as her mind raced to catch up with the heart that had chosen him.

Eventually, they took their seats again, but Brayden kept his arm around her, which was fine with Maggie. She wanted only to be close to him.

When the ceremony ended, he said he needed to use the men's room and would be right back. Maggie took advantage of the time he was gone to talk to some of the organization's leaders about Matthews House and to exchange business cards.

"We get together for lunch with other program directors the first Wednesday of every month," one of the women told her. "You're more than welcome to join us."

"I'd love to."

"Great. I'll email you the info."

"Please do."

"I work with a child who would absolutely love your equine therapy program, and I think it would do wonders for his self-confidence. Are you willing to work with children outside your own program?"

Brayden returned in time to hear the question. "I am if it's okay with Maggie. She's the boss."

"That'd be fine with me. Call me to make arrangements."

Maggie knew that Brayden was ready to go, but appreciated that he was patient while she talked to the others about networking opportunities.

"We've heard such amazing things about your program," another woman said. "We'd love to see your facility sometime, if that's possible."

"Any time. We can do one of the monthly lunches there sometime, if you'd like."

"That'd be great."

Maggie left the event feeling like she'd made some friends and begun to set up the professional network that would be so helpful to her going forward. "That was great," she said to Brayden when they were out of the ballroom. "Those are just the kinds of connections I need."

"I'm so glad you got the chance to meet some people. My mom loved working with them. She said they're the perfect group because they care so much about the kids they serve. It's not just a job to them, but a cause."

"I can see how they would look at it that way. Matthews House has never felt like a 'regular job' to me, and it's not only because I work for my sister and brother-in-law. It's because I know that even on the worst days, we're doing something important to help people who really need it."

"That's right, but tonight, you're off duty."

"Until we get home, you mean."

"Nope. I mean until tomorrow afternoon when the kids get home from school."

"What're you talking about?"

He pulled a room key from his pocket and showed it to her. "Remember that toothbrush I told you to bring?"

Maggie gasped. "We're *staying* here?"

"Yep."

"But the house, I need to… They'll be wondering…"

"Teresa knows you won't be back tonight."

"Oh." Maggie wasn't sure how she felt about him telling one of their colleagues that they'd be spending the night together.

"She said she thinks it's great because you haven't had a full night off since you started months ago, and she said to tell you not to worry about a thing. She's got you covered."

"This is rather sneaky of you, Brayden."

"I realize that, Maggie, but I thought you might enjoy the night away." He directed her into a small alcove off the hallway, and with his back blocking the view of anyone going by, he kissed her neck, jaw and lips. "We don't have to stay if you don't want to, but before you decide, you ought to know there's a huge tub in the room, I ordered champagne, and there'll be room service in the morning—"

Maggie wrapped her arms around his neck and drew him into a kiss. "Sold."

"What did it for you? The room service?"

She shook her head. "It's that I get to enjoy all those things with you."

"So this is a good surprise, then?"

"A very good surprise. Did you check us into a fancy hotel with no luggage?"

"Maybe?"

Maggie laughed. "That's the definition of a booty call."

He flattened his hand on her ass and squeezed. "I can live with that as long as it's your booty calling."

"Can we go check out the room now?"

"Absolutely." He kissed her again before resting his forehead against hers. "Maggie…"

"Hmmm?"

"Is this real? Are you real?"

"I've been wondering the very same thing about you."

"It's the most real thing I've ever had, and all I want is more of it—and you."

"Me, too."

He took hold of her hand. "Let's go upstairs."

BRAYDEN HAD EXPECTED tonight to be a gut punch, and in many ways, it had been. Seeing the photos of his mom alive and well and laughing with the kids she'd loved so much was a brutal reminder of what he'd lost. But being there with Maggie had made it far more bearable than it would've been otherwise.

Being with Maggie made everything better. He thought she was beautiful all the time, but she'd blown him away with how she looked tonight. When he saw her standing there by the truck, he'd thought for a second he was dreaming. Everything about her appealed to him, from the way she handled the residents and staff to their shared love of horses and her dedication to the program they were building together.

She did it for him in a way that no other woman ever had. She was his dream girl, and he'd wanted their first real date to be memorable for both of them. Which was why he'd used the last of his credit card limit to reserve a room at the Hermitage so he could make tonight special for her.

He'd be getting his first paycheck from Matthews House next week, and that would give him room to breathe. In the meantime, tonight was a major splurge, but well worth it to make her happy and to give her a badly needed break from her responsibilities at the house.

They took the elevator to the fifth floor and followed the signs to room five twenty-five.

Brayden used the key card to gain entry and held the door so she could go ahead of him into the elegant room with a king-size bed, sitting area and marble bathroom.

"This is gorgeous, Brayden," Maggie said as she took it all in.

"Your dad builds incredible hotels. You've probably seen them all."

Maggie came to him, put her hands on his hips and looked up at him. "This one is special, the best hotel I've ever been in because I'm here with you."

She was so sweet, so adorable, so everything.

Brayden raised his hands to her face and tipped it up to receive his kiss. He could kiss her for hours and never get enough. In fact, that's exactly what he wanted to do now that they had all night to spend together.

A knock on the door briefly interrupted his plans. "Hold that thought."

"Holding."

Brayden went to the door and let in the room service waiter, who'd brought champagne and chocolate. He signed the slip and included a gratuity. "Thanks very much."

"Have a nice evening, folks."

He followed the man to the door, closed it and locked it since they were in for the night. When he turned back to the room, he saw that Maggie had kicked off her shoes and was checking out the view from the window. From behind her, he put his hands on her shoulders. "What're you thinking about over here?"

"That I can almost see home from here."

"I should've taken you farther away than Nashville."

"No, this is perfect." She leaned back against him. "Thank you for giving me the best reason to take a break."

"Is this the best reason?"

Turning to face him, she said, "You're the best reason I've ever had."

"Same."

As he stared into her stunning blue eyes, he wondered if she felt anywhere near what he did, because if she did… God, he couldn't even bring himself to hope for that. "How about some champagne?"

"I never say no to champagne."

He went to pop the cork and filled glasses for both of them. "They also brought chocolate."

"Yum."

She drank the champagne and checked out the selection of chocolates. "You want one?"

He put his glass on a table, removed his jacket and folded it over a chair, sat on the bed and kicked off his shoes. "Sure. Pick one for me."

Maggie stepped between his legs and fed a chocolate to him.

"Mmm, that's good."

"Uh-huh."

They shared her glass of champagne, then dropped the glass to the carpeted floor as they fell back on the bed in a kiss that tasted of chocolate and champagne. Their heads bumped, and they laughed and then kissed some more while tugging at clothes.

"How in the hell do I get this thing off you?" he asked, frustrated by the jumpsuit.

"I gotta stand up."

Brayden let her up, and when he tried to help with buttons, she pushed his hands away. He groaned dramatically, which made her laugh.

"Get that shirt off," she said. "And the pants can go, too. You won't be needing them for a while."

Brayden's fingers were like thumbs as he tried to hurry. All day, he'd been looking forward to right now, when they'd have hours alone to spend together. In bed. Naked. That couldn't happen fast enough for him as he pulled a strip of condoms from his pocket, tossed them on the bed, kicked off his pants and underwear, nearly falling over in his haste.

Maggie covered her mouth, but her eyes danced with laughter.

"It's not funny."

"It *is* funny."

He sat on the bed, crooked his finger at her, and she stepped into the space between his legs. "You forgot a few things," he said, using his chin to point to the bra and panties she'd left on. "You want some help with that?"

"Sure." She turned away from him, and that was when he saw that she was wearing a thong.

He sucked in a sharp breath at the sight of black fabric disappearing between supple cheeks. "Maggie…"

"Hmm?"

"Are you trying to stop my heart?"

"Nope."

He cupped and squeezed her cheeks. "Well, you just about did."

"I couldn't have panty lines."

"I agree entirely. Panty lines are the devil."

Brayden loved to make her laugh. He unhooked her black bra and slid the straps down over her arms until the garment fell to the floor. Maggie started to turn around, but he stopped her. "Hang on a minute." He stood, pushed his cock into the softness between her cheeks and reached around to cup her breasts and tease her nipples.

She pressed back against him and made him see stars.

Christ have mercy, he wanted her like he'd never wanted anything or anyone—ever. This kind of desire was all new to him, something he'd heard about happening to other people, but he'd never experienced it until he met Maggie and suddenly understood. He'd basically blown off most of a Key West vacation so he could talk to her, and if that wasn't a sign that his life had taken an unexpected turn, he didn't know what was.

He kissed the back of her neck and caressed her breasts until her legs were trembling. Locking one arm around her ribs, he flattened the other hand over her belly, sliding it down between her legs.

Gasping, she leaned into him as he played with her through the silk of her panties. He worked on her until she was breathing hard and moving with him, and then he retreated, pushed his hand inside her panties and finished her off in two strokes. He slid the panties down her legs and held her while she stepped out of them. As she turned to face him, he grabbed a condom and rolled it on.

He guided her onto his lap so she straddled him, her arms curled around his neck and her breasts pressed to his chest. "Is this okay?"

She nodded, lifted herself up and took him in, coming down on him slowly until he was fully buried in her.

His hands cupped her bottom and held on as she set the pace, forcing him to follow her lead. He was more than happy to follow her anywhere she wanted to take him.

CHAPTER 25

*M*aggie slept like a dead woman. She hadn't slept like that in months, since before she moved to Tennessee. Maybe it'd been before Ethan attacked her. When she woke, sunshine peeked in through the curtains, and she had no idea what time it was. Hopefully, the kids had gotten off to school without a problem and everything was all right at the house. She had to assume Teresa would call her if anything came up that she couldn't handle.

Expelling a deep breath, she burrowed deeper into the luxurious bed linens and wallowed in contentment as she thought about the night with Brayden. She dozed until the scent of coffee and bacon had her sitting up in bed.

"Morning, Sleeping Beauty."

She pushed the mass of hair back off her face to take in the delicious sight of him sitting at the table wearing only his underwear as he read the paper. "Morning. What time is it?"

"Almost ten."

"No way."

"Yes way."

"Wow. I've been convinced lately that I'd never again sleep later than six thirty."

"Now you know you still can."

Maggie found his discarded dress shirt and put it on before getting out of bed to use the bathroom and the toothbrush he'd told her to bring. Sneaky devil. She loved that he'd planned this amazing night away from it all for her. After she used the bathroom, brushed her teeth and tried to straighten her wild hair, she went to him and wrapped her arms around him from behind the chair.

"Thank you so much for this. I had no idea how much I needed it until you made it happen."

He reached for her hand. "It was *entirely* my pleasure."

Maggie smiled as she kissed his neck. "Do I smell bacon?"

"You do. It's not as good as Mitch's, but it'll do." He poured her a cup of coffee, stirred in the cream she liked and handed it to her.

"Thank you." She sat in the other seat at the table and took the first sip of coffee, which was one of her favorite moments of the day. "Have you been up for long?" Maggie noted the heavy, dark stubble on his jaw that appeared every morning and gave him a rough, sexy, untamed look that she loved on him—almost as much as the clean-shaven version. She could stare at his face all day, every day and never get tired of the view.

"What're you looking at over there?"

"Scruffy Brayden."

He rubbed at the stubble on his jaw. "Drives me crazy."

"I like it."

"Yeah?"

"Uh-huh."

"Maybe I'll keep it if you like it."

"Not if it drives you crazy."

"We'll take it under advisement."

Maggie devoured the bacon and cheese omelet he'd ordered for her as if she hadn't seen food in a month. "Did you already eat?" She couldn't stop looking at his beautiful chest and cut abs.

"Yeah, I was starving. You wore me out."

She snorted with laughter. "I'd say it was quite the other way around. I was minding my business at three a.m. when I was rudely awakened by a man who'd already had the goods twice."

"The goods are *so* good, he needed more."

That sexy little smile of his would be her undoing. All he had to do was look at her the way he was right then, and she was a goner. The moment was interrupted when Maggie's phone chimed with a text.

"I should check that."

"Go ahead."

She got up and crossed the room to the chair where she'd left her purse. In all the months she'd been in charge at Matthews House, she'd never been out of touch this long. Maggie pulled out the phone and realized there were several texts from Teresa, and as she read them, her heart sank.

Sorry to disturb your time away. I thought you'd want to know that Trey was released from jail last night, and Corey must've snuck out before we set the alarm. I realized she was gone this morning. The gate reported an Uber pickup right around ten. We checked her room, and her things are gone.

"Ugh," Maggie said.

"What's wrong?"

She filled him in as she texted Teresa, the only other person on the staff who had a key to the office. *Go into my office and pull up her file. Get me the last known address for her.*

Already did. Here you go. She sent a photo containing the info.

I'm on it.

Is Brayden still with you? You shouldn't go there alone.

Yes, he's here.

Be careful.

Maggie put down the phone, picked up her clothes from the floor and headed for the shower. If only she'd been there, she might've been able to stop Corey from leaving. Damn it! She should've been there! As she stood under the hot water, Maggie took a minute to formulate a plan. Corey shouldn't be out running around less than two weeks after major surgery. And what if Trey hurt her again?

Brayden stepped into the shower and rested his hands on her shoulders. "I know what you're thinking, and you need to stop blaming yourself. She was determined to see him, and you couldn't have stopped her even if you'd been there."

"You don't know that."

"Yes, I do, and when you take a minute to breathe, you'll know it, too."

"How can she go running back to him after what he did to her and their baby?"

"I don't know, but she would've found a way back to him whether you'd been there or not. Maybe she wouldn't have left last night, but you couldn't force her to stay if she didn't want to."

Maggie sagged into the warm comfort he provided.

He propped his chin on her shoulder. "You're not going to save them all, Maggie, no matter how hard you try."

"I want to save them all. I want them to be safe and secure and happy."

"I know, honey, but people are going to do what they're going to do, and you can't stop them from making bad decisions."

"So I shouldn't go after her?"

"I didn't say that. We can go by and check on her, but you need to prepare yourself for the fact that she's not going to want to go back to Matthews House, even if that's the best thing for her right now."

"She's not even two weeks out from major surgery."

"I know."

They finished showering, got dressed, called down for his truck and were on their way to Corey's twenty minutes after Maggie received the text from Teresa, following the GPS to an address north of downtown Nashville.

The closer they got to the address, the more nervous Maggie became about Corey's safety. She'd been gone more than twelve hours at that point. A lot could happen in that much time. Brayden took a right turn into a run-down apartment complex, and Maggie's heart stopped when she saw police and fire vehicles in the parking lot. "Oh my God."

She got out of the truck and ran for the first cop car she could get to. "I'm looking for the woman who lives in six twenty-two."

"We transported her to Nashville General," the officer said.

"Is she... What happened?"

"Are you a relative?"

"No, a friend."

"I'm not at liberty to say."

Maggie turned to go back to the truck and nearly ran into Brayden, who grasped her arms. "She's back in the hospital," she told him in a flat tone that was in direct contrast to how she felt inside. She wanted to rage and scream over this turn of events. But that wouldn't help Corey. "Nashville General."

He took her hand. "Come on." Brayden led her back to his truck and helped her into the passenger seat.

"Breathe," he said as he drove faster than he probably should have to get them to the hospital.

Maggie forced air into her lungs. Even as she told herself this wasn't her fault, that there was nothing she could've done to keep Corey from going back to Trey if that was what she really wanted to do, she still felt responsible somehow.

Brayden pulled up to the emergency entrance. "Go ahead. I'll find you."

Maggie jumped out of the truck and ran inside, wishing she had something other than heels for this mission. "I'm looking for Corey Gellar."

"Are you a family member?" the nurse working the desk asked.

"No, I'm the director of the shelter where she's been staying. She listed me as a contact when she was here recently to give birth." Maggie showed her Matthews House ID, thankful she had it with her. "I'm not aware of any family in the area."

"Have a seat. I'll see what I can do."

Maggie didn't want to have a seat, but having no other choice, she found two empty seats in the crowded waiting room and waved to Brayden when he came in a few minutes later.

"What'd they say?"

"That I have to wait."

239

He took her hand. "Breathe, Maggie. Just keep breathing and stop blaming yourself."

"I'm trying."

They waited a long time, maybe more than an hour, while Maggie vibrated with tension and anxiety, feeling as if she was going to explode if she didn't hear something soon. Finally, a woman came into the waiting room and asked for the family of Corey Gellar.

Maggie shot up and went to her. "I'm Maggie Harrington, the director of Matthews House where Ms. Gellar was staying until last night. Another member of my team and I are here for her."

"You can come on back."

Maggie signaled for Brayden to come with her, and they followed the woman through the double doors, where they were shown to a small room that had a table with four chairs around it and nothing else inside. Her heart fell when a police officer entered the room.

"A doctor will be right in," the nurse said as she stepped out.

Brayden's hands on Maggie's shoulders helped to keep her calm as she braced herself for what she was going to hear.

"What happened?" Maggie asked the cop.

"We received a call at eight twenty this morning from a neighbor who heard screaming coming from the apartment next door. When we arrived, we found the front door open and Ms. Gellar bleeding and unconscious on the floor. We think she'd been there for quite some time before we arrived."

Maggie processed the information with a growing feeling of dread. "And her boyfriend…"

"We're looking for him."

"He… He's done this before. He just got out of jail."

"We're very familiar with Mr. Williams. He has a long history with our department."

Maggie wanted to break down, but she held it together because Corey needed her to be strong.

A woman in a white coat came into the now-crowded room and introduced herself as Dr. Halstead.

"How is she?" Maggie asked.

"Have a seat," the doctor said as she sat at the table.

Maggie sat across from her.

"I understand Ms. Gellar put you on her list of contacts when she was here to deliver her baby."

"Yes, she has no family in the area. She's been staying at our facility."

"I'm sorry to have to tell you she was badly beaten and is in very critical condition."

Maggie whimpered.

Brayden sat next to her and put his arm around her.

"We've taken her up to surgery to contend with some internal bleeding and the reopening of her previous surgical site."

At that news, Maggie dropped her head into her hands. "Is she going to be okay?"

"We don't know yet. Our primary concern is a rather significant head injury."

This could not be happening.

The next few hours seemed to unfold in slow motion as Maggie and Brayden waited for news. At two, she suggested Brayden go to the house to carry on as planned with the kids and the riding lessons.

"I wouldn't feel right leaving you here alone."

"I'm all right. The kids will be disappointed if we cancel."

"I'll come right back after."

"Ask Teresa to send me some jeans and sneakers?"

He kissed her forehead. "I'll take care of it, and I'll be back as soon as I can."

"Thanks again for the great night."

"I'm sorry it ended here."

She offered him a weak smile. "A wise person once told me that we can't control what other people do."

"Keep reminding yourself of that." He kissed her cheek and got up to leave.

Maggie watched him go, thankful for him and the support he offered so easily, as if it was the most natural thing in the world for him to want to be there for her. She recalled something her mother

241

once told her when she was mourning the loss of the more serious of her two college relationships. *He's out there,* she'd said, *and when you find him, you'll know it because he's there for you, he listens to you, he sees you. The right guy makes you feel like the most important thing in his world. Wait for that guy, and when he shows up, make sure you notice.*

Was Brayden that guy? The one she'd hoped to find someday? He checked all the boxes on her mother's list, and suddenly, more than anything, she wanted to talk to her mom about him and Corey and Debbie. She found a secluded corner, away from the main waiting area, and put through the call.

Her mom answered on the third ring, sounding like she'd run for the phone. "Hey, this is a nice surprise."

"Are you busy?"

"Just doing some yoga before I have to pick up the boys."

"I can call you later."

"Now is fine. What's up?"

Maggie's throat closed, and she couldn't breathe or speak.

"Maggie? Are you all right?"

"Yeah." She forced herself to calm down and do what Brayden had told her to do all morning: breathe.

"What's wrong, Maggie?"

"I... I think this job might be too much for me." The words, once spoken, could never be stuffed back into the jar where she'd kept them contained for months.

"Why do you say that? From what I've heard, you're doing a brilliant job."

"One of the moms died last week."

"I know. Have you heard what happened?"

"Her mom told me she had an enlarged heart."

"So she was probably a ticking time bomb. You have to know there was nothing you could've done to prevent her death, right?"

"How do I know that for sure?"

"Maggie! It's not your fault."

She wallowed in the comfort of her mother's emphatic words. "Last night, I stayed in town with a friend."

"I assume you're allowed a night off every now and then."

"Yes, but while I was gone, one of the residents checked herself out to return to the man who beat her so badly, their baby was born prematurely. He got released from jail yesterday, and today, I'm at the ER waiting to hear if she's going to survive the head injury she received when he beat her again—so badly, she's in surgery." Her voice caught on a sob.

"Sweetheart, I'm so sorry that happened to someone you care about."

"She's so young and has no one."

"Which is why she went running back to him the first chance she got. He's her someone, for better or worse."

"Why does it make all the sense when you put it that way?"

"It'll never make sense to you because you're not in her relationship. Maybe at one point, before it went bad, he was the first person to ever truly care about her. Maybe she's still hoping to find that guy in him again."

"I hope she's done looking for that in him after this."

"You need to prepare yourself for the possibility that she'll continue to go back to him. You can only do what you can, honey. You can't live their lives for them. You can only try to make their lives easier and more comfortable while they figure it out for themselves."

Maggie absorbed her mother's words of wisdom, letting the comforting sound of her voice wash over her. "Thank you for listening."

"The job isn't too much for you, Mags. It's that your heart is too big to handle the hurt sometimes. It's always been that way. Your dad and I were very concerned about whether the job would break your big, beautiful heart."

"You were? You guys talked about that?"

"Here's a newsflash you can share with your sisters. We talk about you guys all the time."

Maggie laughed. "Why am I not surprised?"

"Are you all right, honey?"

"I suppose I will be. I'm really worried about Corey."

"I'll say a prayer for her—and for you."

"Thanks, Mom."

"So about this 'friend' you stayed in town with... Anything you want to tell me about her or *him?*"

"You still suck at subtlety."

"So my daughters tell me."

"His name is Brayden, which you know because Jill and Kate have big mouths, and I think I love him."

Clare gasped. "You do? Really?"

"I think so. He's amazing, smart, sweet, talented and quite possibly the sexiest dude I've ever met."

"Oh, well..."

Maggie laughed again. "You asked."

"This is truly wonderful news. How does he feel?"

"I don't know. It's still early days, but he arranged the night away for me, which was really sweet." Maggie told her about the fundraiser they'd attended and about him accepting the award on behalf of his late mother.

"How long ago did he lose her?"

"A couple of months ago in a car accident."

"The poor guy. It's still new."

"Yes, and she was his only family."

"Oh dear. Well, I'm glad he has you and that you have him."

"Don't get too excited yet, and don't tell Dad."

"I don't keep things from him. You know that."

"You guys are *divorced.* Why can't you act like it once in a while?"

Clare cracked up laughing. "We're not divorced when it comes to our beloved daughters."

"I'll tell him when I'm ready to, Mom. Seriously, don't tell him. He'll fly here to give Brayden an inquisition."

"You're right. He probably would."

"So keep it between us for now. I promise I'll tell him when the time is right."

"Fine. I'll keep your secrets. For now."

"How's the wedding stuff?" Maggie asked, because she wanted to keep her mom on the phone for a little while longer.

"It's all done but the waiting. Andi made it super easy on us. She's got it down to a science after all these years of overseeing weddings at the hotel. Although she said she's never helped to plan a wedding for one of her own kids."

"Does it bug you when she refers to us that way?"

"Nah, I got over that years ago when I realized how lucky we were that you girls had her to lean on when I couldn't be there for you."

"Sometimes all that seems like a million years ago, and then other times, it feels like it happened last week."

"I know what you mean. Even after all these years, it's still weird to me sometimes that I'm married to Aidan and not your father."

"That's because you missed the part where your first marriage ended."

"Very true. I want to add that I love Aidan madly. Wouldn't want you to think otherwise."

"I know you do."

"I missed a lot during those years."

Clare had often said how she left three girls behind and woke up from her coma to three young women who'd nearly finished growing up without their mother.

"I don't mean to resurrect difficult memories. Sorry."

"It's all right. It's our story, and we own it. And besides, it all worked out the way it was meant to. I honestly believe that."

Maggie sat up straighter when she saw Corey's doctor come through the double doors to the waiting room. "Mom, I have to go. I'll text you later."

"Hang in there, Mags. I love you."

"Love you, too."

245

CHAPTER 26

*M*aggie stashed the phone in her pocket and approached the doctor. "Is there news about Corey?"

"Come on back."

With a sinking feeling full of dread, Maggie followed her to the same room they'd been in earlier.

The doctor closed the door. "She came through the surgery and is in recovery. We did a CT scan and saw no sign of bleeding in her brain."

"That's good news, right?"

"Very good news."

"Is she conscious?"

"Not yet, but we're more optimistic after seeing the scans. It's a wait-and-see thing for now. She's not out of the woods yet, but she's better than she was."

"Can I see her?"

"When we get her settled in a room. If you give me your number, I'll have one of the nurses call you."

"Thank you so much." Maggie gave the doctor her phone number and returned to the waiting room to text Brayden, Teresa and Arnelle, updating them on Corey's condition.

Each of them responded with relief and pleas for Maggie to keep them informed. Since she had a little time, she went to the cafeteria, bought a cup of coffee and took it to a bench outside the emergency entrance, where she tipped her face into the warm sunshine and thought about what Brayden and her mom had said about the things she could control and the things she couldn't.

In time, hopefully she'd get better about not taking the setbacks suffered by her clientele so personally. Or maybe she wouldn't. Maybe she would always take their setbacks to heart and feel responsible when their program failed to make a difference for someone they tried to help.

Her phone rang, and she took the call from Kate. "Hey."

"I heard about Corey. How is she? Are you all right?"

Maggie told her sister what she knew.

"I can tell you're blaming yourself, Maggie, and it's not your fault."

"I wish I was home last night. Maybe I could've kept her from leaving."

"If she was determined to go to him, nothing could've stopped her. Not even you. When we hired you for this job, we never expected you to be on duty twenty-four hours a day. Everyone is entitled to time off and time away, including you."

"Thanks. I know. I just wish this hadn't happened."

"I know, but I need you to tell me you understand it's not your fault."

"It's not my fault."

"All we can do, Mags, is provide the tools. We can't make our residents use them. And this is why they sign the release absolving us of responsibility for them. Because they're adults and can do whatever they want, even if it's not what we'd advise them to do."

Maggie recalled how Ashton had absolutely insisted on what he called the hold-harmless release form. Everyone who entered the facility signed it to protect the owners and staff from liability in situations like this one and what'd happened to Debbie.

"Thanks for calling and reminding me of what my job is and what it isn't."

"You're doing so great. The fact that you care like you do is the most important thing to the residents. That's what they need most. Someone who cares."

"True. We do give them that."

"Yes, you do. So how was your date with Brayden?"

"It was really great. He arranged for us to stay in the city after the fundraiser."

"That's so sweet. I love that he did that. And of course you're beating yourself up for being there rather than at home when Corey left."

"I was. I'm better now. I talked to Brayden and Mom and now you, and you all said the same things. It's a learning curve for me on how to deal when things go sideways. I met some people at the fundraiser last night, and they invited me to join their networking group. I think it'll help to have actual contact with other people in this field, rather than just relying on online support."

"I agree. It'll be good for you to be connected to others in the field. You're doing everything right, Mags, despite a really rough couple of weeks. Why don't you and Brayden come for dinner so you can have some Poppy time? That'll make you feel better."

"I'd love to. Let me see what time I get out of here. I'll let you know."

"Either way, it's fine—and it's an open invite. You know that."

"I do. Thanks for the support."

"Love you so much, and I'm so, *so* proud of you."

Kate's kind words brought tears to Maggie's eyes. "Thanks. Means a lot. Love you, too."

"Text me later."

"I will."

Two hours after Maggie saw the doctor, she received a call that Corey had been taken to a room in the ICU. The nurse gave her the room number. "You need to be prepared that she looks pretty banged up, but she's stable and was awake for a short time, which is very good news."

"That's great. Thank you. I'll be up soon."

Maggie texted the room number to Brayden and asked him to update the others.

Got it, he replied. *Will be there soon.*

Maggie also sent a quick update to her mom as she took the elevator to the third floor, where she requested entry to the ICU. The nurse who let her in showed her to Corey's room.

Maggie stepped into the room and gasped at the bruises that covered the young woman's face, arms and neck. Tears filled Maggie's eyes and slid down her cheeks. She would never understand how someone could do such a thing to another human being, especially someone they'd once professed to love.

Her heart broke for Corey. She'd been through so much. Maggie laid her hand on Corey's shoulder and gently brushed the hair back from her face, which was so swollen, she might not have recognized the girl if she hadn't known it was her.

Corey's left eye was swollen shut.

Her right eye opened. She grimaced when she saw Maggie. "Sorry," she said, licking dry lips.

"Take it easy. Don't try to talk."

"Shouldn't have…"

"Shhh. You're going to be okay."

"Hurts."

"I know."

Corey dozed off again, and the next time she woke, she seemed surprised that Maggie was still there. The nurse had come in and said she could have a little bit of water, so Maggie held the straw for her as she drank through swollen, split lips.

The small effort expended to take a sip left her depleted.

Maggie put the cup back on the table, wishing there was something she could do besides stand there and be mostly helpless.

"Maggie."

"Yes?"

Corey took a deep breath, let it out and closed her eyes. "I think I'd like you to call my mom."

"I can do that. Do you know her number?"

Corey gave a slight nod that she seemed to immediately regret, and keeping her eyes closed, she recited the number.

"What do you want me to tell her?" Maggie asked.

"Everything."

"I'll be right back." Maggie went into the waiting room to place the call to Corey's mother. The woman didn't answer, so Maggie left a message. "This is Maggie Harrington, a friend of Corey's in Nashville. Could you please give me a call?" She gave her phone number and ended the call, hoping she would hear from the woman sooner rather than later.

She answered a few other texts, including one from Karen in Arizona, who reported that Debbie's kids had made a smooth transition to their new school and were doing as well as could be expected.

Thank you for the update. Please give the kids our love and keep in touch.

She also checked her email on her phone and found a message sent last night from a sergeant in the Nashville Police Department letting her know that Trey had made bail and would be released.

Maggie blew out a deep sigh. If only she'd seen that message last night, Corey might not be in the ICU. She was about to return to Corey's room when her phone rang with a call from Corey's mom.

"This is Maggie."

"This is Corey's mother, Brianne, returning your call. Have you seen Corey?"

"I have."

"Is she all right? I haven't heard from her in months."

"She's all right, but she's in the hospital."

"Oh my God. Because of him? I told her he was no good. She never listens to me."

"She's been through a lot, and I think she could use your support. She's fully aware that she should've listened to you."

"What happened?"

Maggie told her everything she knew as gently as she possibly could.

"I had no idea she was pregnant," Brianne said, sounding tearful after having heard the whole story. "Where is she now?"

"In the ICU of Nashville General Hospital."

"I'm on my way. I'll be there in less than two hours."

"I'll stay until you get here."

"Thank you so much for calling."

"No problem. I'll see you soon." As Maggie ended the call, she received a text from Brayden.

I'm outside the ICU.

She went out to let him in and led him to the waiting room.

He held a cloth shopping bag. "Change of clothes."

"Bless you."

After putting the bag on a chair, he held out his arms to her.

Maggie walked into his embrace and let him surround her with his strength and the scent of leather, horses and sunshine that she'd forever associate with him.

"How is she?"

"Awake, alert and in a lot of pain. She looks dreadful. Her entire face is bruised, one eye swollen shut, her lips split."

"Motherfucker," he muttered under his breath as he tightened his hold on her. "And how are you?"

"Better than I was. I talked to my mom and Kate, and they said the same things you did. I'm realizing it's going to be a process toward accepting there's only so much I can do for them. They have to be willing to do the rest."

"That's exactly right."

Maggie pulled back to look up at him. "How did the riding lessons go?"

"Good," he said, smiling. "Travis is a natural. He's going to be my star student. Reminds me a lot of myself at that age. Jimmy and Lily are a little overeager. I had a talk with them about making sure they're following the rules of the stables and not acting up around the horses. They're all great kids. Some are just more natural around the horses than others, which is usually the case."

Maggie rested her forehead against his chest for another minute. "I'm going back in with Corey for a bit. Her mom will be here in the next couple of hours. I can get an Uber home if you don't want to wait."

He kissed the top of her head. "I'll wait."

Maggie smiled up at him. "And I shall reward you with dinner at my sister's if you're up for that."

"Works for me. It'll be good for you to see them after the day you've had."

Wait for a man who truly sees you, and when he appears, make sure you notice.

She went up on tiptoes to kiss him. "I really, *really* like you."

His smile was the best thing ever, as was his obvious pleasure in hearing that. "Is that right?"

Maggie nodded.

"That's good, because I really, really, *really* like you."

"That's a lot of reallys."

He kissed her. "Go take care of Corey. I'll be here."

OVER THE NEXT WEEK, Brayden was there. At the hospital, at home, at the stables, at her sister's house, in the car and in bed. He seemed to know what she needed before she needed it. Maggie began to understand what it was like to have a true partner, someone she could lean on in the bad times, laugh with in the good times and count on to have her back.

Maggie was completely and absolutely in love with him, but she didn't know whether he felt the same about her, so she kept her feelings to herself even as the words wanted to burst forth from her lips every time she was around him. She was almost certain he loved her, too.

He was due to arrive at Kate's to meet her any minute, and she couldn't wait to see him after having been apart most of the day while Kate's hair-and-makeup goddesses prepared her and Jill for Buddy's fundraiser.

"Thank you so much for getting me out of this one, Poppy," Kate said to the baby in her arms as she stood by in jeans and a ponytail to watch the proceedings. She'd wanted to be with them while they got ready, but had said repeatedly how glad she was to not have to go.

"Poppy said, 'You're welcome, Mommy,'" Jill said.

"She knows Mommy has had her fill of formal occasions and would be very happy to never go to another one."

"Mommy is a drag," Jill said with a teasing grin for Kate.

"Happy to be a drag if I get to stay home with my sweet Poppy."

"And her daddy," Reid said as he came into the room to check on them. "You ladies look gorgeous."

"We do look rather awesome," Jill joked, striking a pose next to Maggie.

Jill wore a midnight-blue gown, while Maggie was in red. They'd declined Kate's offer of a stylist and had shopped for their own dresses on a recent Saturday.

"Hot damn," Ashton said when he joined them, wearing a black tuxedo. He pointed to Jill. "I'll take that one."

"Good, because the other one is all mine."

Maggie hadn't seen Brayden follow Ashton into the room, so she wasn't prepared for what he said or how he looked in a tux.

"Y'all clean up rather well," Reid said.

Brayden came over to Maggie, put his arm around her and kissed her cheek. "You look incredible."

"I could say the same to you. The tux is hot." She reached up to touch the stubble on his jaw. "The entire package is hot."

"Likewise." They stared at each other for a long moment full of yearning.

At least that was what it was for her. The eight hours since she'd woken up with him had dragged, and she wished they had nowhere to be and nothing to do but be together. She checked her phone and found a text from Corey.

Thank you so much for everything, Maggie. I'm going to be released tomorrow, and I'm going home with my mom. Thanks for bringing my stuff here, for being there for me through the worst of times. I'm sorry I disappointed you all by going back to Trey. I won't make that mistake again. I promise. Someday, when I have my shit together, I want to come back to Matthews and see you guys. You saved my life. I won't forget you.

Maggie blinked back tears as she read the heartfelt text. *I'm so happy you're going home and feeling stronger. We're always here for you. Text me any time, and please do come visit. You'll always be welcome at Matthews. xoxo*

"You okay, Mags?" Kate asked.

"Yeah, just got a sweet text from Corey. She's being released from the hospital tomorrow and going home with her mom."

"I'm so glad to hear she's well enough to go home."

"I know. Me, too. And she said she's done with Trey."

"That's a relief."

Maggie shut off her phone and stashed it in her purse, determined to have a real night off. Teresa was on duty and more than capable of handling anything that came up.

"Are you guys ready?" Ashton asked. He'd drawn the designated-driver card and was taking them in Reid's SUV.

"Ready when you are," Jill said.

"You kids have a nice time," Kate said. "Don't stay out too late."

"And use a condom," Reid added, making them all laugh.

"Shut up, Dad," Ashton said.

"Yeah, shut up, Dad," Brayden said.

Maggie loved the way Brayden fit in, as if he'd always been part of them. That was just another on the long list of reasons she loved him. Her heart was so full of love for him, her sisters, her new niece and her new life. For all its many complications and heartbreaks, the job was also rewarding in ways she was discovering every day. Such as earlier when Travis had thanked her so profusely for the riding lessons.

"It's the most fun I've ever had. Ever."

Having learned to take the victories where she could find them, she carried the little boy's joy with her as Ashton drove them into town.

CHAPTER 27

aggie, Brayden, Jill and Ashton walked the red carpet and posed for photographers, who recognized them as Kate's sisters, probably due to the recent interview they'd done together.

"Who's your date, Maggie?"

"Oh, um, this is Brayden."

His hand on her back made her feel safe and loved and supported. Being with him made everything better, more fun than it would've been without him, and tonight was no different. Buddy's gala was all about fun. After dinner and a performance by their famous hosts, the doors to a second ballroom opened to a carnival street fair, complete with every imaginable game, as well as cotton candy, peanuts, popcorn, funnel cakes and a massive chocolate fountain in the middle of the huge room.

"Holy crap," Brayden said, his eyes lighting up. "This is *awesome*."

"Buddy doesn't screw around," Ashton said. "Last year, the games brought in three hundred thousand dollars."

"Shut up," Brayden said. "That's insane."

"I know. Let's go do our part."

They played every game: Pick a Duck, Water Coin Drop, Balloon

Pop, Gone Fishing, Beanbag Toss and Spin the Wheel. Maggie learned that Brayden excelled at the shooting games, hitting every target—even the moving ones—and winning her three huge stuffed animals.

"Froggie is going to be so jealous when I bring these guys home," Maggie said, struggling under the weight of her prizes.

After a couple of hours of games and way too much cotton candy, Jill came up to them, carrying stuffed animals under each arm. "Are you guys about ready to head home?"

"One more game." Brayden directed Maggie toward the ring toss. "I'm really good at this one."

"You're good at all of them!"

"You ain't seen nothing yet, baby. Check me out here. My gramps taught me how to rope when I was six, and I never miss."

Maggie watched as he deftly put eight rings around eight bottles, impressing even the weary-looking guy running the game.

"You can pick any prize from the top shelf," he said to Brayden.

"I want the jewelry."

The man took down a gaudy set of gold costume jewelry with huge pink stones and handed it over to him. "Nice job. No one ever gets them all."

"Thanks." Brayden ripped the various pieces off the cardboard one by one and put them on Maggie: crown, dangling earrings, necklace, bracelet and ring, which he slid onto the third finger of her left hand before kissing the back of her hand.

She was rendered breathless by the intensity he applied to his task.

Then he looked her dead in the eye and kissed her before whispering, "You are my queen."

Maggie nearly swooned as she dropped the stuffed animals, wrapped her arms around his neck and kissed him square on the lips, right in the middle of the fairway full of people. She couldn't care less who saw them. Who had time for such concerns when the man she loved had adorned her in jewels and called her his queen?

"Um, guys," Ashton said, clearing his throat. "Hello?"

"We may need to call the paramedics to bring the jaws of life to pry them apart," Jill said.

Maggie heard them, but didn't want to end the best kiss of her life. Not yet.

Brayden smiled against her lips and pulled back slowly, seeming as dazzled as Maggie felt.

"Nice bling," Jill said.

"You want me to win you some, sweetie?" Ashton asked.

Brayden scoffed. "Um, no offense, lawyer boy, but you couldn't win that prize."

"Wanna make a bet?"

"Absolutely."

Jill rolled her eyes at Maggie as they stepped back to let the guys have their testosterone-fueled moment.

Brayden went first and once again hooked all eight rings.

Maggie clapped for him. "Well done, babe!"

"The bar is set pretty high, love," Jill said to Ashton. "Don't let me down."

"Give me a kiss for luck," Ashton said.

Jill laid a long one on him. "Go get 'em, tiger."

Ashton got the first seven while Jill acted like a varsity cheerleader at homecoming. He held the last ring and eyed the bottles shrewdly before releasing the ring and just missing.

Brayden let out a triumphant shout and fist-pumped the air. "We'll take another set of the jewelry for my girlfriend's sister, please."

While Maggie processed Brayden referring to her as his "girl-friend," Jill consoled Ashton.

"You were so close, baby."

"I want a do-over," Ashton said.

"Next year," Brayden replied with a cocky smile. "Take the time you need to practice."

Ashton flashed a good-natured grin. "Fuck you."

Brayden laughed so hard, he had tears in his eyes, and Maggie soaked it all in—the fun, the teasing, the love, the friendship and the bone-deep happiness unlike anything she'd ever known. He collected her discarded animals, tucked one under each of his arms and handed the other to her, winking at her as they followed Jill and Ashton to the exit where Buddy and Taylor were holding court.

"Thank you for such a great night." Jill hugged them both. "Best fundraiser ever."

"Glad y'all enjoyed it," Taylor said. "Your sister sponsors the carnival, but she does it behind the scenes. That part was her idea a couple of years ago, and it's been a huge success."

Maggie recalled the carnival that had come to Newport's First Beach every spring and how much Kate had looked forward to it. She loved that Kate had brought that beloved childhood memory to Buddy and Taylor's fundraiser, and that she'd done it anonymously.

"Thanks so much for having us." Maggie hugged Buddy and Taylor. "We had a total blast."

"So glad you could come," Buddy said. "Kate is so, so happy to have her sisters with her. If she's happy, we're happy."

Ashton shook hands with Buddy. "You need to take another look at the ring toss game. I think it's rigged."

Brayden let out a loud guffaw. "Rigged, my ass. Go get another manicure. It might help your aim."

Buddy busted up laughing. "I *love* him. You want to join our monthly poker game?"

Brayden seemed flabbergasted by the offer. "Oh, um, sure. That'd be fun."

"I'll bet he cheats at that, too," Ashton said.

Brayden gave him a shove that had them all heading for the door.

Maggie loved the way he and Ashton bickered all the way to the car, like two friends who'd known each other forever. She'd always accepted that she could never have a serious relationship with a man her parents and sisters didn't like, but she was also realizing how important it would be that Reid and Ashton liked her partner, too, since she spent so much time with them.

Ashton liked Brayden, or he wouldn't be giving him shit, and vice versa.

They filled the back of Reid's SUV with huge stuffed animals and headed out of town.

The minute they were in the car, Brayden had reached for Maggie and brought her close enough to kiss.

"Are they getting busy in my dad's car?" Ashton asked Jill.

"Looks that way to me."

"Keep it in your pants back there."

"F off," Brayden muttered. "And drive the car. I need to get home. Quickly."

Maggie giggled and curled her hand around his neck to bring him back for more. Kissing him had become her favorite thing to do.

"Break it up, kids," Jill said quite some time later. "We're home."

Maggie pulled away from Brayden, surprised to see they were back at Kate's. "Thanks for driving, Ashton."

"I'd say it was my pleasure, but I think it was probably more yours."

"For sure. See you!"

Brayden got Maggie's animals out of the back of the SUV and put them in the backseat of his truck. "We'll get your car tomorrow." With his hands on her hips, he lifted her into the passenger seat and stole another heated kiss before buckling her in and shutting the door.

Best night ever. She touched her fingers to the thick chain around her neck and was struck with a fun idea as she waited for him to get in the truck.

As he drove them home, he kept a tight grip on her hand. "Tonight was so awesome. I had the best time. Thanks for asking me to go."

"It was a blast."

"I can't believe Buddy Longstreet asked me to join his poker game."

"He likes you. They all do."

"As long as you do, I'm good."

"I like you, Brayden." *I love you, Brayden. I love you so much, I feel dizzy from trying to contain my overwhelming love for you.*

At home, they went into the main house, and Maggie set the alarm before leading Brayden to her apartment, where they spent every night together. Since everyone they worked with seemed thrilled to see them together, Maggie had decided to take one of her mother's

259

best pieces of advice—to build a bridge and get over the fact that she was dating a man who technically worked for her.

She had faith that he was every bit the professional she was, and had walked across the bridge into the land of "I don't give a fuck what anyone else thinks." The thought made her giggle.

"What's so funny?"

"How far I've fallen from caring that the others might know we're sleeping together. I've crossed the bridge into the land of 'I don't give a fuck.'"

Smiling, he put his hands on her hips and kissed her. "I love it there. It's the best land ever. It's like Oz."

"Yes, only better because it's real."

His hands slid down to cup her ass and pull her in tight against his erection. "Mmm, so real and so good."

"Hold that thought for just a second, will you?"

"As long as it's only one second."

"You gotta let me go."

"Don't wanna." He kissed her neck and lips before letting her go. "Be very, very quick before I suffer a hard-on-induced stroke."

Maggie laughed as she turned her back to him, pointing to the zipper. "That is not a thing."

He unzipped her and kissed his way down her back, taking a gentle bite of the top of her left cheek. "It's gonna be a thing if you don't give me some relief soon. It's not healthy to be this hard for this long."

She flashed a grin over her shoulder as she walked away from him. "Hold on to your horses, cowboy."

"I'm holding on by a thread."

Maggie went into her bedroom, closed the door and removed everything except for her new jewelry. After a quick trip to the bathroom to brush her teeth, she lit two candles on her bedside table and stretched out across the bed in a provocative pose. "Come on in."

The door opened so fast, he must've been standing on the other side of it waiting for the green light. He'd stripped down to only his pants, which were unbuttoned.

"Oh yes," he said, eyes glittering with appreciation. "Yes, yes, *yes*."

"I believe that's my line."

"You're so cute and so funny and so sexy, and I lo—"

Maggie held her breath.

He crawled onto the bed. "I love being with you so much."

She started breathing again and held out her arms to him. "I love being with you, too."

He held her close, burying his face in her hair. "I've never loved being with anyone the way I love being with you."

Maggie released a deep sigh of relief. He loved her, too, but he probably felt the same way she did about saying the words so soon. "Same goes, cowboy. You're one in a million."

After that, there were no more words, only deep kisses, soft caresses, fiery passion and love. So much love.

And in the morning, they woke to Brayden's worst nightmare come true.

BRAYDEN CAME AWAKE SLOWLY, luxuriating for a few extra minutes in the soft sweetness of Maggie's body snuggled up to him. After years of touch-and-go encounters with women, he'd fallen into the habit of collecting his boots and going home after sex, preferring to sleep by himself. But like everything else, that'd changed since he'd met Maggie. After only a couple of weeks with her, the idea of sleeping alone had become inconceivable.

She was still sound asleep, so he kissed her shoulder and got out of bed.

As he picked up his pants off the floor and dress shirt off the coffee table, he thought about last night and how perfect it had been. Walking into the bedroom to find her naked except for the gaudy jewelry he'd won for her had been one of the best moments of his life. It'd been so great, he'd nearly told her he loved her.

Which he did. Hell yes, he loved her. How could he not?

But it was too soon to be throwing big words like that around, or so he thought. How was he supposed to know when the time was right to say those words? He'd never been in love before. Not like this. This… Everything about it, about her, was different. When she smiled at him, the unrest he'd lived with inside him for so long settled, and a feeling of peace and contentment came over him that he wanted to hold on to with everything he had.

When he was dressed, he ventured into the kitchen for some of Mitch's coffee. He should've brought some clothes to Maggie's apartment so he wouldn't have to do the walk of shame in last night's tuxedo. Oh well. It was only Mitch, and he loved that Brayden and Maggie were together.

Mitch worked seven days a week, even though Maggie told him he should take a day off. He said he didn't want to, that he got bored sitting around at home and that work was fun for him. He'd confided in Brayden that he and his wife had been unable to have kids of their own, and he loved being around the kids at the house.

"Morning," Brayden said when he walked into the kitchen, which was quieter than usual since it was Sunday.

"Morning."

Brayden made a straight line to the coffeemaker.

"How was the thing last night?"

"Really fun. We had a great time."

"That's good."

Brayden filled a mug, stirred in cream and took the first life-affirming sip before turning toward Mitch.

The other man was looking at him with dread etched into his normally stoic expression.

"What?"

"There's some shit online."

Four words that conveyed a world of angst, and before he even understood what Mitch was talking about, Brayden somehow knew this news would change everything for him—again. "What kind of shit?"

"One of the entertainment sites posted a picture of the four of you, and how Maggie and her sister Jill were representing Kate at Buddy and Taylor's annual shindig."

"Okay…"

"Someone commented on it that they knew you from juvie, that you nearly beat a guy to death, and now you're hanging out with Kate Harrington's sister. He gave an interview—"

Brayden held up his hand. He'd heard enough. He put down the coffee cup and walked out of the house, crossing to the stables with an increasingly fast stride. He had to get out of there, but he couldn't leave without Sunday. So he saddled her quickly, efficiently, and led her outside.

Fuck, he couldn't ride without boots.

He put her back in cross ties and ran upstairs, changing into jeans, a work shirt and boots as fast as he possibly could and was racing back down the stairs a second later.

Derek came out of his apartment. "Brayden? What's the matter?"

"Nothing. Nothing is the matter." He felt dead inside. All the love he'd felt for Maggie when he woke had dried up and died along with every hope and dream he'd ever had for himself. People would know what he did, and they wouldn't let their kids anywhere near him. His career and livelihood were ruined along with the reputation he'd worked so hard to establish. Maggie's family would rightfully freak out when they found out what he'd done and wouldn't want her to see him again.

He had to go, and he had to go right now.

Brayden mounted Sunday and pointed her toward the path that led to the back road off the Matthews property, urging her on to get him out of there as fast as possible. He'd worry about sending for his truck, trailer and other belongings later. For now, being gone was his only priority.

As he left the yard, he heard Mitch calling him, but he didn't stop and didn't look back at the place where he'd been so happy.

There was nothing left there for him but memories he'd carry with him forever.

$\mathcal{M}$aggie woke to Mitch screaming Brayden's name. She shook off the cobwebs and sat up, trying to get her bearings. Something was wrong. Mitch didn't yell like that. She went into the bathroom to get washed and dressed as fast as she could and went out into the kitchen to find Mitch and Derek there, both looking grim.

"What's wrong?" Part of her didn't want to know. She didn't want anything to dim the light that burned so brightly inside her after a magnificent evening with the man she loved.

"Brayden is gone."

"Gone where?" she asked, confused.

The two men exchanged glances that took Maggie's nerves to the breaking point. "Will one of you please tell me what the hell is going on?"

"There was stuff online," Mitch said haltingly, seeming pained by every word. "Someone he was in juvie with recognized him in a photo—"

In two seconds, Maggie put the pieces together. "Where'd he go?"

"Took off on Sunday about ten minutes ago."

"Derek, help me get Thunder ready. Hurry." While he headed for the door, Maggie ran back to her apartment and shoved her feet into riding boots, jammed her phone into her back pocket and was running through the kitchen thirty seconds later.

"Be careful, Maggie," Mitch called after her.

She waved to indicate she'd heard him. Derek, bless him, had Thunder waiting for her in the driveway. He held the reins while she swung up into the saddle.

"He went that way," Derek said, pointing to the trail behind the stables. "Probably headed for the back road off the property."

"Thank you." She directed Thunder and gave him his head, hoping the old guy still had gas in his tank, because they were going to need all the gas they could get, not to mention all the love in the world to get Brayden through this. And she would get him through it, because there was no way she was going to lose him.

No way in hell.

She rode like her life depended on it, because it did. Life without Brayden was unimaginable after the blissful weeks they'd spent together.

Thunder gave her everything he had and more than she would've imagined possible, and within fifteen minutes, she caught sight of Brayden ahead of her, heading toward the property line, where a gate stood between him and freedom.

Thankfully, he had to dismount to open the gate, which gave her the chance to catch up to him. "Brayden, stop."

He didn't look at her or in any way acknowledge that she was there or had spoken.

Maggie leaned over and grabbed Sunday's reins, a risky move that nearly unseated her. She managed to barely escape a bad fall by a matter of inches but held on tight to Brayden's horse, knowing he'd never leave without Sunday.

An hour ago, she would've bet her life he wouldn't leave without her, either. She would've been wrong about that.

"Let her go, Maggie."

"Not until you talk to me."

"Nothing to say." He never looked at her or even glanced in her direction, devastation and heartbreak radiating from him.

"Brayden, please. We can get through this."

"Are you *insane*? We cannot 'get through this.' My life is ruined, and I'll be damned if I'll take you down with me. Now give me my fucking horse and go home. There's nothing more to say."

"I have something else to say." Maggie forced herself to bite back the pain at his harshly spoken words. "I love you. I'm completely and totally in love with you, and there's nothing you could want or need that I wouldn't try to find a way to get for you. My sister and Buddy will know what to do. They handle shit like this all the time. Please don't go. Let's fight our way through this. When people hear your side of the story—"

"*No.*" He said the single word so emphatically that it reverberated through her like a shotgun blast.

"That's it? Just no?"

He finally looked at her. "What will your father say when he finds out you're sleeping with a man who nearly killed someone?"

"When he finds out *why*, he'll understand. Everyone will."

Brayden shook his head and ran a trembling hand over the stubble on his jaw. "They won't get it, and everything you and your sister and brother-in-law are building here will be ruined, Maggie."

She took a chance and let go of Sunday before dismounting Thunder, who was still breathing hard and sweating. She'd take care of him as soon as she got through to Brayden. Approaching him the way she would a horse who hadn't been tamed, she put her hands on his chest and looked up at him.

"I love you."

He closed his eyes, exhaled and dropped his forehead to rest against hers. "Let me go, Maggie. It's what's best for you."

Relieved to see some of the fight go out of him, she said, "I love you. We'll figure it out. Stay with me."

He didn't say yes, but he didn't move to leave, either.

Maggie held on to him with one hand while she pulled her phone from her pocket and called Kate.

"Thank God you called. My publicist called me an hour ago. I've been trying to reach you ever since."

"My phone must've been on vibrate. I didn't hear it. We need your help and Buddy's and anyone else you can rally."

"Is it true? Did he nearly kill a man?"

"He did, but when you hear the whole story, you'll know why. Please trust me on this, Kate."

"I do trust you, and I've already asked my publicist and Buddy's to come here immediately. Buddy and Taylor are coming, too. How soon can you get here?"

"Less than an hour."

"We'll be here."

Maggie remembered her car was at Kate's and didn't think Brayden was in any condition to drive them in his truck. "Do me a favor? Send Ashton to get us and tell him to hurry."

"I will. And, Maggie, you should know. I've already heard from Dad. I tried to talk him out of coming here, but you know how he is."

Maggie closed her eyes, having little doubt her dad was already en route. "Yeah, I do. I'll see you soon."

"Your dad is coming here," Brayden said in a dead-sounding tone. "Because he's freaking out about your new boyfriend being a violent felon. You don't need to put yourself through this, Maggie. Let me go. I promised you if it ever got untenable between us, I'd leave. Let me keep my promise to you."

"No."

"Just no?"

She looked up at him, hoping he could see how much she loved him. "Just no." Taking hold of both his hands, she looked into the tortured face of the man who'd become the most important person in her life. "*Fight*, Brayden. Fight for you, for me. *Fight for us.*"

He gave the subtlest of reluctant nods, but that was all she needed.

Aware that she'd won the first battle in a war that was only just beginning, she said, "Let's go home."

. . .

267

AFTER TURNING over the horses to Derek to be cared for, they embarked on a tense, silent ride with Ashton in the Mercedes Kate had bought for Jill, which, unlike Ashton's car, had a backseat. It was hard to believe that less than twelve hours ago, Brayden and Ashton had been messing with each other the way longtime friends did. Now they were both rigidly quiet while Maggie sat in the back, trying to stay calm and focused for her sake and Brayden's.

Judging by the extra cars in the driveway, the people Kate had summoned had already arrived. Maggie also recognized Buddy's black Escalade.

Her stomach was in her throat as she took hold of Brayden's hand and followed Ashton inside.

Everyone was in the great room, where Kate sat on the sofa with Poppy while Reid stood behind her, looking every bit as tense as his son. Ashton went to Jill, who'd been pacing the big room, and put his arms around her to keep her still.

Maggie realized her brother-in-law and future brother-in-law had gone into protector mode, looking out for her, even if she didn't need their protection. She was one million percent sure she had nothing to fear from Brayden, that no one had anything to fear from him. Now she just had to convince everyone else of that.

Without her morning jolt of caffeine, she was running on desperation and certainty that fighting for Brayden, his reputation and their relationship was worth any sacrifice she had to make.

"I'll give you the highlights." Maggie spoke for him because she sensed he was in no condition to speak for himself after being so blindsided. "Brayden has always had a special affinity for horses and a natural way with them, dating back to his earliest childhood. He and his mother lived on his grandfather's ranch. His grandfather taught him everything he knows about horses and instilled in him a love for them along with a healthy respect for them. He taught him to trust his instincts and follow his gut when it came to horses and life. His grandfather died when Brayden was thirteen. A short time later, his mother fell for and married a former rodeo star and brought him home to live on the ranch, thinking he could help them keep their heads above water.

"Brayden took an immediate dislike to Clive. Every instinct he had told him his stepfather was a bad man, but his mother needed the help and fancied herself in love with the guy, so Brayden made himself scarce around the place, coming home only to care for the horses. When he was fifteen, he came home one day after school to find Clive beating the horses with a bullwhip. He was giving special attention to the horse that had belonged to Brayden's grandfather because he knew that horse was Brayden's favorite. He'd timed his attack for when he knew Brayden would be there to care for the horses and made sure he'd see them suffering."

Kate wiped away tears while Jill shook her head in dismay.

Buddy muttered, "Son of a bitch," under his breath.

"Brayden didn't think. He acted. He jumped the fence and beat the hell out of the man who'd made his life a living hell even before he attacked Brayden's beloved horses. Thankfully, his mother came home before he actually killed Clive. Brayden served three years in juvenile detention, followed by five years of probation upon his release. His mother sold the ranch and the horses to pay for lawyers to defend Brayden and divorced Clive. She went on to become a fierce advocate for other children and recently died in a car accident, leaving Brayden with no remaining family. *I* am his family now, and I'll fight for him with everything I have." She looked to the people she didn't know, who were sitting on sofas and chairs. "Tell me what we need to do."

"We need to get his side of the story out there immediately," one of the women said.

"We'll do it through my social media," Kate said.

"And mine," Buddy said.

"And mine," Taylor added.

"You guys don't have to do that," Brayden said, his expression pained.

"It's happening." Kate gave him a look that shut down his objections. "Lenore, you heard the story. Write it up."

The woman typing on a laptop nodded. "Already on it."

"Add this." Kate waited for the other woman to let her know she was ready: "Brayden Thomas has the support of me and my entire family. I'm honored to employ a man with his skills and dedication in charge of the equine therapy program at Matthews House and to have a man of his integrity dating my sister. Juvenile records are sealed for a reason, and the breach of Brayden's privacy is outrageous. I won't have anything more to say about this situation and ask that you respect my sister's privacy. Neither she nor Brayden are public figures and should be treated as the private citizens that they are."

Maggie had never loved her sister more than she did in that moment. "Thank you, Kate," she said softly, blinking back tears.

"Don't thank me. None of this would be happening if we hadn't done that stupid interview. They wouldn't have even known who you were, and I should've kept it that way. I'm sorry, Maggie, and Brayden."

"This isn't your fault, Kate," Brayden said. "It happened, and I own what I did. If I had it to do over again, I'd do the same exact thing."

Lenore eyed him over horn-rimmed glasses. "Don't say that to anyone outside this room."

For the first time since the shit had hit the fan, Brayden cracked a small smile. "Got it."

That small smile made Maggie want to weep from the hope it gave her.

They worked on the statement for an hour, tweaking it until everyone was happy with it, particularly Brayden. It was his story and needed to be told correctly.

"You're sure about this?" Brayden asked Kate, his gaze encompassing Buddy and Taylor.

"Absolutely," Kate said, speaking for the three of them. "Release it, Lenore." To Brayden, Kate said, "Lenore works for all three of us."

"Y'all are impressive," he said, clearly wowed by them.

"We get shit done," Taylor said.

"Thank you," he said softly. "Thank you all so much."

"You have a family with us, Brayden," Jill said. "We've got your back."

Sensing he was overwhelmed, Maggie put her arm around him and brought his head to rest on her shoulder.

"Now you just have to get past Jack," Reid said. "You poor bastard."

WITH THE STATEMENT issued and blowing up Instagram, the others got busy making food and coffee and Bloody Marys. They carried on as if everything were normal, when Brayden's life had spun so far out of control, he had no idea what to make of everything that'd happened in the last couple of hours. He had no idea what "normal" was anymore.

People knew what he'd done. Before this day was out, *everyone* would know what he'd done. Maggie's family knew, and they'd gone to battle for him, risking their own reputations to restore his.

No one had ever done anything like that for him.

And Maggie, dear God, Maggie… Calling her a queen hadn't given her enough credit. She was an empress, and he loved her madly. It occurred to him that he'd forgotten to tell her that earlier when she was pouring her heart out to him. As soon as he got a second alone with her, he would fix that.

Hanging over everything was the imminent arrival of her father, who was apparently known for dropping everything and jumping on a plane any time his daughters encountered trouble.

He was the trouble that Maggie had encountered, and now Jack Harrington was on his way to Nashville to make sure he was good enough for Maggie—or to have him killed.

Of course he wasn't good enough for her. He'd always known that, but damned if he'd been able to keep his distance from her, even knowing she could do so much better than him.

Bringing a mug of coffee with her, she sat next to him on the sofa. "How you holding up?"

"Okay. I guess."

"Lenore said people are responding well to the posts."

"That's good."

"I know it's a lot to process, but maybe it's better this way. People know. Life goes on. You no longer have secrets to protect."

"Maybe, but they were my secrets to tell or not to tell. I bet I know exactly who it was that blabbed."

"It doesn't matter who it was. The damage was done, and we did what we could to repair it."

"You did more than anyone has ever done for me in my life, Maggie, except for maybe my mom."

She sipped her coffee and turned those potent blue eyes on him over the rim of her mug. "I told you why earlier."

"We need to talk about that."

"We will. Later. But you should know that if I had it to do again, I wouldn't change a thing."

He smiled at the way she'd turned his words around on him. "So much I want to say to you."

"We'll get to that. After we see my dad."

"How bad is that gonna be?"

"Hard telling. He's mellowed a bit in his old age—"

"Who you calling old, Mags?"

Maggie nearly jumped out of her skin when she realized her dad was standing behind them. "Jeez, how'd you get here so fast?" She handed her mug to Brayden and got up to greet her dad with a hug and kiss.

"Never mind that. What's this about me mellowing in my old age?"

"Be nice, Dad. I mean it. This is Brayden Thomas. Brayden, my dad, Jack Harrington."

Brayden stood to shake his hand, making eye contact the way his grandfather had taught him. The man was tall with dark hair sprinkled with gray, handsome and formidable. "Good to meet you, sir. I'm sorry it's happening under these circumstances." Brayden couldn't believe how much Jill looked like her dad. Maggie resembled him, too, but Jill was him all over again.

"Yes, the circumstances are somewhat unfortunate," Jack said.

"Dad, you need to know the full story."

"I already know it. I saw Kate's post."

Maggie's mouth dropped open. "*You* know what *Instagram* is?"

Jack gave her a withering look. "I live with a teenager and two preteens. I know what Instagram is, and when two of my daughters text me links to something I should see before I 'come in hot,' I'm also capable of doing what I'm told."

"We both said the same thing," Jill said to Kate as they joined them.

The sisters exchanged a high five, obviously pleased with themselves. Brayden would be forever grateful to them as well as Buddy and Taylor for what they'd done for him today. But Maggie… She was the one who'd made it happen, and his gratitude for her couldn't be measured or summed up in mere words.

"I told you he'd mellowed in his old age," Maggie said. "He never used to do what he was told."

Jack gave Maggie a stern look that managed to also convey amusement and boundless love. "Brayden," he said, "let's take a walk."

"Dad—"

"I'd like to talk to Brayden alone."

Brayden knew it was time to man up and fight for her the way she'd fought for him. "It's fine, Maggie. Lead the way, sir."

"My name is Jack. Call me that."

"Yes, sir. I mean Jack, sir."

"It's okay," Reid said. "You get used to him, and once you do, he's not so scary."

"You," Jack said, pointing at Reid, "shut your mouth. Not only did you marry my daughter after I told you to 'keep an eye on her,' you also made me a grandfather. Where is my sweet Poppy anyway?"

"She's napping, Dad," Kate said. "You can see her in a bit."

"Excellent. Brayden, let's walk."

Brayden grimaced at Maggie.

"Be strong, grasshopper." Maggie affected a comically serious expression. "As far as we know, he hasn't bitten anyone in a while, and he's up-to-date on all his shots."

Jack rolled his eyes at her. "Don't listen to my daughters, Brayden. They don't know me at all."

CHAPTER 29

*B*rayden followed Jack out the French doors that led to Kate's thousand-acre backyard. It occurred to him that there were a lot of places to hide a body out there, but then he recalled how Maggie had come for him earlier and had faith she'd do it again, if it came to that…

For a long time, they only walked. Brayden wondered if Jack was taking him far enough from the house that the gunshot wouldn't be audible. And then he snorted under his breath at the direction his thoughts were taking.

"Care to share the joke?" Jack asked.

"I was wondering if you're taking me far enough from the house that they won't hear the gunshot."

Jack chuckled. "You figured out my plan." They walked past an A-frame log cabin, a smaller version of the main house, as they headed toward a thicket of trees. "That's the bunkhouse Reid built before we all came last Christmas for their wedding."

"Wow. It's huge."

"There're a lot of us."

"I'm starting to realize that."

"Do you have a big family?"

"Nope. It was just me, my mom and my grandfather. He died when I was thirteen, and I lost her recently."

"I heard that. I'm really sorry."

"Thanks."

"I understand you have a way with horses."

"So I'm told. That comes right from my gramps. He taught me everything I know."

"Maggie has loved horses since she was a little girl. Begged and pleaded with us for lessons for years before we finally relented. She was such a tiny little thing. I had nightmares about her being crushed by a falling horse. But Maggie, being Maggie, was completely fearless. She jumped up on that first horse like it was no big deal and took off like she'd been riding all her life. The instructor had to run after her because she was supposed to walk before she ran, but by the time he caught up to her, it was already too late."

"Why am I not surprised?"

"Not only is she fearless, she has the biggest heart of anyone I've ever known. Her mother and I were very concerned about her taking the job at Matthews House, because we knew it would be tough on her when things don't go as planned."

"It has been. She cares so much about the women and kids she works with."

"I know," Jack said with a sigh. "If Maggie cares about you, you're a lucky guy."

"I've never felt luckier in my entire life than I have since I met her."

"Is that right?"

"Yes. Sir."

Jack stopped walking and turned to face Brayden. His intense gray eyes reminded Brayden of Jill when she was in what Maggie and Kate called *lawyer mode*. "Do you love my daughter?"

Brayden thought of the way Maggie had fought for him earlier. He could give her no less than she'd given him, which was everything. "I love her more than anything in this world, even my horse. When you get to know me better, you'll understand there's no higher honor I could give to Maggie than to put her before my horse. She's the most incredible person I've ever met. I want nothing more than to marry her and make a life with her."

Jack nodded, seeming pleased by Brayden's answer. "And you're a convicted felon."

Brayden looked him in the eye. "I am, sir. I mean Jack. Sir. I was convicted of a felony as a juvenile. I served time in juvenile detention and five years of probation afterward. I've been trying to get my record expunged, but it hasn't happened yet."

"Hmm." Jack took off walking again.

Brayden followed, trying to ascertain what that "hmm" had meant. Was Jack going to tell him to stay the hell away from his daughter? Because Brayden wasn't sure he could do that, not after learning earlier that she loved him, too. Before he'd known that for sure, he'd thought he could leave and not look back. Now everything had changed once again.

This day reminded him of four others that had changed his entire life forever—when his grandfather died, when he'd assaulted Clive, when his mother died and when he'd met Maggie and had been immediately attracted to her.

"I want you to know that I don't regret what I did to my stepfather. I regret the pain it caused my mother, but I'd do it again if the circumstances were the same." Maybe he was a fool to say such a thing to Maggie's father, but it was the truth.

"When I first heard about the stuff online, I'll admit I freaked out."

"I can understand why."

"My freak-out switch is set sort of low where my kids are concerned. I'd like to think I've gotten better about rolling with the highs and lows of fatherhood, but when one of my kids is in trouble, I act first and think second." Jack glanced over at him. "Did Maggie tell you about what happened when Kate and Reid were first together?"

"I've heard the highlights."

"Then you know he was my good friend from college, and when I heard he'd taken up with my eighteen-year-old daughter... Well, you can imagine I didn't handle that well."

"Who would?"

"I made a lot of assumptions during that time, only to find out later that I'd been wrong about most of it. While I was thinking that my old friend had taken advantage of my daughter, I missed the fact that she was truly in love with him. I wasn't the reason they split the first time they were together, but I certainly didn't help by failing to see the complete picture.

"She's happier than I've ever seen her since they've been back together. Would I have chosen a man twenty-eight years older for her? Hell no. Can I deny that he loves her with his whole heart? Absolutely no question in my mind about that."

After another period of silence, Jack said, "After hearing your full story, I understand why you did what you did. I don't like that you did it, but I get *why* you did it." He stopped and turned toward Brayden again. "Do I need to worry about my daughter's safety with you?"

"God, no. I'd never..." The thought of anything or anyone hurting Maggie killed him. "No, you don't need to worry about her safety. I give you my word on that."

"And her big, open, trusting heart will be safe with you, too?"

"Yes, sir. You have my word on that, too."

Jack nodded, seeming satisfied. "Well," he said, "that saves me a bullet."

MAGGIE WAS DYING the entire time they were gone. She stood with her nose pressed to the window facing the direction they'd taken, intently watching, hoping her father wasn't being too hard on Brayden. He'd already had a rough enough day without Jack piling on.

Her nerves were stretched to their absolute limit. When she thought about the way she'd begged him to stay, told him how much she loved him...

She sighed deeply.

"It's going to be all right," Jill said when she joined Maggie at the window.

"You sound awfully sure of that."

"It will be. He loves you. That's obvious to all of us. You fought for him, and now he's going to fight for you."

"He was going to leave before."

"Because he thought that was best for you, not because it was what he wanted."

Maggie glanced at her sister. "When did you get so smart about these things?"

"As the oldest and wisest, I've always been smart about all things, as you surely know by now."

Maggie laughed and leaned into her sister's loving embrace, the way she had all her life. She simply couldn't imagine a world without Jill and Kate supporting and loving her. Sure, they'd fought like sisters did growing up, but after their mother's accident, they'd come together to survive it. Having them close by again was such a joy to her.

"You don't think Dad would actually run him off, do you?" Maggie asked.

"Nah. He's just making sure Brayden is worthy of you."

"He is."

"We know that, but Dad needs to see it for himself. It's what he does."

"It was a lot more fun when he was doing it to you and Kate."

Jill laughed. "I'm sure it was." She gave Maggie an extra squeeze. "Let's go play with Poppy. She'll keep your mind off it."

Not even her beloved niece could distract Maggie. "You go ahead. I'm going to stay here."

"Keep breathing, Mags."

"I'm trying."

While she waited, she read texts from her mom, Andi and Eric, all of whom had seen Kate's post about Brayden and were sending love and support to Maggie.

Can't wait to meet this guy, Eric said. *Kate and Jill say he's cool, but I need to see for myself before I decide if he's good enough for you.*

Maggie smiled as she realized that Eric was just like their dad in that way, even though they weren't biologically related. Nurture trumped biology when it came to her dad and Eric, who were the epitome of the expression *two peas in a pod.*

Hang in there, honey, Clare had written. *This, too, shall pass. I heard Dad was on his way. Sending you love and best wishes for your visit with your father. Haha!*

Hugs and love, Mags, Andi said. *Sorry about your dad. I tried to tell him to stay home and mind his own business, but you know how he is. LOL. I'm here if you need me. Always.*

Maggie put her phone back in her pocket. She would reply to the messages later. For now, all she could do was stare at the tree line and wait.

A little while later, Reid silently handed her a glass of iced tea with a lemon wedge.

"Thank you," she said.

"I've been where Brayden is right now. If I got through it, he will, too."

"I suppose that's true."

"After me, a little old felony is nothing."

Maggie laughed when she wouldn't have thought it possible.

"At the end of the day, your dad just wants to be sure his girls are happy, healthy, safe and well loved. You can't blame a guy for that."

"Spoken like the father of a daughter."

"I have a whole new appreciation for your dad since Poppy was born. I hope I can be half the father to her that your dad is to you and your sisters."

"You're going to be great."

Reid nodded toward the window. "Here they come. Looks like Brayden still has all his limbs."

When she saw Brayden, her heart gave a happy lurch.

"Play it cool, darlin'," Reid said as he kissed the top of her head and left her.

279

Maggie tried to follow his advice. She really did, but she couldn't play it cool when it came to Brayden. She went to the mudroom door to greet them.

When he saw her there, Brayden gave her a wink and a smile that filled her with relief.

He was okay. They were okay. It was going to be okay.

They brought the smell of fresh air and spring grass with them.

Brayden came directly to her, put his arm around her and pulled her in close to him. That he did that right in front of her dad said a lot about what'd been decided between them.

Jack glanced from Maggie to Brayden and back to Maggie again. "I'm happy for you, Mags."

She stepped forward to hug her dad. "I'd say thanks for coming, but…"

"I'll always come. That's one of the few things in life you can absolutely count on."

Maggie held on tight to the man who'd been her first love, her anchor and touchstone. "Love you, Dad."

"Love you, too, sweetheart."

MAGGIE WANTED to take Brayden and get the hell out of there so they could be alone. But her dad had come so far, and Jill was making dinner, so they stuck around long enough to eat and be polite. The second the last dish was in the dishwasher, Maggie said, "We have to go."

"You lasted about two hours longer than I would have," Kate said. "Go. Be with your man. Recover from this day, and make some plans."

"And invite him to my wedding," Jill said.

"I will. In case I forget to tell you, I have no idea what I'd do without you guys."

"Likewise," Kate said. "Harrington sisters forever."

"We need to start a hashtag," Jill said.

Maggie enveloped them in a group hug. "Love you so much."

"Love you more," Kate said. "You were our first baby. Don't ever forget that."

"How could I when you'll never let me forget?"

Brayden came into the kitchen and stopped short when he saw the three of them clinging to each other. "Oh, um, sorry to interrupt."

"You're not," Maggie said. "We were just saying goodbye. You ready to go?"

"Whenever you are."

"Brayden," Jill said, "I was thinking that Ashton and I might be able to help you get your juvenile record expunged. We'd be happy to try if you think it would help."

"I'll take all the help I can get with that. I've been trying to do it on my own for years and getting nowhere."

"We'll see what we can do."

"Thank you so much."

They said their goodbyes and thank-yous and were on their way a few minutes later in Maggie's car, which had been left at Kate's the day before. Brayden offered to drive, and she happily handed him the keys.

"Are they talking about us back there?" he asked, holding her hand the way he always did in the car.

"What do you think?"

"We gave them enough for a year today."

"It won't last long. My dad has six children. Something else will knock us off the front page. He doesn't know yet that Eric wants to go into the Peace Corps rather than go to college. That news is gonna drop any minute."

"How do you feel about that?"

"I think it'll be great for him. He's applied to teach English as a second language as well as American Sign Language to other Peace Corps volunteers. He's heard there's a bit of a demand for that."

"But his parents will freak."

"Probably. He got into Northwestern in Chicago, which is where Andi is from. Her mom and aunt would be nearby. Andi was happy with that plan."

"And now he's going to upend it."

"Looks that way." She glanced at him. "Will you please tell me what my dad had to say before I die from wanting to know?"

"It was fine. He told me about when Reid and Kate first got together and how he feels like he didn't handle that as well as he could have. He's trying to learn from his mistakes."

"Wow. That's highly evolved for him."

"He did come right out and say, 'You're a convicted felon.'"

"Ugh."

"He said he understood what I did and why, and I told him I'd do it again under the same circumstances. That led to him asking if he needed to be worried about me harming you."

"No," she said, aghast. "He did *not* ask that."

"Of course he did, and I don't blame him, Maggie. He was making sure his beautiful daughter would be safe with me. I assured him you will be. Always."

"Always is an awfully long time."

He brought their joined hands to his lips and kissed the back of hers. "Won't be long enough for me."

Maggie shivered from the promise she heard in the gruffly spoken words.

They got home just as the sun was heading for the tops of the trees in the distance.

"Let's walk," he said after parking her car behind the stables.

They set out in the direction they usually took to ride, but after having worked the horses hard earlier, they left them to rest.

Brayden put his arm around Maggie and matched his stride to hers. "What a day."

"One we won't forget. That's for sure."

"I'll never forget the way you came after me, or how strong you were when I was falling apart."

"I was falling apart on the inside."

"I never would've guessed that."

"Well, it's true. I was so afraid you'd ride away, and I'd never see you again."

"You made it impossible for me to leave, even if I still think that would've been the best thing for you."

"No, it wouldn't have."

They walked into the woods, down the path to the clearing by the pond, where they sat on the grass to watch the sunset.

"There's something I didn't get a chance to tell you earlier, but it's something you should know."

Maggie glanced at him warily. "I'm almost afraid to ask."

"This is actually something good. The best thing ever, in fact."

"What?"

"I love you, too. I have for a while now. I was dying to tell you, but I kept thinking it was too soon."

They were among the best words Maggie had ever heard. "I was the same. Dying to tell you, but afraid to freak you out with too much too soon."

"I could never have too much of you, sweet Maggie." He kissed her then with hours of desperate need and desire coming together in an explosive burst of passion that left them both reeling when they finally came up for air. "*Whoa.*"

Maggie laughed at the astounded face he made.

"We should get married," Brayden said.

"*What?*"

"You heard me. We should get married and live together and run this program of yours together and have beautiful dark-haired babies together. We should have everything. I love you. You love me. Your dad didn't kill me. What else is there?"

"Nothing," Maggie said, her heart so full of love and excitement, she feared it would burst. "That's everything I've ever wanted."

"Is that a yes?"

She couldn't believe this was happening. "Are you really asking me?"

He got up on his knees and reached for her hand. "Maggie Harrington, I love you. I'll always love you, my dream girl, the one I thought I'd never find. For the rest of my life, I'll remember the way you chased after me, stared me down and forced me to fight for myself and for us. Will you please marry me and live with me and let me help you change people's lives in this incredible place and father your children and be part of your amazing if overly involved family?"

Maggie laughed through her tears. "Yes, Brayden. That's a yes. Yes to everything."

*D*ressed in a black tuxedo, Jack Harrington walked through the ornate main doors to the Infinity Newport Hotel he and Jamie had designed and built a dozen years ago. His only job today had been to get his three sons into their tuxes and deliver them to the hotel by two o'clock. They'd made it with minutes to spare.

After reminding them to behave and do what they were told, he turned the boys over to a member of Andi's staff and then exhaled as he took in the huge staircase that provided the centerpiece of the hotel's lobby. At the landing halfway up, it split into two sets of stairs, one leading to each of the hotel's wings.

He'd proposed to Andi at the top of those stairs, by the big window that overlooked Narragansett Bay, and had married her here on the same day their twin boys arrived. What a day that had been, and what a day this one promised to be.

He'd been an emotional wreck since Eric graduated from high school and started making preparations to leave for Thailand. *Ugh,* that was really, *really* far from home, but Jack had been trying to make peace with it and support his son's decision, even if his heart was breaking at the thought of his precious boy being so far away. Letting go continued to be his greatest challenge as a dad. Maybe he'd have the hang of it by the time the twins left home.

The wedding weekend had kicked off with an informal cookout for the entire extended family at Clare and Aidan's home on Thursday night, followed by a fantastic rehearsal dinner hosted by Reid at the Tennis Hall of Fame last night. And today, Jack would be expected to give away another of his precious daughters.

He'd gone round and round with Jill and finally convinced her to allow the father of the bride to pay for the wedding. She hadn't wanted that, but he'd insisted, and she'd ultimately relented because she understood it was something he wanted to do for her.

It was all too much for one doting dad to handle. His kids had grown up so fast, were *still* growing up too fast. How was it possible that the twins would be *eleven* in August?

His sister, Frannie, and her husband, Jamie, came in through the main doors with their twins, Owen and Olivia, who'd recently turned twelve.

"Uncle Jack." Olivia rushed over to him. "Listen to the sound my dress makes when I swirl!"

Both kids had Frannie's red hair, and Jamie referred to the three of them as his gingers.

"I love that. You're stunning, sweetheart."

Owen struck a pose. "I got a new suit."

"Handsome as ever, my friend." Owen and Jack exchanged the elaborate handshake Owen had created for them a year ago.

"Come on, guys," Frannie said to the kids. "Let's go figure out where you need to be."

Jill had asked Owen and Olivia to hand out programs to all the guests.

"See you out there," Jack said as Frannie took off with the kids.

"How you holding up?" Jamie asked.

"Oh, you know. Just another day."

"Right," Jamie said, laughing. The tall blond bastard barely had a gray hair, unlike Jack, who had three times as many kids and the gray hair to prove it. "Just another day. Our baby girl Jill is *getting married*."

"I know. I can't deal. And Maggie right behind her."

"My heart can't take it. I can only imagine how you must feel. And Eric, going to *Thailand*."

"Ugh, don't remind me." His son would be teaching English to Thai students and ASL to other American volunteers for the next two years. After many late nights and long debates, Jack and Andi had agreed to Eric's plan in exchange for his promise to go to college upon his return. "Just like when Kate wanted to go to Nashville. Remember?"

Jamie grimaced. "How could I ever forget? Look at what became of that. I have to believe Eric will do great."

"It's just so frightening to think of him being so far away." Eric had never let his disability define or limit him, and Jack couldn't bear to hold him back from chasing his dreams. But he would worry about him every day that he was gone.

"I know, but it'll go by fast, like everything else has."

"I hope so."

"It will."

Aidan's brothers Brandon and Colin arrived with their wives, Daphne and Meredith, as well as Brandon's daughter Michaela and her husband, Josh. Brandon pushed his mother, Colleen O'Malley, in a wheelchair. Every one of her snow-white hairs was in place, and her nails had been painted pink, the same color as her house in Chatham, Massachusetts, or so Jack had been told by his girls.

Jack and Jamie greeted them all with handshakes and kisses. Since Aidan married Clare, the O'Malley family had been good to Jack's girls, which made them family to him, too.

Jack bent to kiss the cheek of Colleen O'Malley. "It's so lovely to see you, Colleen. You're looking well."

"I'm hanging in there," she said in the delightful brogue of Ireland. "My grandchildren keep me young."

"I hear the whole gang is coming today," Jack said.

"I'm afraid so. I'll apologize in advance for the unruly mob of O'Malleys. I did what I could with them."

Jack laughed and directed them on how to find the south veranda, where the wedding would take place in forty minutes.

God, forty minutes until Jill got *married*. Wasn't it five minutes ago she'd been dancing at her first recital and learning to sail? "I suppose we should get in there before they send out a search party for me."

Jamie nudged him in the right direction, as usual. "Let's go."

As they walked through the hotel, Jack saw memories in every nook and corner of the place. He'd worked on this project during the most difficult time in his life, had met Andi because of this place and had his life changed forever by a series of events that continued to feel surreal even after all the time that had passed.

He was proud of the family he'd created with Andi, Clare and Aidan. They had worked together as a team to support the three girls he and Clare shared as well as the children they'd had with new spouses. People told him and Clare they were the gold standard for how to do divorce right. He didn't see it that way. They had simply put their children first—all their children—and the result was one big happy family that gathered today for Jill's wedding.

One of the wedding staffers directed him to the room where Jill waited for him with Clare and Andi. He'd done this "giving away the bride" thing once before, so he'd expected to be better able to cope with it this time around. He'd been wrong about that. Seeing Jill in her wedding dress stopped his heart. The dress was simple yet elegant, matching the understated style of the gorgeous bride who wore it.

"You're stunning, sweetheart."

"Thank you, Dad."

"You ready for this, kiddo?"

"I can't wait."

Jack hugged Clare, holding on for a long moment that belonged only to them as they prepared to watch their eldest daughter tie the knot. "We done good with this one," Jack whispered.

Clare pulled back from him, laughing and dabbing at tears. "We done good with all of them."

He nodded and kissed her cheek before turning to Andi, who held out her arms to him. "You got this, Daddy?"

"Oh sure. No biggie."

Andi, who knew him better than anyone ever had, laughed as he'd expected her to. "Right. Whatever you say, stud."

"See you out there?"

"I'll be waiting for you, love. Make me proud."

"I'll try."

After Clare and Andi left the room, Jack extended his arm to Jill. "Shall we do this?"

"Yes, please." She curled her right hand through his arm, took her bouquet from the wedding planner and smiled up at him, incandescent with joy. "Love you, Daddy."

He fought back tears. "Love you more, my sweet girl."

JILL HAD ORCHESTRATED every aspect of this day, and when everyone was in place, the ceremony began with Brayden escorting Clare to her seat in the front row, followed by Eric escorting Andi and Owen escorting Frannie, who had stepped up for Jill and her sisters during the dreadful years following their mother's accident. Jack was deeply touched to see that his sister had been given the same courtesy as Jill's mother and stepmother.

Jack's parents, Jamie's parents, Clare's mother, Andi's mother and aunt, Martha Longstreet and Colleen O'Malley were seated in the row behind Clare and Andi, all of them wearing honorary corsages. His girls were lucky to be loved by such an amazing group of grandparents.

One of the hotel's musicians provided the music for the ceremony because Jill hadn't wanted any of her famous guests to worry about performing. Kate, Buddy and Taylor would do a set together at the reception instead, and everyone was looking forward to that.

Ashton appeared at the front of the gathering with his father and Buddy by his side.

Ashley, Chloe and Georgia Longstreet and their brother, Harry, the siblings of Ashton's heart, as he'd introduced them at the rehearsal dinner, were the first members of the wedding party to appear from a room across the hall, followed by their mother, Taylor, who was one of Jill's attendants. The women in the wedding party had been asked to wear shades of purple. They carried bouquets made of lilacs and other purple and white flowers.

Jill's brothers followed: Eric, Rob and John Harrington, along with Max and Nick O'Malley, all of them cute as could be in their tuxedos.

Jack noticed that Rob's hair could use a combing, and John's bow tie had gotten crooked at some point, but oh well. Too late now.

Next came Maggie, looking impossibly beautiful in an off-the-shoulder lilac gown and sporting a sparkling new diamond ring on her left hand. She caught his eye and flashed a saucy grin at him before continuing down the aisle.

Brayden stood off to the side, his gaze fixed on Maggie, smiling as she came toward him. The more time Jack spent with the two of them, the more comfortable he was with Maggie's choice for a husband. Brayden was a good guy, and he made Maggie deliriously happy. That was all that mattered to Jack.

Kate was next, her gown a darker shade of purple than Maggie's. Instead of a bouquet, she carried Poppy, who wore a dress covered in purple pansies and a crown made of baby's breath. His gorgeous middle daughter had become even more so since becoming a mother. Kate radiated pure joy as she made her way down the aisle toward her husband, who lit up with delight at the sight of his wife and daughter.

True love, Jack thought. All his girls had found true love, and he couldn't be happier about that, even if none of it had happened the way he'd thought it would.

Jack escorted Jill to the start of the aisle, where they met up with Aidan, who would accompany them.

"This is one of the greatest honors of my life." Aidan's tearful gaze encompassed them both. "Thank you for asking me."

Jack smiled at Clare's husband, who, against all odds, had become his close friend. "We wouldn't have it any other way, would we, Jill?"

"Absolutely not." She tucked her left hand into Aidan's elbow and held her bouquet of white roses and lilies in the right hand that was looped through Jack's arm.

Ashton watched Jill come toward him, smiling through his tears.

As Jack and Aidan walked their girl to meet her groom, everyone Jack loved was there, gathered in the place that had changed his life forever. He couldn't ask for anything more.

PHEW! So there you have it! I finally wrote Maggie's book, and I can't begin to properly articulate the emotional journey this book took me on as I wallowed in memories of the earliest days in my author career. It was such an incredible joy for me to be back once again with Jack and his family—and to write the epilogue from his point of view. I was so giddy when I came up with the idea of ending the series where it began with him. Ahhhh, all the feels, I tell you! ALL. THE. FEELS!

For the readers who've asked me relentlessly for YEARS to write this book, thank you for never giving up on one more Treading Water book. While I know at times the wait seemed interminable, I'm so glad I held off until I could do this story justice. I hope you love it as much as I do. And yes, **this is the end for this series**, so don't start asking for another book! Lalalala, I can't hear you! LOL

Special thanks to my fabulous assistant, chief operating officer and dear friend, Julie Cupp, who has been on this ride with me so long that she read *Treading Water* as I was writing it in 2004-2005. Back then, we were colleagues on the day job. Neither of us could've imagined then what we were starting with that book or how it would link our lives the way it has. Julie, you can't quit me! Thank you for everything always.

Thanks also to the rest of the amazing team who support me every day: Lisa Cafferty, CPA, Holly Sullivan, Nikki Haley, Ashley Lopez and Tia Kelly. Thank you, Dan, Emily and Jake, who've also been on the Treading Water ride with me since the early 2000s, when they first understood that a man named Jack Harrington had joined our family—and was apparently here to stay. To my late parents, George and Barbara Sullivan, who always knew that someday I'd write a book and never let me give up on that dream, even when it seemed so far out of reach as to be laughable. I am who I am today entirely because of them.

A huge shout-out to my chief executive beta readers, Anne Woodall and Kara Conrad, both of whom have been with me from the beginning and help me so much with every book and even between books. To the Treading Water Series beta readers: Gwen, Kasey, Tammy, Melanie, Kelly and Mona, thank you for checking the details for me. I'm so happy to have you guys on the team! To my amazing editors, Linda Ingmanson and Joyce Lamb, thank you for always finding time for me when I come calling, and to Tracey Suppo for reading as I wrote this book and for cheering me on. You're the best!

I had so much fun visiting Joye M. Briggs and her daughter, Emily Cournoyer, cofounders of Yellow Horse, Inc. in Ashaway, Rhode Island, to learn about equine-assisted therapies and programs. I so appreciate the time and information Joye and Emily provided. Thank you, ladies! I also want to mention my "baby" cousin and close friend, Jennifer Barrera, who basically did Maggie's job in this book for thirteen years as the program director of Lucy's Hearth, a shelter for families in crisis in our hometown of Middletown, RI. Jennifer's dedication to her clientele very much inspired Maggie's journey in this book, and I thank Jen for her valuable input into this story.

Last but most certainly not least, thank you to the readers who've made every dream I've ever had come true. I'd be nowhere without your unwavering support of me and my books. I love you all so much, even when you're begging me to write a book for seven years! HAHA! Especially then. It's always nice to feel wanted, and you always make me feel wanted. Thank you so much for everything.

Much love,
Marie

ALSO BY MARIE FORCE

Contemporary Romances Available from Marie Force

The Treading Water Series

Book 1: Treading Water

Book 2: Marking Time

Book 3: Starting Over

Book 4: Coming Home

Book 5: Finding Forever

The Gansett Island Series

Book 1: Maid for Love (*Maddie & Mac*)

Book 2: Fool for Love (*Joe & Janey*)

Book 3: Ready for Love (*Luke & Sydney*)

Book 4: Falling for Love (*Grant & Stephanie*)

Book 5: Hoping for Love (*Evan & Grace*)

Book 6: Season for Love (*Owen & Laura*)

Book 7: Longing for Love (*Blaine & Tiffany*)

Book 8: Waiting for Love (*Adam & Abby*)

Book 9: Time for Love (*David & Daisy*)

Book 10: Meant for Love (*Jenny & Alex*)

Book 10.5: Chance for Love, A Gansett Island Novella (*Jared & Lizzie*)

Book 11: Gansett After Dark (*Owen & Laura*)

Book 12: Kisses After Dark (*Shane & Katie*)

Book 13: Love After Dark (*Paul & Hope*)

Book 14: Celebration After Dark (*Big Mac & Linda*)

Book 15: Desire After Dark (*Slim & Erin*)

Book 16: Light After Dark (*Mallory & Quinn*)

Book 17: Victoria & Shannon (Episode 1)

Book 18: Kevin & Chelsea (Episode 2)

A Gansett Island Christmas Novella

Book 19: Mine After Dark (*Riley & Nikki*)

Book 20: Yours After Dark (*Finn & Chloe*)

Book 21: Trouble After Dark (*Deacon & Julia*)

Book 22: Rescue After Dark (*Mason & Jordan*)

The Green Mountain Series

Book 1: All You Need Is Love (*Will & Cameron*)

Book 2: I Want to Hold Your Hand (*Nolan & Hannah*)

Book 3: I Saw Her Standing There (*Colton & Lucy*)

Book 4: And I Love Her (*Hunter & Megan*)

Novella: You'll Be Mine (*Will & Cam's Wedding*)

Book 5: It's Only Love (*Gavin & Ella*)

Book 6: Ain't She Sweet (*Tyler & Charlotte*)

The Butler, Vermont Series

(Continuation of Green Mountain)

Book 1: Every Little Thing (*Grayson & Emma*)

Book 2: Can't Buy Me Love (*Mary & Patrick*)

Book 3: Here Comes the Sun (*Wade & Mia*)

Book 4: Till There Was You (*Lucas & Dani*)

Single Titles

Five Years Gone

One Year Home

Sex Machine

Sex God

Georgia on My Mind

True North

The Fall

The Wreck

Love at First Flight

Everyone Loves a Hero

Line of Scrimmage

The Quantum Series

Book 1: Virtuous *(Flynn & Natalie)*

Book 2: Valorous *(Flynn & Natalie)*

Book 3: Victorious *(Flynn & Natalie)*

Book 4: Rapturous *(Addie & Hayden)*

Book 5: Ravenous *(Jasper & Ellie)*

Book 6: Delirious *(Kristian & Aileen)*

Book 7: Outrageous *(Emmett & Leah)*

Book 8: Famous *(Marlowe)*

Romantic Suspense Novels Available from Marie Force

The Fatal Series

One Night With You, *A Fatal Series Prequel Novella*

Book 1: Fatal Affair

Book 2: Fatal Justice

Book 3: Fatal Consequences

Book 3.5: Fatal Destiny *The Wedding Novella*

Book 4: Fatal Flaw

Book 5: Fatal Deception

Book 6: Fatal Mistake

Book 7: Fatal Jeopardy

Book 8: Fatal Scandal

Book 9: Fatal Frenzy

Historical Romance Available from Marie Force

The Gilded Series

ABOUT THE AUTHOR

Marie Force is the *New York Times* bestselling author of contemporary romance, romantic suspense and erotic romance. Her series include Gansett Island, Fatal, Treading Water, Butler Vermont and Quantum.

Her books have sold nearly 10 million copies worldwide, have been translated into more than a dozen languages and have appeared on the *New York Times* bestseller list more than 30 times. She is also a *USA Today* and *Wall Street Journal* bestseller, as well as a Speigel bestseller in Germany.

Her goals in life are simple—to finish raising two happy, healthy, productive young adults, to keep writing books for as long as she possibly can and to never be on a flight that makes the news.

Join Marie's mailing list on her website at marieforce.com for news about new books and upcoming appearances in your area. Follow her on Facebook at *www.Facebook.com/MarieForceAuthor* and on Instagram at *www.instagram.com/marieforceauthor/*. Contact Marie at *marie@marieforce.com*.

Made in the USA
Middletown, DE
19 March 2020

86814125R00169